# The Forgotten Girl

JESSICA SORENSEN

First Paperback Edition: May 2014



For information:
jessicasorensen.com

Cover Design and Photography: Mae I Design
http://www.maeidesign.com/

*The Fogotten Girl*
ISBN: 978-1494776909

## Prologue

The heart is fascinating. It pumps blood through the veins. Feeds us. Starves us. It's steady when we're steady. Is erratic when we're erratic. When it goes silent, everything inside us stops. Stills. When we're alive, it's the fuel to that life. It drives the adrenaline. Soars it through us. Makes us able to do more than we're normally capable of.

The same thing goes for when we're afraid. Fear. It's as potent as life and the more afraid we are, the faster our hearts beat.

Right now, my heart feels like it's going to explode out of my chest as I stare at the dark sky, rain pouring down as lightning bolts slap against the earth, barely able to turn my head. My hair, clothes and skin are drenched, and my eyes blink fiercely against the fierce raindrops, making it difficult to see. However, I can make out the tips of pine trees and a massive steel water tower nearby... and there's a glow in the distance like fire...

Glass is scattered around my head, a halo of piercing thorns, cutting into my scalp. The puddles on the pavement ripple against my back. Lights shine on me from somewhere and blood trickles from my forehead into my eyes.

I don't know how I got here, where here is, or who I am. I know nothing except I'm lying in the middle of the road. My arms are kinked and twisted above my head and my legs are cut up and sprawled out in an unnatural position.

There's something clutched in the palm of my hand. It's metal with sharp edges that are splitting open my trembling palm. I should let it go, but I can't find the will to unfold my fingers from it. I want to hold onto it—need to. Just thinking about letting go sends my heart slamming against my chest *faster, faster, faster*. I'm scared... alive... scared... dead. I can't tell which one.

*I feel dead.*

The thought sends a strange calmness to my chest and my heart gradually slows, the cold becoming comforting. *Death*. Is the thought of dying calming me? Or is my heart dying? Am I'm dying? I'm not sure whether to keep trying to breathe or to just let go. Do I want to die? Why does it feel like the answer is yes and no?

I attempt to turn my head, to look around and figure out where I am. Blinking several times, the rain washes the blood away from my eyes. With a lot of effort, I manage to slant my head to the left, but immediately regret it when I'm blinded by a light. *Is that death?*

Headlights of a car parked in the middle of the road... I'm lying in the middle of the road and there's a car just off to the side of me. Wait. Was I hit by a car? Is that why I'm here? *Why can't I remember?*

I attempt to flip over onto my stomach so I can get to my feet, but my legs, arms and torso aren't having any part of it.

*Someone help me!*

I open my mouth to scream, but the rain drowns me, flooding my mouth and lungs. I shut my eyes and listen to the descending rhythm of my heart. Slower. Vanishing. Icy, cold water rivers over me, but I'm so warm inside. *Numb*.

The rain is soundless. I think I might be dying...

"Can you hear me?" A voice drifts through the stillness. I'm uncertain if it came from inside my head or outside in the rain. I know it, though... I think.

With effort, I open my eyes again. It's darker than I remember it being, the lightning fickle as the clouds thin. That's when I notice one of the headlights is blocked out by something... a tall figure standing in the leftover drizzle of rain.

"Who's... there?" My voice is hoarse, feeble, helpless.

The stranger doesn't respond, just walks toward me. Boots crunch against the wet pavement, splashing through puddles. With each step, my heart quickens. *Thump. Thump. Thump.* Blood crashes through my body.

I can feel the rain again. The cold. Feel the blood running down my head. Pain. So much pain. I should get up and move, but I'm still immobile and suddenly they're standing right above me. I can't see their face through the veil and the light hitting the back of them, but my heartbeat quickens with every second they stare at me. Fear. I think I'm afraid. Of them? Of dying?

"Who… are… you…?" I croak, my body quivering.

"You're going to be okay, Maddie."

The name makes me feel hollow. Maddie? Who's Maddie? Who am I?

The person continues to stare for a while before crouching down beside me. I have the strangest compulsion to reach up and claw their eyes out, hurt them, but I can't lift my arms. They lean over me, sheltering my face from the rain with theirs. I still can't see their expression or facial features, but I know they're watching me, studying my wounds.

My heart thrashes. *Quicker. Quicker. Quicker.* My chest moves with it, gasping for air. I can't hear, see, think. *Who am I?*

"Who are you?" I manage to say again. "Do I… do I know you?"

The person silently assesses me with their head tilted to the side. Putting a cigarette into their mouth, they then strike a match and light it, puffing on it a few times before pulling it out of their mouth. Then they reach over me, their fingers seeking my hand, smoke dancing into my face and nostrils.

Then he utters softly, “Wait, you’re not her.”

*Not who?* I start to shake, scream, try to move. My heart racing so fast inside my chest it aches deep inside my muscles. My adrenaline soars, blood rushes through my body. It’s too much. I get dizzy, and the world becomes colors and shapes that I can’t make sense of... I can’t make sense of anything. But I do feel the touch of fingers on my hand as he pries my fingers open easily, despite my desperation to hold onto it.

The object falls out of grasp. *Plink*. It hits the pavement.

My heart slams against my chest so hard it knocks the breath out of me. I suck in an inhale and scream as loud as I can. Pain surges through me, filling my head. It feels like I’m splitting in half, becoming someone else, part of me dying. *Kill him.*

I lift my hand up toward the stranger as he watches me through the dark, unafraid. When my fingers graze his neck, I fold them around the base and squeeze, strangling him. He doesn’t fight back; just remains crouched beside me, as if saying: *Go ahead. Do it. Kill me.* And I do until I open my mouth and finally get my scream out, the pain in it evident, burning its way through my body.

"I don't want to be here anymore!"

"It's going to be okay," he whispers as he gasps for air. "I promise."

But he's wrong. Because moments later, the rain drowns me out and everything goes black.

## Chapter 1
## Maddie

*Six years later…*

I'm considering killing my therapist. Leaning over his mahogany desk, clubbing him over the head with the smiley face paperweight, and then watch him fall out of his chair and onto the floor. I would calmly get up and stroll over to him then crouching beside him, my fingers would enfold around his neck and I'd squeeze, watching his veins bulge until he gasped his last breath.

I wonder how pallid his face would be toward the end. If his veins would be more defined against his peachy complexion. If a plea would escape his lips. *Please don't do it. I have a family. I don't want to die. I'm so sorry, Maddie, for making you sit through this endless torture of therapy sessions, making you feel more insane with each one.*

The only thing I'm not positive about is if I'd get cold feet halfway through—if Maddie would regain control again and back out, my good shining through the evil. Perhaps dark and morbid thoughts were never supposed to be lived out; they were just put there to torture me daily.

Still, I wonder what I'm capable of. It feels like there's so much more to me than just living my ordinary life day in and day out. There has to be more. I wonder all the time what the more is.

Fear it.

I might find out soon if my therapist keeps asking me questions about what's going on inside my head. Too much pushing and I'll finally break down and tell him what's really going on in the darkest crevices of my mind. That Lily, the person hidden inside me, is encouraging me to do dark and twisted things. That she hates getting annoyed and right now, he's annoying her to no end. But, if I told him that, then I'd actually have to explain who Lily is and that could be more complex than explaining my murderous thoughts. Besides, even I sometimes don't understand who Lily is.

I never wanted to be this way—feel this kind of darkness rotting within me, an open wound that won't heal. What I want is to be normal and for a split second, I was. For ten, glorious seconds when I opened up my eyes in the hospital, I was no one.

But then she spoke to me.

*"Maddie, are you awake yet?"*

A name that can mean purity, innocence, beauty, Lily probably doesn't seem like such a terrible person to be. A flower commonly used at weddings, which represents happy times, full of smiles, kisses, and hearts—the name screams good and pure. Of course, it's also the most common flower used at funerals.

They were one of the first things I had laid eyes on after I woke up after the accident.

I'd opened my eyes, so tangled, lost and scared. I couldn't remember anything before lying in the road—still can't. My name. Where I was. How I got to the hospital bed. Anything about my childhood. It was almost like I'd been reborn.

I'd lifted my hand up in front of my face and turned it over; the way it moved was fascinating because my arm felt disconnected from my body and my body detached from my mind. There had been a bandage around my palm, wrapping the cut I got from the item I was grasping onto in the road—I never did find out what it was—and the hand that had strangled the man. A hand that felt like it had a mind of its own, capable of so many frightening things.

My eyes had finally left my hand and wandered along the hospital room. There was a single window where light peeked in and shined brightly along the walls. Beside the bed was a black and purple vase full of blooming lilies, which were too unsettling to look at. Too perfect—too flawless. Too clashing with the room. And the scent… it drove my senses mad and made me sick every time I got a huge whiff of the potent scent.

There was something else about the flowers, too. I couldn't quite put my finger on what exactly it was that made me want to smell them then shred the petals and make them go away like they reminded of something beautifully painful. I'd only felt inner peace with them when they started to wilt a couple of weeks later, yet there was still this strange sensation of loss when they were gone, just how I felt.

Dying, life slipping away, unnourished, despite the steadiness of my heart. Maddie was withering and someone else was growing in her place, her words alarming, yet familiar. I decided that I needed to give the voice a name to differentiate between the two of us, so I started calling her Lily after the dead flowers. It felt fitting and the voice seemed to agree with me. I'm not even sure why I chose the name. Whether it was because the flowers beside my bed were dying and that I wished she'd die along with them, or if it was simply a name that had surfaced from somewhere deep in my mind. Whatever the reason, the name seemed fitting and Lily was born.

"Maddie, did you hear anything I just said?" Preston Wrightson, my therapist since this all began almost six years ago, waves his hand in front of my face. There's a sharpened pencil in his hand and I flinch back when it nearly pokes my eye out. "Sorry," he apologizes, quickly withdrawing his hand. "You were zoning out on me again."

I'm in a strange mood today, which I usually am when I'm at therapy. Being a combination of Maddie and Lily, it makes my mood unstable, more depressed, more struggling to find a balance, but I think that stems from my dislike toward Preston.

"As much as I think I could rock the pirate look," I say, forcing my fake light tone out as I touch my eye that survived a near puncture, "maybe you should start working on your depth perception before you go waving around sharp objects."

He sighs, that *oh Maddie and your sarcasm* sigh. "I really wish you'd tell me where you go when you space off like that." He pauses, waiting for a response he'll never receive.

"Me, too," I reply evasively. If I ever did tell him where I went—what I was thinking—I'd be in a straightjacket. So round and round we go on the merry-go-round where nothing happens, the one I live on every single day. Madness. Insanity. It drives me crazy, but I still keep my secrets and he still tries to pry them out of me, despite almost six years of failure.

He sighs again then looks down at the folder in front of him, the one that carries years of notes about me. I can only imagine what they say. Difficult. Uncooperative. Confused. Childish. It makes me sick to think about, what he could possibly see inside me, if he can see underneath the steel shell I've created around myself, but is keeping it to himself.

After reading some of the notes over, he sighs for the third time, then closes the folder. There's disapproval in his expression when he glances up at me.

"Maddie, you've barely spoken today at all." He overlaps his hands on the desk, scooting his office chair forward. "It seems like for the last couple of visits, you've kind of regressed, and your mother mentioned you've been distant and distracted at home. Is there anything going on in your life that's been different? Or maybe your nightmares have been getting worse?"

"I hate that you talk to my mother so much," I say, dodging the subject. Yes, my nightmares are bad, but that's not what's wrong with me. What's wrong is that Lily's been gaining more control over me, so I feel like I'm more bad than good anymore. I'm trying to fight it, but I've been fighting it for years and I'm starting to get tired. There's been a few times where I've zoned out and I swear to God she's taken over, but I can't prove it yet. "I wish you'd stop. She's not your patient. I am."

"I know you are, but that's not what we're talking about at the moment," he replies. "Please answer my question. Are your nightmares getting worse?"

I bring my foot up onto the chair, hug my knee to my chest, and rest my chin on top of it. "Maybe I don't have anything to say anymore." I pause, contemplatively. I need a detour from my nightmares. I don't want to talk about how every night, late at night, and sometimes even during the day, I see things that normal people never would. Blood. Screams. Fire. My hands taking the lives of others.

I open my mouth to say… well, I'm not even sure what, but the darkness within me takes hold and I'm no longer just Maddie. "Or maybe it's just your dazzling, prince charming looks that have me all distracted. Perhaps that boy band combo you got going on." I lift my hand and gesture at his blond hair, blue eyes, dimples, GQ suited, boyish good looks that I'm sure many women are drawn to. "It's very hard to form words when I pretty much have my own Ken doll right in front of me." I've actually always despised Ken dolls or at least, I think I did.

After the accident, my mom gave me boxes of my old stuff, full of things like toys, drawings, clay vases and sculptures. There were a few Barbie and Ken dolls in it and all the Ken doll's heads were ripped off. I wonder what it means. What was going on through my head when I did it? Whether I popped the heads off the doll because I thought he cheated on Barbie or something, or if maybe I just enjoyed the act of popping off his head.

Preston frowns as he squirms uncomfortably in his chair. "I thought we discussed that you can't flirt or flatter me anymore. It's wrong and I can't allow it." He's been saying that for years and yet, he never actually does anything about it.

"Oh, it's not flattery, Preston," I say, lowering my foot to the floor and leaning forward in the chair, tucking a strand of my chin-length black hair behind my ear. “Because I’m not a fan of Ken dolls.” Under no control of my own, I wink at him. Actually wink. Jesus.

He shakes his head, reaching for his pencil again. “Please stop that.”

“Sorry.” There’s a hint of sincerity in my voice. I’m so confused at this point. Who’s really in control over me? Maddie? Lily? It is nearly impossible to tell anymore.

He scratches down some notes on a piece of yellow legal paper. “You say you don’t like Ken dolls, but how do you know that for sure?” he asks. I’m not quite sure if he’s using Ken doll as a metaphor or not, but regardless, I find it amusing. “Is it because of something you remember? Or is it just a hunch you have?”

“A hunch that I don’t like plastic, blond haired, anatomically incorrect dolls?” I ask and when he nods, completely serious, Lily orders for me to have fun with him. Play a game with him, like cat and mouse. I’m conflicted whether to listen to her—always am—but in the end, I begrudgingly give in. “Well, I’m not sure if it’s a memory per se,” I tap my finger on my chin, “so much as a dream I keep having?”

“Is it different from the dream you normally have?” he asks and I nod. Curiosity crosses his expression. “And what happens in this dream?”

“Headless dolls are walking around everywhere.”

“And are the dolls doing anything in particular as they walk around?”

"Yeah, they're biting each other, like zombies." I slant forward, cup my hand to the side of my mouth, and lower my voice. "And the strange part is, that whenever I wake up, I have the strangest desire to go find a doll and eat it."

He looks disgusted for the briefest second and then his repulsion shifts to irritation as I relax back in my chair, crossing my leg. Lily quiets down as she gets the satisfaction she desires and I can sit lighter because of it.

"Relax. I'm just fucking with you, Preston."

He frowns disapprovingly. "Maddie, you know as well as I do that every time you lie, it makes it harder for me to believe you."

"Maybe that's what I want."

"No, I think it's your way of avoiding the truth and what you're most afraid of."

"I don't know what you mean," I say calmly, despite the fear within me. *Did he finally discover my secret?*

He gives me a sympathetic look. "I know it's hard to think about, but it has to bother you—the fact that you may never truly remember anything before the accident."

I relax, but try to appear heartbroken on the outside because that's what he expects me to do. "But the idea that I might scares me." I press my hand to my heart, like it aches to speak of, when really I feel nothing at all. It's so hard to explain what it's like. Not knowing anything about yourself, yet I'm supposed to be at a point in my life where I've got it all figured out. I don't have anything figured out. Not even my name. Sometimes, not even who I am...

He nods understandingly. "That's an understandable fear. I'm sure anyone in your situation would probably feel the same way."

Oh, I doubt anyone is feeling how I feel most days, except for maybe serial killers. And maybe a dominatrix.

"So what do you suggest I do?" I ask, lowering my hand from my heart and sitting back in the chair. "To help calm the fear?"

"Talk about it," he suggests, thrumming his fingers on top of the folder. "It's what we really need to start working on during these sessions. Talking and communicating."

"You say that all the time, yet we never get anywhere," I mutter. Sometimes I wonder why I keep coming to these sessions, now that I'm an adult. The only reason I ever started was because my mother made me after the accident. She was worried about my heath due to the trauma I'd been through, even though I can't even remember most of it. "But how am I supposed to talk about things with someone I don't trust?"

"You don't trust me?" he asks. "After all these years?"

I look at him. Eyes so full of concern. So nice. Polite. It seems perfectly reasonable that I'd like and trust him, but Lily won't allow it. "You have to earn trust, just like you said. And so far, I feel like you haven't."

He sits up straight in the chair. "You can trust me. Anything that's said in here is strictly confidential." I swear it's like he's waiting for a confession.

"I know that." I scratch at the back of my neck. *Yeah, you say that now, but I'm sure the feeling would change the moment my real thoughts spill out of me.*

He opens his mouth to say something, but his eyes skim over my face and he must see something that makes him hesitate. I wonder what it is. My facade? Lily? What does he see in me? I wish I knew. Understood. What's living inside me? The thoughts of harming people. Killing them. The way Lily controls me at times and how sometimes I just want to give into her because fighting is physically and emotionally draining.

"How about we switch to a hypnotherapy session?" he says, setting his pen and folder aside on his desk.

"We're really going to do that?" My expression sinks at the idea of being under and having no control over myself—over Lily. "I thought you were joking when you suggested that last time."

"Why would I joke about that, Maddie?"

"Because it never worked when you tried a few years ago, so there's no point in trying it again."

"This method is a little different than the one we used a few years ago," he says, rolling up his sleeves like he's preparing to fight.

"What's your different method? Beating me up?" I joke to distract myself from what's about to happen.

He gives me the fourth look of disappointment for the day. "No, Maddie. I'm not going to beat you up." His voice is tolerant. "Look, if you don't want to do this, you don't have to. You don't have to do anything in here that you don't want to. You know that." He pushes his chair back from his desk. "But I'd really like it if you did."

I consider what he said with hesitancy. "You really think it might help bring my memories back?"

"Possibly. There've been a few recorded cases that this particular hypnotherapy has helped patients with memory loss." He begins rummaging around in his desk drawer, digging around through countless amounts of pens and neon sticky notes until he finds an iPod.

Optimism. It's something I don't have when it comes to my memories returning to me. My amnesia didn't come from just a bump to the head. I have Psychogenic Amnesia, which more than likely means there was some sort of stress factor that played a part in why I have no idea who the hell I was before the age of fifteen.

I shrug and get to my feet, being tolerant with Preston because I know if I don't do this, he'll just bug me until I do. It's been done a handful of other times to me and he never can get me to go under. "If that's what you think will help, then I'll give it a go." I amble toward the leather lounge chair in the corner of the room and he follows me with a notepad and pencil in hand. "But I'm a total pessimist that this—or anything else—will ever work."

"Pessimism isn't going to help you improve either." He sits down in a chair and places the notepad on his lap, close enough now that I can smell cigarette smoke on him. "Let's try to think positive."

"Wow, you really are a Ken doll today, aren't you? All perfect and positive," I mutter, lying down on the lounge chair on my back. I overlap my hands on my stomach and stare up at the ceiling. "Okay, let's get this show on the road," I say in a false cheerful voice. Then I glance over at him. "Was that optimistic enough for you?"

"I guess so." He's getting irritated. I wonder if he gets this way with all of his patients.

Leaning over to the side, he extends his arm toward a package of matches beside a candle. He strikes a match and lights each one then moves his finger to an iPod dock on a nearby shelf. He scrolls through the list of titles then ultimately clicks on a tune that sounds like rain pitter-pattering against a surface.

I hate the sound of rain and the smell of it. I think that's why he chose this one—because it was raining that night—and I don't appreciate him going there. I don't like the sound of rain and everything it represents. My loss of everything.

"Can't we listen to something else?" I squirm in the chair. "Maybe something a little less naturey?"

"Listening to this is an important part of the treatment." He relaxes back in his seat, eyes on me as he puts the end of his pen up to his lips. "I'm trying to take you back to the day of the accident—to the day you lost your memories."

"But I hate remembering that day," I say. It's the most vivid memory I have. I can still feel the coldness of the rain. The blood soaking my hair. The pain in my body. The way my heart thrashed in response to the fear. The car in the street; the car that hit me then took off.

Everyone said I was lucky to have such minimal injuries on my body, considering I'd been hit on a highway where the speed limit is sixty-five. I don't call it luck because part of me doesn't fully believe I was accidentally ran over. What happened though is a mystery.

Maybe I threw myself in front of the car. Maybe I wanted to die. Maybe I'd gotten into some trouble with the strange man. Or maybe I just wanted to forget whoever I was. Maybe this disgustingness that's inside me now was in me then and I just wanted to get rid of it.

"Maddie, relax. Take a deep breath and try to clear your head," Preston advises, taking a deep inhale and exhale himself.

Clear my head? Impossible. How can I when someone else is living inside it? I shut my eyes anyway.

*Pitter-patter. Pitter-patter. Pitter-patter.* The rain from the speakers flows and surrounds me until it gives me a headache.

"Just relax," Preston says softly through the rhythm of the rainfall. Now *he's* giving me a headache. "Breathe in and out."

I suck in a breath of air and let it out.

In and out.

Over and over again.

Pitter-patter... Pitter-patter... Pitter-patter... the rain is falling... Through it, there's a spark of light. I've seen it before. Heard the voice that whispers help. Seen the flames. Burning... burning... burning... and burning me along with them.

## Chapter 2
## Maddie

"What just happened?" I open my eyes and rub them with the palms of my hand. I'm still lying in the lounge chair, the sound of rain flowing from the speakers, this strange sense of lost time floating around inside my head.

Preston is staring at me with a quizzical expression, pen in hand, the tip pressed to the paper. "I think you fell asleep." He scratches his head then reaches over and silences the rainfall sounds. "Do you feel different? Remember anything at all?"

I shake my head, pushing myself up into sitting position, swinging my legs over the edge of the chair, and planting my feet on the floor. "Nope. My mind's still as blank as ever, although I'm tired as hell." I pause, rubbing my eyes again. God, I feel like I'm hung-over; my head is throbbing and my eyes feel like they're on fire.

Glancing at the clock, I notice my session has ended. I push to my feet. "Well, this has been extremely great, Preston. Seriously, the powernap was amazing, but it's time for me to go."

"Wait. Are you sure nothing happened at all?" he asks as I pick up my bag from off the floor beside the door. "You didn't see anything… maybe something you thought was a dream?"

"Nope, other than I got a good, dreamless nap, zilch happened," I lie as Preston gets up from his chair and wanders back over to his desk. "How long was I out for?"

He checks his watch. "About ten minutes." He lets his arms fall to the side. "Although I'm extremely disappointed, I have to say I'm not surprised. The studies I read through said in the beginning a lot of patients simply got drowsy. Hopefully next time we can progress further into it."

"Next time?" Sighing, I turn around to face him. He's standing behind his desk, loosening his tie as he gathers papers on his desk into a stack. "We're doing this again? Really, Preston? I thought we decided a long time ago that hypnotherapy was not the way to go."

"I know, but this way is different and I'd like to keep trying it, just for a little while." Flicking the top button of his shirt, he undoes the collar. His finger must snag the button though, because it ends up falling off and onto his desk. He doesn't seem to notice however, taking off his tie completely and setting it aside. "But only if it's okay with you."

I want to say no, but I'm distracted by the button. *Pick it up. Pick it up!* A sickness of mine. The need to pick up every single fallen button. "I guess so," I mumble, sliding the handle of my bag onto my shoulder, trying to ignore the compulsion to pick up the button.

*Pick it up,* Lily entices.

*No fucking way,* I reply. *I already told you, it's crazy to do that.*

*Everyone's crazy in their own way.*

"Good, I'm glad you're onboard with this," Preston says, turning around to search through a stack of papers on the filing cabinet behind the desk while I zone in on the button.

*Pick it up. Pick it up. Pick it up.*

Shaking my head at myself, I quickly reach over the desk and snatch up the button before he can turn around. I stuff it into my pocket. As always, I wonder why I do it, but never have been able to stop myself.

"This hypnotherapy is a little controversial," Preston continues, oblivious to what I just did as he faces me with a paper in his hand, "but I think at this point in your recovery, controversial methods might be the only options."

"Whatever you think. You are the doctor after all." I point to his PhD on the wall, black bold letters with his name on it, nonchalant as can be, like I didn't just steal a button like a psychopathic button kleptomaniac. "Or at least, according to that you are."

He offers me a small smile. "I'll see you next Tuesday, Maddie."

I wave as I walk out the door, keeping a neutral expression until I get outside and into the open. Then I breathe for the first time today, because soon, I'll be at work and I won't have to try so hard to hide Lily anymore.

## Chapter 3
## Maddie

I once spent an entire day doing research about "voices in my head." The findings where alarming. Psychosis. Schizophrenia. Multiple Personality Disorder. I'm sure if I told Preston, he'd crack open my head and give me a diagnosis but, that would mean living with the results. I'd no longer be able to hide the insanity—I'd have to accept what was wrong with me. So, I try to keep Lily locked up the best that I can, only letting her out when I know it won't harm anyone. Like when I go to work.

After my therapy session, I go home to watch the channel nine news at six o'clock, a habit of mine that started while I was in the hospital. It's the local station and, living in the small town of Grove, Wyoming, not too much goes on. Fire at the old millhouse, lost bike, found bike, car accident down on 5th Monroe and Maple drive. No injuries, just damage to the cars, which is causing traffic to back up. Alternative route suggestions. Then, a quick clip on how to make pumpkin spice cake. Laughs, smiles, laughs.

*Yeah, get on with the good stuff*, Lily whispers.

The brief five minutes when the station gives a section to a more global headline, the brief insight to the grimier stuff, well, usually anyway. Today ends up being a brief update on the disappearance of a girl, but there's no details other than she's been gone for a week and is still missing. "*Keep an eye out everyone. And if you have any information at all, call this number.*"

"Maddie, would you turn that off," my mother shouts from the kitchen. "I hate it when you watch the news. Please, find something else to watch." She says this every day. I'm not sure what bothers her about it, but for some reason, she seems dead set on me not watching the news.

I click off the television halfway through the clip. It's nearing five thirty, so I decide to go into my room to change into my go-to-work uniform. It's a little early for work, but if I leave now, I can make a much-needed extra stop on the way.

My room is a very stressful place. My mother decided to put up every single photo of me she could find, hoping it would spark my memory. All of them were taken before the age of thirteen because I got really camera shy when I hit my teenage years, something revealed to me in one of my mom's stories she loves to tell about me.

There are some of just me, some with her, and none with my father. Some of them are torn, like she ripped someone out of the photo. All the photos feel like pieces of paper to me, nothing more. And it makes me uncomfortable that I have to stare at multiple versions of myself every time I step in there, always feeling like I'm being watched by myself.

I turn on some music and then rummage through my dresser for something to wear, occasionally glancing over the walls and ceiling, cringing at how happy I look in most of the photos; all sunshine and rainbows, like there was no bad in the world. But there is. Just turn on the news. Just live inside my head for five minutes.

Sometimes, the girl in the photos doesn't even look like me when I stare at her long enough. Like she's just someone who shared the same face, but had different thoughts and values.

After selecting an outfit, I close my dresser and start getting dressed. Slacks and a button down shirt, done up all the way to my chin. Black hair combed and gelled into place, so it's plastered straight at the side of my defined cheekbones. Minimal makeup, so my freckles are visible. No jewelry. Hideous loafers. This was how I dressed before the accident, I've been told. And the dresser full of stuffy and boring attire confirmed this. That this is who I am. *Maddie Ashford. Boring. Simple. Preppy. Conservative. I am Maddie and I look like a banker.*

*You were a good girl, Maddie.*

*You always did what was right.*

*Always followed the rules.*

*Never got into trouble.*

I glance in the mirror, seeing the girl my mother described to me after I'd woken up and asked who I was, yet at the same time, not seeing. Honestly, I look confused—always do. Like I'm trapped behind a face I don't recognize.

*I am hiding behind a mask.*

*I'm hiding behind my amnesia.*

*I'm hiding.*

*Lost.*

*Lost.*

*Lost.*

*Drifting.*

Part of me wishes I could be that girl she described, but most of me knows that I can't be that person. Sighing at the thought, I pick up my discarded pants and reach into the pocket, retrieving the button I stole from Preston earlier today. I hate that I do it. In fact, it makes me sick that every time I see a stray button, I have to collect it. Not any fallen button either, just ones off people's shirts, like some sort of strange OCD habit.

It's not a new habit either, something I discovered one day going through my old boxes of stuff. I came across a wooden box one day that was full of buttons in various colors, shapes and sizes. I thought about asking my mother why I had it, but quite honestly, it's something I feel like I should keep a secret. Crazy, like Lily.

Going into my closet, I stand up on my tiptoes and grab the box from the top shelf. Lifting the lid, I drop the new button into it, feeling a brief moment of gratification; but the feeling goes away the instant I put the lid on, as if I'm shutting a door closed that carries secrets to myself.

After I put the box back on the shelf, I go into the kitchen, where my mom is cooking over the stove. The air smells like chocolate and cinnamon and there's dough all over the countertops. She has her apron on, the fabric covered in melted chocolate and flour. There's even some in her greying hair.

She has her back to me, but hears me come in and peers over her shoulder. "Oh, you're ready early today," she says as she skims over my outfit and gives me an approving look. "You look very nice, Maddie." She walks up and smoothes the invisible wrinkles in my shirt.

I give her a tight smile as she brushes her hand over my head, putting some of my stray hairs into place. "Thanks."

I sometimes wonder if she still sees her little girl when she looks at me, the one I don't know, but who she likes to remind me once existed. That needs to be taken care of.

My mom's not a terrible person. She's nice, caring, giving, although she worries about me way too much and is very controlling. But any faults of hers can be blamed on her twenty-one year old daughter still living with her who can't remember anything before the age of fifteen.

It's not like I want to be living with her still, but every time I suggest moving out, she says I need to act more responsibly. But I feel like I am. I have a job. I can dress myself. Make decisions. Granted, maybe they're not always the best. However, I'm not incompetent and I wish she'd realize that. Although, sometimes I think she does know it and she just has issues with letting me go.

I'm the only child and my father passed away when I was seven, something told to me in a very rushed story. "*He died in a car accident*," my mother told me when I asked her once. "*That's all you need to know*." Then she dismissed the conversation by leaving the room. I'm guessing it's too painful for her to talk about, so I don't bring it up, even though Lily tries to get me to all the time.

"Did you remember to pack your scarf and gloves just in case it snows tonight and the car won't start?" my mother asks, interrupting my thoughts. She's packing a bag of cookies for me like I'm going to school and she needs to make my lunch. "I hate that you work clear out in the middle of nowhere."

"Yes, Mother." The possibility of it snowing is slim to none, but arguing with her does no good, something I've learned over the last few years.

"And you remembered to put your paycheck in your purse so you can deposit it, right?" She hands me the bag of cookies with worry all over her weathered face.

I nod, patting my purse as I drop the bag of cookies into it, trying to resist the urge to mess around with the collar on the shirt that's so tight I feel like I'm being strangled. "Yes, I have everything I need, so can I please go to work now?"

Her worry increases, making more lines appear on her face. I saw pictures of her a few years before my accident and there were hardly any lines at all, but six months after, wrinkles were flourishing all over. "Maddie, since you're leaving early, can you please stop by and put that check in this time? If you keep forgetting, then it's going to expire and then it isn't going to be any good anymore."

"I know that." I reach for my coat draped on the back of the kitchen chair. "And I promise I'll put it in." But I won't because I'm making a stop somewhere else, the same stop I make every couple of days, the one stop that makes being two people just a little bit easier.

"I'm worried about you, Maddie," she says. "You've been so irresponsible lately. With the checks. Coming home late. It's so unlike you and it worries me that maybe something's going on with you that you're not telling anyone." She stares me straight in the eyes without blinking and it wigs me out.

"Nothing's going on." *Unlike you. Seriously?* I bite down on my lip, trying to stop myself from saying it, but the urge overpowers me. "How do I know for sure if it's unlike me," I sputter. "I mean, are you really sure that six years ago I wasn't irresponsible? Maybe I'm returning to my old self again."

She either looks horrified or extremely angry—. I can't one-hundred percent tell which one, but thank God it gets her to blink again. "Let's get one thing straight," she snaps. "You were never irresponsible. You never talked back. Never did anything wrong. You were the perfect daughter and never think otherwise."

I want to drop it, but Lily is persistent. "No matter how many times you say that, it seems highly implausible. No one is perfect." I should just stop there. She seems frazzled and usually I don't try to push her buttons, but I'm not sure I'm really myself at the moment. Lily feels very powerful, Maddie really tired, and I'm starting to wonder if the hypnotherapy set something off. "Besides, you say all these things about me—that I was responsible, never talked back, a good girl—yet it doesn't feel like that's my nature."

"Maddie Asherford." Her tone carries a warning as she reaches to turn the oven timer off as it buzzes. "You're a good person. You're just confused because you can't remember anything—all the good stuff you did." She pauses. "Preston said you've been a little uncooperative the last few sessions. Is there anything you want to talk about?" she asks, reaching out and petting my head again. "Anything at all."

Anger flares up inside me. "Preston's not supposed to be talking to you about what goes on in therapy," I say in a low tone that startles us both. I'm not even sure why this is bothering me so much. "It's confidential."

She flinches at the tone of my voice and her hand stops moving over my head, but remains there. "I asked him to tell me today if you were doing okay or not, considering you've been a little out of it at home."

"You have no right!" My voice cuts through the air like a knife as I tighten my jaw and lean against the countertop.

"I have every right, Maddie. And you won't talk to me like that. I'm your mother and everything I do is to help you, whether you can see that or not." There's this plea in her eyes, begging me to stop. "Please start trying to act like the daughter I used to know again. It feels like I haven't seen her in weeks."

I want to say a million things to her, tell her everything. How I feel. How I walk around in this world, being told what I was, how I used to act, yet no one understands that that person doesn't exist anymore. She died the moment she woke up in the street;

bloody, mangled, and a bundle of confusion. And that I don't believe I was ever a good person considering how fucked up I am now. I think, like humans in general, she believes what she wants to believe because it helps her sleep at night and be able to get out of bed in the morning.

"Fine, Mother. I'm a good girl and I'll do what I'm told." It's the biggest bunch of bullshit. I can only be what I can be and right now, that's a mixture of a lost girl named Maddie, who wonders why she ran out in front of the car in the first place; and a girl named Lily who wants to believe that I chose to forget all of my memories for a reason. Someone who is good and bad. Who rebels, yet sometimes wants to obey. Breaks rules and follows. Craves danger and fears it. Basks in the darkness and embraces the craziness living inside her, and who sometimes cries over it.

My mom looks partially convinced then hugs me and returns to the kitchen to take out the next sheet of cookies from the oven. "Call me if you need anything."

"I will," I say, stepping toward the door, the toe of my shoe slipping into the sunlight, me inching my way to freedom.

Lily starts to stir inside me. *Let me out. Let me out. I need to breathe.*

I take another step and then another, waiting for my mom to say anything else. When she starts to hum under her breath, picking up the spatula on the countertop to scoop the cookies up, I know that the conversation has ended and I'm dismissed.

I swing open the back door and hurry outside into the frosted driveway where my car is parked. I try to keep Lily still inside me for just a few minutes longer. Try to keep myself contained just enough so that I can get out of the driveway and down the road to the corner. She's restless, and by the time I'm pulling into the driveway of a quaint antique shop on the corner, I'm practically hyperventilating in my seat to get out of these stuffy clothes and into something else.

The lights are off in the building, the closed sign up. I leave the engine running as I hop into the backseat, tousling my fingers through my hair, freeing my gel sustained locks. I pick out a nasty clump of it and flick it onto the floor. Then I kick my shoes off, remove my pants, and unbutton the stuffy shirt, breathing the fresh air in with each button unfastened. When I shuck it all off, I feel like I've shed off all my skin and air can finally get to my pores, only it still feels like there's a layer of dirt on my skin, filthy, disgusting. *I can breathe again.* I feel both disgusted and pleased with myself for feeling this way. Confliction. It's become my middle name.

Beneath the banker-like attire, I'm wearing a short, tight, black *Metallica* shirt and leather pants. I'm a biker chick today and maybe tomorrow, I'll be mod. I change my look quite frequently. Play different characters, trying to discover my true identity, waiting to feel a spark inside me that says, *hey, that has to be me*. But as usual, I feel disconnected, so I'm guessing I wasn't a biker badass in my previous life.

After I adjust the shirt into place over the massive scar on my side, I get back into the driver's seat. Road rash, I was told, scraped quite a few layers off my ribs and left a massive, gnarly scar about the size of my fist. It's sort of hideous, but there are worse things in life.

I also have one on the palm of my hand where I was gripping the object that cut open my skin. It kind of looks like a burn mark with these weird diamond shaped patterns attached to a long thing line that teethes out at the bottom. When I squint closely at it, I can almost make out the number fourteen in the center of it.

Once my outfit's in place, I reach under the seat of the car and grab the duffel bag I keep hidden there. I take out my leather collar and matching bracelets, hoop earrings, and my lace-up boots. After I put them all on, I apply red lipstick and kohl eyeliner and then grab my pack of cigarettes, feeling inner peace for the first time today, free.

Glancing in the rearview mirror, the confusion in my eyes from earlier has settled as I light up my cigarette. Smoke encircles my face. I'm smiling at the same time tears are rolling down my face. I feel darkened. Sedated. Just like my soul. But as I pull away, heading to my secret spot to see my secret friend, I feel even more hope of some sort of peace for the day because where I'm going I can be anyone. Good or bad.

## Chapter 4
## Maddie

I discovered this place about a year after the accident. I was having a hard day because I felt like I was about to fall out of my skin. I'd spent hours listening to my mother recollect memories of me as a child, good ones. Her eyes were so full of hope and, by the time she was done, I wanted to end it all. Throw myself out the window or run into the street again. Not exist in the confusion that had taken over me. But I talked myself out of it—or Lily did, anyway.

Despite it all, I had to get out of the house and away from my mother's smothering, so I took a joyride. I was sixteen and technically didn't have my driver's license yet, but I could drive. And boy did I drive. Up and down the town, through the neighborhoods. But it wasn't enough.

I needed to go someplace further, away from everything, where I could breathe again. So I headed down the highway toward the foothills with no real destination in mind and ended up on a turnout on a dirt road that wove through the trees. The area seemed familiar, but then again, all the foothills looked the same.

Eventually, the road came to a dead end, where the trees opened up a little and I got a full view of the town below. Nearby, surrounded by dead grass and dying flowers, was a log cabin. I found it fascinating to look at, out there in the trees, untouched. It was beautifully haunting and I instantly fell in love with it and everything that it represented. And my love for the place only grew when I discovered Ryland living in it, a guy who seemed just about as broken as me.

At first, he didn't seem too fond of me just walking into his house. Quite honestly, I'd thought it was vacant when I'd entered and was startled by the fact that someone was living in the minimally furnished house. Except, Ryland is a minimal person, something I quickly found out and thankfully, I quickly wore on him enough for him to let me keep visiting, because the cabin—he is my sanctuary.

On my way up to the cabin today, I pick up takeout for Ryland and me to eat. After I pick up the food, I make the ten-minute drive up the hill, my heart leaping with excitement the closer I get. It's the only time my pulse ever does that—usually it's out of fear.

By the time I spot the cabin, I feel elated. Whole. At peace with myself, whoever I might be. I park the car just a ways off then slip on my jacket and grab the bag of food before climbing out of the car. I take my time walking through the dried out grass, the cool breeze caressing my cheeks and whispering through my hair. I feel a sense of tranquility up here with the town below, in the distance, where I have to live my life as someone I don't think I am.

"I didn't think you'd show up." As soon as I hear Ryland's voice floating from the cracked window of the cabin, a smile touches my lips. A real one, too, not the fake one I show everyone else.

Even though I can't see him, only hear him, I know he's inside—he's always in there. I pick up my pace across the field, feeling myself getting closer to him.

"I told you I'd be back," I call out. "I'll always come back, Ryland."

"You say that now, but one day, you'll stop coming up here," he utters softly. I see his shadow cast across the window as I approach the front door. There are bits of logs and bricks piled out front in the yard and the entire house looks like it needs a bit of maintenance, but to me, it just makes it look more welcoming—ruined, rundown, imperfect.

"Never." I duck my head below the low porch and step inside, the floorboards creaking beneath my shoes. The roof showers a bit of dust on my head and I brush some off my hair as I walk toward the living room where there's a rocking chair and a fireplace, along with a window. Rays of sunlight glimmer through the glass as I take a seat on the rug on the floor.

I set the bag down and relax back on my hands, tipping my head back and basking in the warmth of the sunlight through the window as it kisses my face. I wait for Ryland to come to me—always do. He's skittish, something I learned when I first met him and he barely would talk to me or stand near me. He has social anxiety and a bit of agoraphobia because of something that has happened to him in his life—he's never given me the exact details, only that he never can leave this place. He's not crazy or anything, despite what some people might think. I've been coming up here for six years to visit him and he only makes me feel safe and welcome.

"I brought you food," I entice, without opening my eyes. "You better hurry up before it gets cold."

I hear him chuckle, this low chuckle that makes me shiver in ways I'm not comfortable with, whether I'm Maddie or Lily, because it confuses me. No one makes me feel the way that Ryland does and it seems like every time I come up here, he brings out another new emotion I have to spend days figuring out. And by the time I've figured it out, a new ones arose.

"You really think I mind if my food is cold?" he asks. I feel the warmth of the sunlight leave my face and I know he's right in front of me.

I peek open my eyes and smile up at him. "Took you long enough."

He shakes his head, almost smiling, but it doesn't reach his eyes—never does. "That's because I was hoping you'd leave me."

"When will you start realizing you're good enough for me to visit," I say to him as I sit up, taking in the sight of him.

He's always wearing a plaid shirt with missing buttons over a t-shirt and his jeans are so worn there's several holes all over them. He's around my age with sandy, untamed hair that flips up near his ears and hangs in his eyes. His eyes are actually strange in a fascinating way. Two different colors if you look closely; one green and the other a greenish blue, almost like he could be two different people completely, depending on which angle you look at him. His legs are long, body lean. He has smudges of dirty skin through the holes in his clothes.

If I was an artist, I'd draw him all the time, something I actually looked into after the accident when I felt this dire need to sketch. Turns out, I was never an artist, or at least, said my fucked up doodle of what was supposed to be a tree and some flowers, but sort of looked like a garden gnome stepping on ants when I closed one eye and stared at it.

"When will you realize I'm not good enough for you to waste your time with? You really should let me go," he replies. I stare at him and he stares back. There's this unspoken rule that whoever looks away first, loses. He always loses. Finally he sighs, sitting down on the air mattress beside me. "Fine, you win for today."

I grin. "I always win." I nudge the food bag toward him and he reluctantly takes it, putting it on his lap without opening it up.

He gazes off at the window across from us. Through it, I can see the quiet city below and the leafless trees. "Sometimes, I feel like it's moving farther away," he utters quietly without taking his eyes off the town.

"Maybe that means you should go down there," I say, taking in his profile, his nose, his lips, the ones that I want to taste, yet I don't at the same time because I'm scared. "Maybe it's time to leave this place."

"I can't." He says it so soundlessly I barely hear him.

"Why not?"

His jaw tightens and then he whispers, "Please don't start today. I'm begging you."

I sigh and give him what he asks. He's the only person I'll do that with.

Silence stretches between us, but it's comfortable. There are some days where I come up here and neither of us says anything at all to each other. Those are near perfect days.

"So, do you want to tell me what's on your mind today?" he asks, opening the takeout bag and peeking inside.

I shake my head and flop back on the mattress, draping my arm over my forehead. “Not really.” I shut my eyes and relax.

*Do you feel that, Maddie?*

*The peace.*

There’s a pause and then he lies down beside me, close enough that I can feel his presence, but far enough that we’re not touching. We’ve actually never touched and I could blame it on the fact that he’s so skittish, but I’d be lying to myself if I did. The real reason is me. I’m afraid—afraid that the peace I get coming here will change somehow if we touch.

“Are you sure? Because you seem sad,” he says.

“I always seem sad,” I remind him. “And so do you.”

Another pause and I secretly hope that he’ll tell me why he’s sad, why he lives here in the middle of nowhere—anything really, because I know nothing about him. I once offered for us to move in together so he wouldn’t have to be so lonely, but he said he couldn’t. So all I can do is cross my fingers that one day, whatever’s keeping him here, will finally let him go.

“It’s getting worse,” I eventually say, cracking the silence. “Lily… It feels like she’s gaining more control over my mind.” It’s amazing how easy it is to talk to him about this stuff, how freeing it is, if only for a moment.

"I don't think you should worry about her so much." He never judges, never seems afraid; accepts me for who I am. "You need to stop fearing who you are and just be yourself."

"But I don't even know who I am," I reply, desperate to reach over and hold his hand, finally touch him. Again, I'm afraid of what will change between us if we touch.... afraid he'll disappear... or maybe I will. "Maddie... Lily... They're supposed to be two different people, but both of them feel like me. God, I sound so crazy."

"Crazy's not always such a bad thing. You can be two people, Maddie, if that's how you feel. Be whoever makes you happy," he says, shifting his weight. I feel the sunlight vanish and when I open my eyes, I find him leaning over me, eyes warm and caring. "And I think everyone's got a little crazy in them, but have a hard time admitting it exists."

"I can't admit it exists," I admit, thinking about what he said. Be whoever makes me happy? I'm not sure who that is. "I can only imagine what would happen if I did."

He acts like he's going to reach out and touch me, but then withdraws his hand back to his side. "You admit it to me."

"But everything's easier with you."

This seems to sadden him. He frowns, forehead creased. I wonder what he's thinking. What he's feeling. I wonder what I'm feeling. More unspoken words pile up between us as he sighs and lies back down beside me. The quiet sinks in, surrounds us, consumes us. I can almost feel us shifting to another place and time, where I'm somewhere different—less confused. He's happy. I'm happy—free.

"She's always quiet when I'm with you," I divulge more of myself. "Lily. She hardly ever says anything to me. I think it's because she likes you… She doesn't like anyone but you."

"And that's a good thing, right?" he asks. "I mean, not the not liking me part, but that she's quiet?"

I want to say yes, but I can't find my voice at the moment. Yes, Lily drives me crazy, makes me feel like I'm crazy; but at the same time, I feel lost without her. Like a part of me dies when she's quiet. I hate the feeling; that I'm drifting away from reality when I'm not insane. Honestly, it makes no sense, yet it does. Even though I hate to admit it, Lily is a part of me. And no matter how much I despise her, she might always be.

## Chapter 5
## Maddie

I leave the cabin and Ryland about an hour later, not to the bank to cash the check and not to the library where my mom thinks I work. I go to my real, Lily approved job down at the *Devil & Angels Bar.* I applied there about five months ago while I was working nights at the library. I was becoming so distracted by the idea of actually stabbing someone that I feared an impulsive murder was in the making. That's when Lily arose and enticed me to go down to the bar and do something more reckless and worth my time. I filled out an application for a dancer/bartender.

Even though I had no experience, the owner took one look at my curves and said I had the ideal look for the thirty to forty-year-olds that generally migrated there. I was hired on the spot and I quit my library job an hour after the interview zealously with a bow as I walked out of the door. I blame the latter on Lily because Maddie felt furious and somewhat embarrassed, like she does now in this slutty outfit. She even tried to convince me to tell my mother or therapist what was going on inside my head, but it never happened, and so my double life began.

I enter the bar where I'm greeted by Bella Anderfells, one of the waitresses/bartenders who I converse with a lot and who started working here a couple of months after I did. I'm actually not positive what our title is. Friendships baffle me and don't seem possible, except for maybe with Ryland and Bella. They are my two exceptions in this world where they are more than just a face and a name, who I don't feel like some strange alien creature around.

"Hey, Maddie," Bella says. She smiles as she strolls out from behind the bar, her cheeks rosy, her blond hair pinned up, her bangs framing her face. She's about twenty years older than me, but looks like she's in her thirties and dresses and acts like she's in her twenties. She told me once she has some sort of disorder that the doctors say make her act younger than she is, because she's trying to grasp onto something she lost when she was younger; her son and the man she was dating died in a fire. She said it so forwardly, so openly, and in a way, I envy her for it. To not fear the fact that she might be a little off. Maybe that's why I like her.

"How's it going, sweetie?" she asks. She kind of reminds me of a Barbie doll and I could see her going well with Preston, arms linked—heads on, of course. She exchanges kisses on the cheeks with me, a ritual she does with everyone she likes, then she backs up and adjusts her red tank top, rearranging it to show more of her cleavage.

"I'm fantastic." And at the moment, I do feel fantastic, like myself—Maddie and Lily are subdued and conjoined into one single person. Serenity. No extra voices. No feeling like I'm being pulled in two directions. Like I have control over myself, a feeling leftover from my visit with Ryland. I know from past experience that the sensation will linger for another hour or so and then the real world will catch up with me and *poof*, I'll be crazy Maddie/Lily again.

Bella picks up a rag and begins wiping the barstools down. "Did you hear about the party going on after hours tonight?"

"I didn't hear about it." I drop my bag behind the counter and then kick it into one of the bottom cubbies. "Who's having it? Glen or River?" Glen's the owner of the place and River is the manager, although it's just a side job for him until he gets out of grad school.

"River? Seriously?" She gapes at me because River hates parties and drinking.

He's a recovering alcoholic, something I discovered by accident one day when I crossed paths with him coming out of an AA meeting down on Broadway. At the time, I was coming out of my support group meeting, which was coincidently next door. He was extremely nervous and somewhat agitated that I suddenly knew something about him that he kept from almost everyone except his brother. He told me to please not tell anyone at the bar. When I asked how he even was able to work at a bar without giving in to his addiction, he simply said that some stuff had happened that made it nearly impossible for him to drink again. *That's what they all say,* I'd thought, but on the outside, I simply smiled. I'd kept his secret just like he'd asked.

After that, he started talking to me all the time during work hours, calling me up to his office for the vaguest reason, like to find out if we needed to order soap. I wasn't stupid. I could see the way that he looked at me. He wanted to fuck me and eventually, he put a move on me. Even though we haven't screwed yet, we still fool around all the time and I know he's waiting for me to give it up, which makes me never want to give it up.

"Maybe River decided to step out of his comfort zone," I say as she shakes her head, giving me a dirty look. "Oh, fine. No more jokes. Whose party is it?"

She continues to wipe the sticky residue that we all pretend is alcohol, when really it's a mixture of that and the residue leftover from sexual encounters that go on after hours at the bar. It's what made this place so intriguing to me in the first place. Dancing/bar until midnight then it shifts to a whorehouse. There are two sides to this place, just like there are two sides to me. I wonder if there are two sides to everything.

"It's one of Glen's acquaintances," she says, making air quotes because acquaintance means some rich guy who comes here to fuck around with women, do drugs, and pretty much everything that's illegal. She tosses the rag onto the countertop and turns to face me. "His name's Leon. I actually knew him in high school. He was arrested for drug trafficking or something, but he pretty much paid everyone off so he could get out of it."

"Leon... That name sounds familiar. Has he been here before?" I slip my jacket off and shove that into the cubby with my bag.

"Not since either one of us started working here." She shakes her head as she plops down onto the stool, props her elbow on the counter, and rests her chin on her hand. "I did hear that he just got acquitted for trafficking."

I try to shake off the unsettling feeling that's rising in my body. A feeling like something's set off a trigger in me, causing the hairs on my arms and neck to stand on end. It happens sometimes, usually when I'm being reintroduced to something from my past.

I glance around the bar to see if there's anything out of the ordinary. There's a guy in the back corner working on the ice machine, but he doesn't look familiar. Other than that, everything looks normal, yet I feel like it's not, like there's something else here I haven't seen before and it's seeing me.

*What is your problem?*

"So he's innocent, then... if he got acquitted?" I wiggle my neck and then pop my knuckles, trying to get myself... Lily—I can't tell who—to settle the fuck down. "I mean, no cops are going to show up and take this place down, right?" I hope not because I need this place.

"Yeah, he's innocent, according to the trial." She pats my arm, like she can sense I'm getting worked up. "Don't worry, Maddie. Everything's going to be okay. Just another day at the bar."

"I know... I just... I just need this job and I don't want anything to ruin it," I say, reaching for two shot glasses.

"The bar will be fine." She glances around then leans over the counter, lowering her voice. "But just to let you know, I've heard rumors that he got in pretty deep with trafficking and that someone tried to kill him and everything. The guy is super hardcore."

"Sounds dangerous and kind of mobsterish," I joke, trying to make myself feel less like I'm about to slip out of my skin, but it's not working.

"Yeah, it does," she says, biting her lip as she deliberates something then mutters, "Although, I do find it really weird that he got mixed up in it at all."

"Why?" I ask. She taps her fingers against the countertop, dazing off at something behind my shoulder and I wave my hand in front of her face. "Earth to Bella."

She blinks out of her trance and then laughs. "Sorry, I was just zoning off, thinking."

"About what?" I grab a bottle of vodka and unscrew the cap.

She shrugs. "High School and stuff. I used to know Leon back then and he never did seem like the type to turn into a criminal." She tucks a strand of her hair behind her ear. "In fact, he was sort of a nerd, even through college."

"So you know him, then?"

"Kind of. I mean, like I said, we went to school together, but we didn't run in the same group or anything. This will be our first time seeing each other in about ten years."

"Well, maybe his being a nerd was just a facade." It makes me wonder what I was like in high school—a good girl like my mom says, or maybe that was my facade. "Sometimes, people aren't what they seem on the outside. Plus, that was over twenty years ago. A lot can change over a couple of decades."

"Yeah, I guess, but still. It's so weird. Like he completely changed into a different person. Like he had this dark side and suddenly it came out of him."

She's making me feel really uncomfortable, to the point that I'm starting to sweat. I feel like I have this giant, crazy sign flashing above my head. I'm about to change the subject when she does it for me.

"All right, enough reminiscing," she says, her upbeat personality returning. "Pour me a drink."

"Okay, what do you want to start off with today?" I ask, setting the glasses down on the bar. The disconcerting feeling inside me, thank God, is cooling down. "Vodka? Whiskey? Tequila?"

"Just water," she replies, tucking a strand of her blond hair behind her ear. "I'm getting burnt out. In fact, I actually went to an AA meeting down on Broadway the other day to confess my sins about how much I've been drinking." She thrums her finger on her bottom lip. "Strangely, they were very unsympathetic."

"That's because AA is a recovery group." I shake my head, reaching for the Vodka. "Not a church."

She rolls her eyes. "You say potato; I say *potato*. Besides, I needed my support group fix."

"You need to stop doing that." I pour two shots of vodka, licking off a few drops that spill onto my hand. "People are really serious about that shit. Trust me. I used to go to one."

"To an AA meeting?"

"To a support group."

"For?"

I tap the side of my head and she nods, getting it. For my amnesia, although I think I could go to a Potential Killers Anonymous if one existed. Maybe there I could finally express what I was carrying around inside me. Maybe I could finally let Lily out for a moment and be okay with it.

"I sometimes forget that you've forgotten." She grins then scoops up the shot glass like she's going to make a toast. "And just so you know, I'm still going to go to the AA meetings. I met a hot guy there and now we're dating. And let me tell ya, the sex is amazing."

"Does he know you're not a recovering alcoholic?"

She bites her lip guiltily. "I haven't had the chance to mention it yet."

"Sure you haven't." I collect the other shot glass, spilling a little of the liquid. "You're so manipulative." *Isn't that the pot calling the kettle black?*

"So are you." She grins before downing her shot then she puts the glass down and goes over to the table area and begins putting down the chairs. I slam my warm-up shot back then begin to get ready to open up the bar, checking the glasses and alcohol bottles to see what all I need to get from the store. Glen usually doesn't show up until the afterhours, if at all, and River is always fashionably late, something he gets away with because he's Glen's baby brother by about twenty years.

After Bella and I get everything set up, I turn the lights and music on, while three of the other waitresses/dancers—Mindy, Sydney, and I think the other's name is Marilynn—get ready to open up. I try to remember names, but waitresses come and go here about as frequently as internet trends. I blame it on the high amount of males touching themselves at the tables and how the waitresses and dancers are just supposed to overlook it and "do our thing."

Sydney is the only waitress that's worked here for over two weeks. She's tall, leggy, and has a heart tattoo on her ankle that matches the little heart buttons on her shirt, that are actually kind of pretty. For a stupid moment, I picture myself plucking them off her shirt. She also doesn't like me at all. No surprise since most women tend to not like my blunt and bold personality. Plus, I think she has a thing for River. Honestly, I'm not even sure what the real foundation of this dislike is for me, other than her first day working here, she took one look at me and made this noise in the back of her throat that sounded an awful lot like disgust. Then she walked away, shaking her head, and that was that. She hates me and has acted upon the loathing several times over the last couple of weeks, including one very intense fight where I discovered that I don't fight like a girl. I kick and punch and can throw down like a guy, something Sydney and her nose didn't appreciate when I crashed my knuckles against it. She actually tried to get me fired, but luckily, Glen likes me.

As Sydney strolls by me today, she mutters under her breath, "Fucking slut. I know what you did the other night."

The other night? I have to think about what I did… Oh, that was the night she caught me and River in his office making out. I don't say anything to her because there's nothing to say.

"You know, you can be such a bitch," she says, picking up the pace just a little as she looks at me from over her shoulder. "I have no idea how River can even touch you. You're fucking pathetic and disgusting. You probably have herpes with how much of a *whore* you are. You've practically slept with everyone in this town."

I'm not a whore. Yes, I have sex, but not that much, and not with just anyone. It's all very high schoolish and I really just want to walk away, but I find myself standing there. The word *whore* has triggered an unexplainable rage within me. One that's so overpowering it drowns everything else around me out. My vision blurs. My hearing pops. My pulse hammers and a figure appears behind Sydney. He's not real—I've seen him before and know he's just an illusion—but every time it happens, it makes me sick to my stomach.

*You're a whore!*

*You're a whore!*

*You're a whore!*

It's not my voice inside my head. Not Lily's. It's male. Baritone. Angry. I've heard it before.

These episodes aren't new to me at all. I sometimes wonder if something from my past sets them off, but since I can't remember anything, I just get angry.

Enraged. It's so thick I can't see. I'm not mad over the insult at this moment, but sometime in my life, I have been. And sometime in my life, I've cowered like a child from the sound of it. I want to do it now, especially with the man staring at me with eyes I can't see and a face that's a shadow. I want to look away, wrap my arms around myself, and pretend to be somewhere else. Surrender and give up.

*You will not. You can't just stand around and let this go on. Take her out. Stop being Maddie.*

"I don't know how," I whisper, my body starting to tremble as I grip onto the chair for support because my knees are about to buckle. The man fades in and out of focus.

*You're a whore!*

*Make her hurt. Like you're hurting. Don't be weak. Make her suffer.*

## Chapter 6
## Lily

As soon as I get control, the imaginary man vanishes because I have more power over the mind than to let the ghost memory remain there, attempting to torment me.

"I'm not a fucking whore," I say in a level voice. Sydney's lucky we're in a crowded place, otherwise, this would all be over within the snap of a finger. "And if you call me that again, you won't be walking away from me." My hands are calmly at my sides, my posture straight, gaze unwavering. I'm in more control than I've ever been, which is good. Maddie is weak and the most undecided person I've ever known. It's no wonder she needs me.

"Excuse me," Sydney says, inching toward me, but then rethinks it and retreats. "What's y-your deal," she stammers, bumping her hip against a chair.

"What's *my* deal?" I press my lips together, deciding how to go about this. If Maddie were completely silent, I'd probably knock her out and walk away from it. Suffer the consequences. It's not like I haven't done that before—suffered. And I can sure as hell do it again.

I take a few calculated steps toward her and slant my head to the side, inspecting blondie. "You really want to know what my deal is? *Really?*" My voice drips with sarcasm.

Sydney's lips part as if she's going to say something, but then she gets this frightened look and starts moving around quickly, practically jogging around the tables, ramming into some of them. All I can think of is tackling her down and enfolding my fingers around her neck. Strangle her, like I did to the man in the road. I want to so badly, but I know I can't, not with four sets of eyes on me.

I have to ball my hands into fists and stab my nails into my palms to contain my inner desires that I don't understand. I draw blood. Cut skin. It feels good, so I plunge my nails deeper into my skin. I don't move even when Sydney disappears into the back room. It's the hardest fucking thing I've ever had to do—not following after her.

*You're a whore!*

The voice is right—I am a whore. That among other things. I'm a sinner. A rebel. A punk. A psychopath, at least according to the voice. It's not like I chose to be this way. Shit has happened that created me. Shit I don't understand and don't really care to. All I care about at the moment is chasing after Sydney, pulling her hair out, making her bleed. Watching her veins pop open. Spilling blood. Making her pay for saying those things to me. Not being weak and letting myself get walked all over. That's Maddie's thing. I'm alive just thinking about it. Finally, I decide to give into it and let Maddie deal with it later. I step forward, ready to go through with it—rip her to shreds.

"You okay?" Bella touches my shoulder and I whirl around, almost hitting her in the face.

She blinks, stunned, surrendering her hands in front of her. I blink, nearly falling to the floor as it feels like a ghost rushes from my body and I've gone back into my hiding place, where I can't be seen. Locked up, just like always.

Story of my life for the last six years, ever since I lost control.

## Chapter 7
## Maddie

"Relax, Maddie." Bella lowers her hands only when I've taken a few breaths and calmed down. "Jesus, you really shouldn't let Sydney get to you. Trust me. It's her mission in life to get a rise out of people."

I nod, still unable to speak, fearing what my voice will sound like—fearing she'll hear Lily in me. Worried that whatever just happened will happen again. I feel a lot of fear at the moment. *What just happened?*

The man is gone. Sydney is gone. I'm shaking, beads of sweat covering my skin, my palms are cut open; my mind racing from the lingering sensation of the voice, from Lily's overwhelming control, from homicidal thoughts, from this crazy feeling of lost time.

I manage to shake it off before I return to the bar with Bella and begin checking the alcohol glasses to see what needs to be refilled, anything to ignore what just happened because it's all I can do at the moment; otherwise, it'll get even harder to breathe.

After making a trip back to the storage room, I go back to the front counter where Bella is standing in front of the register, filing her nails, eyeing Sydney down, who's staring as she flips over a chair from the table and sets it down on the floor. I can't even remember what I said to piss her off so bad. She was insulting me and then, I got mad... Then I...

"You know, I'm really starting to wonder if she has some sort of underlying grudge toward you," Bella remarks as she moves the nail file back and forth across her fingertips. "Like maybe she knew you pre-amnesia and is holding a grudge."

"Yeah, maybe... but why would she know me and not say anything for the last few weeks?" I stare at Sydney, trying to will my mind to make a connection. Do I know her from somewhere? I don't think so... but then again, how can I know? How can I know anything about the past unless someone tells me?

*Maybe she's just not a good person. Did you ever think of that? That some people aren't good.*

"Then again, it could just be because you kicked her ass the first week working here." Bella looks away from Sydney and shakes her head. She reaches for a glass beside the register and takes a long drink. I don't even bother asking what's in it. I already know it's something strong by the way her face twists as she swallows the liquid. Bella is great at pretending to be good, too, when really at heart, she's probably almost as equally as bad as me, well, close anyway. "I should probably unlock the front door, huh?" She changes the subject off Sydney, glancing at the clock on the wall and then at the front door.

"Isn't River supposed to be the one who actually unlocks the place?" I ask, looking up at the picture window above me where River's office is. "I mean, I know he's usually late, but he always gets here in time to unlock."

"Actually, River's up in his office," she says as she rounds the counter and heads to the front door, twirling the keys around on her finger. "He came in early today."

"Really? What's the occasion?" I ask as she flips on the neon open sign. I feel exhausted, on the verge of passing out. Today's been a rough day mentally and I'm not sure how much more I can take. I really should have just skipped out on work and stayed with Ryland.

Bella shrugs, unlocking the door with the key then returning to the bar area to put the keys in the drawer just below the register. "Who knows?" Her eyes sparkle mischievously as she winds around the counter and behind the bar. "Maybe he's excited to see you after your hook-up last night."

I adjust the bottom of my shirt higher as a bald guy comes roaming in the front door. "We didn't hook up last night."

She eyes me over suspiciously as she reaches down the front of her top and rearranges her cleavage so it's pretty much busting out of the shirt. "I know there's something going on between you two, and I wish you'd just fess up so you can give me the juicy details."

"Nothing is going on between us." It's not a lie. Nothing really is going on, at least, not to me. Fun. That's what I consider it. Pure and simple fun because anything else would be wrong. River's a nice guy, but I don't feel nearly as comfortable around him as I do with Ryland. That steady peace I feel up in the cabin is more like unsteady, nervous energy when I'm near River, mainly caused by Lily because she doesn't like him very much. "And maybe he just got here early because he wanted to get a jump on things so he could actually come down and hang out tonight."

She laughs, shaking her head. "You actually think he finally decided after all that studying of people or whatever the hell he does that he actually wanted to be part of society and enter the real world?"

"He studies sociology," I correct her, grabbing my drink and moving for the doorway that leads to the stairway, "which is the study of human social behavior."

"Wow, brainiac," she teases me then turns around as the bald guy strolls up to the counter, asking for a lap dance and laying down a twenty on the countertop. Bella obliges without her cheery mood deflating. She's good at that, either not caring or concealing her emotions—I can't tell for certain which one it is. I flinch a lot and cry about what I do later in the bathroom, that is, when I'm Maddie. Lily owns it.

Turning away from them, I climb up the stairway to the office to see what River's doing, even though I shouldn't. Lily always tells me to stay away from him, that he sees too much in people, and if he looks hard enough, he'll probably see her. She doesn't like him at all, which is part of the reason why I think I haven't had sex with him. But I can't help but go see him; I'm drawn to him like all the sweaty, beer-gutted men that show up here every night are drawn to half-dressed women they can't touch and booze.

When I get to the top of the stairs, the door is wide open. River is sitting behind the desk, his head tipped down as he sorts through the papers. He's the mirror opposite of a Ken doll, but in a good way. I find his floppy brown hair, tattoos, and his hipster style appealing enough that I keep coming back for more.

Honestly, I can't really explain what my attraction is to him. It's not usually like me to continue to hook up with the same guy for a month straight. I usually have one-nighters, even though *I* feel guilty about it—Lily loves them—because I know there's no way I can have a relationship with someone without them eventually stumbling across the madness inside me.

"Knock, knock, knock," I say as I rap my hand on the doorframe, entering the small, very disorganized room that is supposed to be an office, but looks more like a storage room. The window to my right gives an open view of the entire bar and stage area where there's a shiny pole waiting to be danced around.

River quickly glances up, startled by my appearance. "Fuck, you scared the shit out of me." He's wearing a pair of square framed glasses and takes them off to rub his blue eyes. "You have a knack for that. You know that?"

"Sorry," I apologize, wandering into his office that has crooked pictures hanging on the walls, stacks of papers on the desks and overflowing filing cabinets, and the empty energy drink cans and candy wrappers falling out of the overly full garbage can. "So, I thought you guys were going to hire a maid?" I plaster on a playful smile because that's who I have to be around River—playful and flirty. Fun, fake Maddie. "You know, one of those naughty ones, who flashes her ass while she cleans then gives you a happy ending."

He looks around the room with his forehead furrowed, like he's just noticed the mess. "Oh yeah. I think Glen is working on it or something." He blinks then focuses on me, his gaze slowly drinking me in. "I mean, not the naughty maid part; just a normal maid."

"Sure, if you say so." I press back a smile. "You know Glen is never going to hire anyone, right?" I ask, plopping down in the chair in front of the desk and setting my drink on the desk. I cross my legs and tap my fingers on my knee. "He's been saying forever that he's going to hire someone to fix the handle on the freezer door, yet it's been broken longer than I've worked here."

"I'll talk to him," River says. "I think he's just got a lot of other important stuff he's been trying to take care of."

"You know Bella almost got locked in there, right? She was in there for like an hour or something before anyone heard her. The thing is sound proof. Seriously, she could have died and no one would have known." And the cold air would have preserved her body. We would have never smelled the death in the air, breathing it in unknowingly. Vile burns at the back of my throat. God, I wish I could stop.

"Bella's overdramatic," he says, relaxing back in the chair. "*Almost* means she walked in, the door shut, and then she actually had to open it to walk out."

"Wow, hater," I tell him, biting my lip as Lily gets aggravated by the fact that I'm flirting with him—she always does. In fact, she always tunes out whenever River and I are fooling around, which means that anything I do in those moments is clearly under the will of my own—no excuses—which makes Maddie kind of slutty and more and more like Lily everyday. "And here I thought you were all about the love."

"No, you didn't," he says amusedly as he leans forward and crosses his arms on his desk. "You're too smart to think I'm that nice."

"Everyone else does," I tell him, relieved to be up here playfully bantering with him for the moment and getting a break from the voices and ghosts that haunt me. "It might have to do with the fact that you blush when I say 'naughty maid.'"

"I don't blush." He rolls his eyes and gives me a look like I'm the most absurd person in the world. "And I really don't believe that you think I'm nice. And if everyone else does, then everyone else is stupid in my opinion, at least around here."

"Maybe I'm really stupid, too," I say lightly. "You know, you don't even know me. And for all you know, all our conversations have been centered around me memorizing facts on the internet right before we meet up."

"You think you're more mysterious than you are, Maddie, because I do know you," he says, watching my reaction closely, like he does whenever he's associating with anyone. "You're a girl who has a very twisted sense of humor. That is hard to faze. That has a lot of secrets. That doesn't seem to mind giving guys personal dances when a lot of the girls get emotional and complain about it later. That dresses like a different character almost every single day." He relaxes back in his chair again as Lily squirms inside me and starts clawing her way under my skin.

*He sees too much. You need to shut him up.*

"Tell me, who are you today?"

I glance down at my outfit. “I think I was going for badass biker chick.” I elevate my gaze back up at him and force my tone to be upbeat. “Using those stellar sociology skills, are you?”

He shrugs, the corners of his lips quirking. “Perhaps.”

“If I didn’t know any better, I’d think you were trying to impress me.” I almost smile for real.

The corners of his lips quirk with amusement. “Maybe I am. Is it working?”

“Nope.” I give a soft laugh, tucking a fallen strand of my hair behind my ear. “What is your thesis on again? Remind me.”

“I’m still working on it,” he replies then marginally perks up. “Why? Do you want to offer yourself as a test subject?”

“I’ve already told you before, I’d be a very boring test subject,” I say, getting to my feet without even thinking. It’s so abrupt, so sudden, I can barely process doing it.

*You can’t let him study you—can’t let him find out who you really are. They’ll lock us away.*

“Yeah, right,” he says, standing to his own feet and rounding the desk.

I have this baffling compulsion to drop kick him straight in the balls as he invades my personal space, which is odd. It’s not like we haven’t been this close before—we’ve been closer—but the abrupt movement puts my nerves on end and Lily starts scratching at the inside of me, about to tear out of my skin. Maddie is starting to panic, half afraid that Lily will actually puncture through and reveal herself.

"I think you'd be a very interesting test subject, Maddie." He reaches out to touch me, but I flinch back, surprising him. "You're actually one of the most interesting people I've met in a long time."

"Yeah, you say that now." I dodge around him and stride for the door, calm as I can be despite the fact that Lily is stirring inside me. "But one day with me when we're not fooling around and you'd be bored as hell."

"Oh, I doubt that." He backs up and sits on his desk, putting one foot on the floor and letting one dangle. "We could always give it a try and see where it goes."

"I'll tell you what," I reach the doorway and keep my back to him, not wanting to look at him when I say it because I sort of feel guilty for getting drinking involved, "come down tonight and have a few drinks at the after party and you can observe me, but only while we're drinking."

"What after party?"

"The one your brother's friend is having."

"What friend?"

"Leon something or another. The one who got arrested." I glance over my shoulder at him.

He seems puzzled, rubbing his scruffy jawline. "Oh... yeah... I forgot he was going to be out here for a while." He pauses, thinking deeply about something then shakes his head. "So, what if I said okay to your request to drink and join the party?" he replies, getting to his feet. He picks up my drink on the desk and then walks over to me with his eyes fixed on me. "Then what would you do?"

Lily growls at me. She's mad. Enraged. Murderous.

"You can't drink." I arch a brow and look down at the glass in his hand. "You're a recovering alcoholic. Remember?"

"Is that why you offered?" He hands me the glass and I take it from him then he reaches out quickly and strokes my face with his fingers before I have time to back away. "Because you knew I couldn't accept the offer?"

I shake my head.

*Liar. Liar. Pants on fire. You have to do better, Maddie. He'll read you like an open book.*

"Nope." I'm getting thrown off balance.

*Get it together.*

I take a long, slow drink, feeling the burn of the alcohol as I pull myself together. "Honestly, I really don't care if you observe me or not. You can do whatever you want, River." I step out of his touch, feeling a ping of guilt when he looks a little bit hurt.

*Bravo. Way to clean up the mess you just got us into*, Lily says sarcastically.

"Okay, I will then. And sober, if that's okay." He slants against the doorframe, so close I can smell his cologne. "I really don't want to throw eight years of sobriety away."

I should tell him no, and that this is only going to happen if he's as drunk as a Las Vegas tourist stumbling down the strip at two a.m. I should not care about him enough to care. But another voice rises inside me. One that's mine—Maddie's alone—and it's connected to an emotion I didn't know I possessed. Compassion.

*So much for having fun.*

"Fine." I step away from him, my head getting too foggy to think clearly. I need to chill out on the drinking. "You can come observe me, but don't say I didn't warn you when you're about to die of boredom."

*Die of something.*

"Oh, I highly doubt that's going to happen. In fact, I'm pretty sure it'll be the exact opposite." His voice carries a promise of something... I wish I could figure out what. Discovery perhaps? If so, then I'm in some serious trouble.

He steps forward and places a kiss on my lips, taking control over the situation, something he rarely does. Lily snarls and Maddie winces and bites down on River's lip, hard. And the startling part is, she... I like it. River moves back and touches his lip with his fingers, his brows furrowed. I'm not sure if he liked it or is just startled. I'm guessing the latter, since seconds later, he smashes his lips against mine. His tongue slides deep into my mouth and by the time he's pulling away, he's breathing profusely.

"After you get off," he says, breathing heavily and gripping my hips. "You should come up here."

"Maybe…" I look into his eyes and see lust and desire flaring brighter than it ever has. It's startling because I can almost feel it myself; the need to rip off his clothes and touch him all over. It's clear this little relationship thing we're having has been going on for way too long.

I back away from him. "I have to go," I tell him and then leave the office before he can utter a word.

I have a headache and I'm feeling kind of tipsy as I walk down the stairs. Lily is pissed and whispering at me to turn around and strangle River to death, that way there won't be a problem. Maddie feels stupid. I feel like my flesh is cracking apart and I'm about to split open.

By the time I reach the bottom of the stairway, Lily has flipped a switch and is laughing inside my head about how big of a mistake I just made. That if she was in more control, none of this would have happened. I almost wonder if I should just let her come out and clean up my mess. Take over. Finally just be her and see what happens. Let all the darkness and morbid thoughts inside me spill out.

Let myself finally become her.

## Chapter 8
## Lily

I'm not sure how I got control of our body this time, what the purpose is. Something seems off with my freedom or maybe I seem off. I'm a little unsteady compared to usual, which is kind of the point for me existing. I'm the stable one, the one who gets even. The one who takes matters into their own hands, instead of being weak. But I feel weak at the moment, and sick.

Still, I move through the crowd, a silent predator looking for something to do to distract the need to vomit. There's so much sex dripping from everyone in the room, the music with slutty lyrics blaring too loudly as they shout and holler for Sydney who's dancing on the stage. The sight of her brings the anger out briefly, but I won't act on it, not here, not now; but maybe one day, if I'm given the right moment.

I turn away from the stage, ignoring the overly large man who smacks my ass as I down the rest of my drink. With each step, I feel more lightheaded and sick to my stomach, the lights above my head seeming brighter than the norm. When I spot the woman named Bella, I decide to go over there and chat, if for no other reason than to keep my attention focused on something besides the blurry dance going on inside my mind.

"Hey!" Bella raises her hand as I approach her. I'm still trying to figure out if I like her or not. Sometimes it feels like she's as dark as me inside, but there are other times where she seems sketchy and untrustworthy. "Come meet Leon." She points a finger to a man sitting down on a stool beside her.

The hairs on the back of my neck instantly stand on end and it feels like a jolt of static flows across my skin. I stop for a moment, staring at the back of the man whose name makes me feel like my airway is constricting.

Bella keeps waving me over, despite my lack of interest in her. Rolling my eyes, I finally maneuver my way through the crowd and to the bar area, stumbling over my feet a few times.

"Hey," she says, giving me a quick kiss on each cheek, invading my personal space and annoying the crap out of me. "What have you been up to?" she asks, giving me this look like I've just done something she'd like to do.

"Nothing much," I reply, with a hint of slur to my speech.

Bella gets this all-knowing smile that I don't understand—no one understands me. "Would that nothing much be a certain someone who has an office with a view."

She glances over her shoulder at the window above us, which reminds me of how irritated I am with the man standing up there, looking down at us, a shadow in front of the glass; I can still tell that it has to be River. Always watching. Always looking at me. I swear he knows, no matter what Maddie says. He knows who I am and needs to be taken care of.

"I don't know." I stare at the window until my eyes start to sting then I drop my gaze at Leon, my skin tingling with an eerie sensation I don't like. "Is this Leon?" I finally ask, just so he'll have to turn around and I can see his face.

*You're a whore!* I swear I hear it aloud, but maybe it's in my head.

"Oh, yeah. I forgot introductions." Bella picks up a beer and gestures at Leon. "Maddie, this is Leon." She motions her hand at me. "Leon, this is Maddie."

He slowly turns around in the barstool with a smile plastered on his face. He's wearing a baseball cap low on his forehead, his eyes shadowed, and between that, my blurry vision and the dim lighting, I can't see his face very well. "Pleasure to meet you, Maddie." He sticks out his hand for me to shake, his sleeve riding up a little and I detect the dark lines of a tattoo on his wrist, that of a dragon with fire blazing from its mouth.

"It's a pleasure to meet you, Leon," I say. I think he has brown hair, his eyes look black, and his face is rough. "Do I... know... you...?" My voice sounds like an echo in my head.

"You're a whore," I swear I hear someone whisper from nearby, but I keep my eyes on the Leon, feeling as if I look away, I'm giving up my power over myself and I'll fade into the dizziness.

He gives a low chuckle. "I don't think so." He says something else, but I can't make out what it is, his lips move, his eyes studying, hand on mine, but nothing makes sense.

There are people in the room, but I feel none of them, almost like I'm surrounded by dead bodies. I should be okay with the idea—I usually am. Calm. Cool. Collected. I don't like to feel out of control. That's Maddie's thing, and if I didn't pick up the other end, I wouldn't have much of a purpose. But right now, I feel like I'm hanging off the edge of a cliff, holding on with one finger.

"Leon's going to be chilling at the bar for a while," Bella says, but her voice sounds far away.

My pulse throbs underneath my flesh. "Oh yeah… that's… nice." My palms sweat… bones ache…

"I'm going to be helping Glen out for a while," Leon says, eyes still fixed on me. "While he takes a few weeks off for vacation."

"That's nice." My eyes start to roll into the back of my head, my legs about to give out. "Will you… excuse me," I say, pulling my hand away from his. He laughs again and it makes me want to slam my fist into his face. Instead, I stumble away toward the stairway, figuring I'll go take care of someone else and get my control back, no matter what it takes.

## Chapter 9
## Maddie

I remember the first time I saw a dead body, the first time since after the accident anyway. I was eighteen and the incident strangely occurred by choice, which probably isn't very common except for maybe a mortician or a detective or a serial killer.

I'd been out back of the diner where I waitressed at, taking my fifth smoke one break of the day. I was going through my 1950s to 60s movie phase, curious to see if perhaps I felt more peace in that era than I did in the current one I was supposedly born into. I proceeded to watch every classic one I could get my hands on and while I was fascinated with the simplicity of the time, I didn't feel particularly moved by anything.

Regardless, I started acting like a character from that time, a hobby of mine since I have no idea what character I really am. One trait a lot of the characters had was they smoked from cigarette holders. It made them seem so dazzling and sophisticated and I found myself obsessing the demure. So I went out and bought a sheath dress and saddle shoes from a vintage store, along with a cigarette holder, jade with a white tip. I wore the outfit for a week straight, everywhere I could, which caused a near panic attack from my mother and scrutiny from my grandmother, yet I kept on wearing it.

I was wearing the get-up the day I saw the body. Standing out back, smoking near the dumpsters, two guys had wandered past the end of the alleyway that led to the main road. They were talking about a crime scene they just passed and how the body was still on the sidewalk.

I don't know why I did it. What really pushed the compulsion to manifest? It's not like I'd spent hours upon hours obsessing over the need to see a dead body, thinking about the dead, or even killing. I hadn't quite gotten to that point yet in my life. But I still found myself putting out my cigarette and walking down the alley to the street where I spotted the blue and red flashing lights of cop cars, but no ambulance. People were gathered in a restless cluster, so that had to be the spot.

Shuffling off the curb, I slowly made my way across the street toward a row of shops on the other side. The crowd was growing in front of Mel's Fine Seafood and I noticed the window on the second floor of the store was broken. Slivers of glass were scattered and covered the sidewalk. Whenever the sunlight above hit them at just the right angle, they'd shimmer like diamonds. The illusion of pretty.

I approached the edge of the people and stopped toward the back. There were some people crying, some whispering about how tragic, some shaking their heads with sadness. I squeezed my way up to the front where two policemen in uniform where standing with their arms out to the side, trying to keep everyone back.

The people were drawn to it, wanting to see, yet not wanting to. Just like me. I was no different from them at the time, except that maybe I couldn't remember a huge time of my life. My emotions were the same, though. Part of me wanted to go back to the diner and continue working as if I hadn't seen anything at all, while the other part of me wanted to stay. I would have blamed the need to see it on Lily, but she was strangely silent. So it was just Maddie, myself, no one and nothing else that made me step forward. I did it on my own.

I couldn't get up close and personal because of the policemen, but I could see a girl, probably around my age, lying just behind them with her arm kinked above her head, her legs sprawled out on a sheet of blood soaked concrete. It was in that moment, I knew this wasn't the first time I'd seen a scene like this. I didn't know when else or who it was, but I knew I'd stood and gazed down at something similar before.

The blood looked like spilled paint, the patterns of splatter and droplets creating a symmetrical abstract painting that told a story of how a girl fell through a window. But that's it. There was no story of what caused her to get to this moment in time, what had happened right before. If she was hurt to begin with or if the glass cut up her skin. If she did this to herself or if someone else did it. I wondered what the story was.

Inching closer, I noticed the girl was missing a shoe. It wasn't anywhere around, either, and part of me wondered if maybe someone had killed her and the killer took it. I had no idea why I'd think such a thing. I didn't watch crime shows. But for the briefest second, I swear I could feel... almost see myself doing something similar once before. Holding someone's shoe after they died and feeling powerful over it. Then I suddenly thought of the box of buttons in my closet that feel like my treasure in a way, and I had to wonder if that's what they're from? As quickly as the image surfaced, it was like a door slammed shut inside my head, blocking it out. I often wondered if it was Lily. If somehow she'd shut the door on me. Why, though? What could she possibly not want me to see?

## Chapter 10
## Maddie

*I can't escape. The fear. It's scorching within me. Fire and smoke. Suffocating like the rain crashing down from the clouds. It drowns me. My soul. I can't outrun it… Can't escape… Can't escape the flames… The fear. Everything I've seen… done… to myself. To him. To her. But I need to… but she tells me I can't. That I have to feel it. There's no other way.*

*Someone is screaming from inside the house, something about someone being a whore. I hate when I hear the screaming because it means something bad is going on. I don't want to move, so I lie there on my side, staring at the wall. The concrete is cold on my skin. I'm sick of how cold it is. I don't want to be in this room anymore. I want to see the sun, smell the rain, breathe fresh air. But I'm a prisoner.*

*I don't want to be a prisoner anymore… Someone help me… please… Let me out… Make all this go away…*

*"Look at me," he whispers and suddenly I'm somewhere else. Not with the man or the screams. I'm safe. "Stop listening to the screams, stop feeling it, and look at me."*

*I tilt my head and see a figure sitting beside me. I can't see their face, but I have this feeling they're smiling at me and it almost makes me smile. They seem so content, even with the screaming, as if it gives them some strange sense of peace instead of pain.*

*"Do you want to play our game?" he asks. "It'll help you not think about him."*

*"I'm not sure it'll help," I whisper, squeezing my eyes shut as I start to fade away back to the man. I wish I could disappear from this place. I miss the outside world so badly. It's been too long since I've seen the grass and trees, the flowers just outside, breathed the fresh air, looked at something other than these same four walls.*

*"We can try to see if it works," the voice pulls me back to the room and the person in the corner gets to their feet and walks over to the boy, gently stroking their fingers through the boy's hair. The boy cringes, but remains focused on me. "You at least have to try and focus on something else besides what he's doing… focus on something else but the pain."*

*"Do you think she'll be okay?" I say softly, reaching my hand toward the boy, almost able to grab him, but not quite.*

*"Of course," the boy says, trying to disregard the person standing next to him, patting his head as if he were a pet. "She's stronger than that—you know that."*

*It makes me smile because he's probably right—she is stronger and deals with it better. I'm sure she's all right—she has to be. That's why she's here, isn't it? To protect me from the bad. To allow me to stay good, unlike the person in the corner who seems pleased by all this.*

*"Don't listen to him," they whisper, strolling around the boy. "You're not stronger. Not yet."*

*"But I am." I sit up, ignoring the person and the screams as I reach for my box of buttons, trying not to think about what they really represent, where they came from, who they belong to. The figure in the corner laughs at me, but I block the laughing out as I count them all one by one, over and over again until the screaming stops.*

I jerk out of the nightmare, gasping for air. My head is pulsating. The taste of stale tequila, blood, and something sour burns inside my throat. My muscles ache. I feel cold, but at the same time, I'm sweating... it almost reminds me of when I was lying in the street, after the car hit me, only I know who I am this time. Maddie. And full Maddie, too, at the moment anyways, since Lily is being strangely quiet, as if she's in some sort of deep slumber.

My cheek is pressed against something icy cold, my hair matted to my forehead, and my hands feel crusty and dry. For a moment, I feel like I'm back in my nightmare. A prisoner again.

It's quiet and I feel so silent inside, so still, so lost, which doesn't make sense. I should be embracing the silence, but I can't. If I couldn't feel my lungs and heart beating erratically inside my chest, I would think I was dead and in my grave, buried underneath the ground. *Where the hell am I?*

I can hear the soft hum of something mechanical and I try to open my eyes, but it feels like they've been sewn shut. They won't lift and my throat is as dry as sand. I need water. Need to wake up. Need to move. But my limbs are rubbery. Useless. I feel dead and for a moment, I contemplate welcoming it.

"Lily, open your eyes and get up. Now." The voice triggers a spark of recollection and my eyes shoot open, jerking me out of my daze. I immediately scan the darkness for the person the voice belongs to, but it's so dark I can't even make out the outlines of anything. I push up from the ground and blink my eyes several times, hoping my vision will adjust, but it doesn't. I worry I've gone blind or something, my eyeballs are on fire.

"Hello!" I call out and my voice echoes back to me. There's a bang from somewhere, but no one responds. I try again, "Who's in here?" Again, recollection sparks in my brain—Déjà vu—but it's like there's a wall blocking me from connecting all the dots.

"Lily, are you doing this?" I whisper under my breath. The only response I get is maddening silence. And the humming. I know I heard a voice. Someone has to be watching me in the darkness, but whom? And where am I?

I can barely remember a single thing about last night. The ceiling lights of the bar flashing… they hurt my eyes... watching people dance... I drank way too much, which is probably why my throat's still dry and my head feels like it's in a fishbowl. I also wasn't alone. I saw Bella, I think… yeah, I can picture her laughing, her drunken laugh, too. There was also someone else… a guy. River? I can't quite see his face in my memories. A shadow, like everything else.

Feeling my way across the floor, I scoot forward on my ass, my limbs and muscles aching in protest. The floor feels like chilled metal and stings at my palms so badly my skin feels like it's tearing open. I keep going until the tips of my fingers brush against the edge of a frosted surface.

I pause, listening for the person whose voice woke me up, but all I can hear is humming. However, the feeling is there inside me, the haunting sensation that I'm being watched. Like when I'm in my room and the photos of my past feel like they're watching my every move.

"I know you're in here, so you might as well say something, you fucking weirdo," I call out. Again, no one replies.

What I need to do is get to my feet. Tucking my legs under me, I slide my fingers up the surface as slivers of frost falling off. I manage to stand up, my knees weak beneath my weight, unsteady, just like the rest of my body and my mind. Thoughts of where I could be race through my psyche.

Claustrophobia sets in. I haven't experienced it in the last six years, but the thickness of the darkness suddenly feels like it's smothering me… I've felt this way before… a long time ago… I can almost feel…

*Let me out! Let me out! God, please, let me out! I don't want to be in the dark anymore.*

*Only if you do what I say.*

A door slams shut in my head, locking out the memory and causing me to jerk back. I need to get out of here. Now. There's got to be a way out of here and a light switch somewhere. Trying to stay calm, I feel my way across the wall, gradually inching sideways. It's strange how hyperaware I am of everything, how it feels like I know exactly what to do to find my way out of the darkness and this frosted, cold as ice room.

My instincts take over and with calculated steps, I move my way around the dark carefully. Whenever my foot or hand brushes against something, I instantly stop and slowly maneuver around it without getting hurt. My eyes stop hurting. I feel more comfortable with each step. A few steps more and my fingers graze against a metal handle.

"Yes," I whisper as I pull the handle down and shove the door open. Breathing in the light and warm air, I stumble out and spin around to see where I was. Shelves with frozen food fill the small area and a light mist from the cold swirls around in the light. A freezer. I was in the freezer at the bar, but that's not the most startling thing about the situation.

There's no one else in there.

It doesn't make sense. I heard a voice. It's what woke me up.

*Are you sure it wasn't just another voice inside your head?* Lily's voice is so clear, so loud and unannounced that I jolt back in surprise and bump my elbow into the wall.

I shut my eyes and try to force my mind to remember what happened. The sequence of events that led me to this moment. Yet, the harder I try, the more distorted everything becomes. Lights... blinding lights… music… drinks… blood on my hands… Suddenly, the doors in my mind are slamming shut with so much force I fall down on the floor. Pain soars through my body and my eyes shoot open as I sit up. That's when I notice the blood. Dried on my skin, it covers the back of my arms, cracked and peeling, like grimy sand.

"Oh my God… what did you do?" My stomach burns, fire, melting me from the inside and works its way up my throat.

I jump to my feet, bolt out of the back area, and run down the hallway to the private restroom. Then I collapse to my knees on the hard tile floor, my head tipping forward as vomit purges from my mouth. My stomach empties out the tequila and whatever else I had last night. Exhausted, I flush the toilet then quickly stand up and start scrubbing the blood off my arms in the sink. I'm in a panic and tears sting at my eyes.

*Keep it together. Don't lose it.*

There are no visible cuts anywhere, so I don't think it's my blood. It's so caked on that I have to scratch at my skin to get it off and by the time I'm done, I am bleeding in certain spots on my arm.

I feel like shit, my stomach churning again, worse than when getting drunk. My legs give out on me and I sink onto the floor, letting my head fall back against the wall as tears stream out of my eyes. I've been drunk before, had killer hangovers, but this feels different. I feel overwhelmingly sick. Time lost. My mind spinning. And the worst part is, I have no idea what I did for almost the entire night. But the ideas are there. All those times, pondering people's murders. What if I… we…

"God, Lily, why?" I whisper in horror. Whatever happened had to be her. It just had to be. And now I'm the one that's going to have to pay for it.

"Maddie."

For a second, I think I'm losing it, hearing yet another voice; save for feeling the presence of another in the doorway. I collect myself and turn my head to the side and find River. He's still wearing the same clothes from the last time I saw him, only wrinkled, and his dark hair is disheveled. He's also giving me a horrified look, his gazed fastened on my arms.

"Jesus." He rushes into the bathroom, his eyes widening even more as he sees the bloody paper towels all over the floor. "What the hell happened to you?"

"You tell me," I say in a hoarse voice, staring down at my arms. "Because I have no idea what went on pretty much after I left your office." As soon as I say it out loud, a voice inside my head screams at me to keep my mouth shut. I want to shout back at the voice and tell it to fuck off, but the burning sensations on my arm from where I scrubbed the blood off makes me keep my lips sealed.

He glances around at the bathroom, which reeks of vomit, then grabs a few paper towels from the dispenser near the sink. Crouching down beside me, he hands me the towels and I dab my mouth off with them while he takes hold of my arm and examines it.

"Where did this come from?" he asks, delicately rubbing his thumb across a bloody spot on my wrist.

"I had stuff on my arms and I scrubbed a little too hard cleaning it off." I slip my arm from his hand and put it to my side, his touch making me feel distant and cold. "God, I feel like shit and the really shitty part is I can't even remember what I did to feel this way."

He watches me intently as if he's seeking a sign that I'm lying to him while I clean my face off with the paper towel. "You really don't remember last night at all?" he questions with skepticism.

I shake my head, balling the paper towel up in my hand. "I really don't, so it would be great if you would enlighten me as to what the hell happened." I'm aiming for a fake, light tone, but fail miserably.

He takes the paper towel from me and chucks it into the trashcan. "I'm not really sure where the blood came from… All I can remember is you and Bella talked, drank, did all that lovely stuff you do; although I think you got a lot more intoxicated than you normally do." He scratches his head. "After about your eighth shot, I sort of lost track of you in the crowd."

"So you have no idea what I did last night either?" My head slumps against the wall again because it's too heavy to hold up. What did I do from the hours of midnight to seven?

*I wouldn't trust him if I were you*, Lily whispers.

"I know you kept saying that the only way you'd let me observe you was for me to be drunk and it made it really, really hard to decline." He contemplates something. "You know, if I didn't know better,

I'd think you wanted to get me drunk on purpose, just so I couldn't observe you with a clear head."

"Why would I do that?" I ask, feigning innocence.

"Well, I'd say I have no idea," he replies, staring at the floor with wariness before sitting down on the stained tile, his hands balanced at his sides so he doesn't touch anything, "but from the little that I saw last night, you have a way with getting people to do what you want." He glances up at me, his expression unreadable. "You know, you're kind of a manipulative person."

"I am not," I lie, raising my head up and straining the best smile I can muster. "I'm a total angel. Ask anyone." I'm trying to be sarcastic, but there's a strain in my voice that matches the ache in my body. *I'm not okay.*

*No, you're not. Especially near him.*

River props his arm on his knee and itches at his tattooed arms so roughly he leaves streaks of red. "Maddie, I've known you for almost two months now and you're not the angel part of this bar."

He reaches for my hair and, with hesitancy, tucks a strand behind my ear, a gesture very unlike him and one very unlike me to kindly receive. I lean back and he jerks away, almost as if I'm on fire. Silence encompasses us as I watch his nails tear apart his flesh with his fingernails. It makes me want to scratch the hell out of myself and see what's hiding underneath the layer of flesh that covers my body.

Finally, I slant forward and grab ahold of his hand, trapping it in mine and forcing him to stop itching. "Would you stop that?" With my free hand, I trace my fingertips down the red marks. "You're scratching the hell out of yourself."

His mouth curves downward, confusion written all over his face as he stares down at the scratches. "You seemed perfectly content last night about scratching me."

*I scratched him... What?*

When I don't say anything, staring at him unfathomably, he adds, "God, you really can't remember anything at all, can you?"

"But apparently you can remember some stuff you're not telling me," I say, still grasping onto his arm to the point he should probably tell me to ease up, but he doesn't, which makes me want to only grip tighter. Hurt him.

"This happened at the beginning of the night before I lost track of you." He holds my gaze firmly. "After you left my office yesterday, you came back up a while later and, well..." He shifts uneasily. "We fooled around quite a bit."

"We did?" *Why can't I remember this*?

*Maybe you should ask him.*

He nods. "How can you not remember...? You weren't that drunk when you came up. At least, I don't think you were."

I rack my brain for any sort of spark of reminiscence, but all I can remember is making it to the bottom of the stairs right after I told him he could study me for the night, tripping over my own feet, then falling to the floor. Then nothing.

"And things got kinky, I'm guessing." I think about how I bit his lip before I walked out of his office and how I liked it, inflicting pain on him.

"Not too bad, but..." He glances down at his arms and then at my fingertips digging into his skin. "You did get a little rough." His voice cracks and I can tell he wants me to let his wrist go. It makes Lily not want to let it go. Hold onto it forever until he cries out my name.

Bits and pieces float back to me.

*"God, you're so fucking amazing." River kisses me deeply as I straddle him in his office chair, gripping onto him, stabbing my nails into his flesh. Lines form on his skin. Dots of blood drip out... I love the sight of it. This is who I am. I'm sick. Twisted. Deranged. And I fucking love it because if I don't love it, then I have to fear it. Accept or drown in self-hatred. I'll never let fear own me—never let anyone control or hurt me. I want to hurt him. And I can because I'm*

*wild, reckless Lily, who doesn't give a shit. Strong. Even a little deranged, which was who I was supposed to be in the first place.*

*I rock my hips against River and he groans, his hand sliding down the front of my neck to my breast. I'll admit it, despite my distrust for him, it still feels so good. Makes my body yearn for more. But right as he's about to brush his fingers across my nipple, I snatch his wrist and bite his bottom lip. This time, he moans out in pain and I feel satisfied. In control. I almost own him. But not completely. I need to own him completely to feel in control again.*

The memory starts to become hazy as I straighten up my posture. "Did you like it?" I ask River, my lips moving on their own accord, completely separated from my mind. I'm not Maddie at the moment. Not Lily either. But some weird in between person where both of us have control.

He seems apprehensive with my question, like he wants to pull his hand away, but doesn't dare. "I don't know, Maddie. It was different."

My brow meticulously arches. "Different good or different bad? Tell me, River, did you like it when I was rough?" My tone is demanding and I press my fingertips roughly into his wrist, until I can feel his pulse hammering, hammering, hammering. *He's afraid.*

*Good.*

*But I feel wrong for making him afraid. For hurting him.*

*That's because you're weak. You need to be stronger, like me.*

*Pitter-patter... pitter-patter... pitter-patter... I can feel the rain falling... hear the thunder... feel the fear... Feel it... it's clutching on to me and I want nothing more than to not feel it.*

*Let me help you,* Lily coaxes. *Let me show you how to be immune to the pain.*

"Maddie, you're hurting me." The sound of pain in River's voice snaps me back to reality and I jolt back, releasing my hold on him.

"I'm sorry." *Get up and leave. No more questions.* "I need to get home." I practically jump to my feet as I summon up every ounce of energy I have to shove Lily away.

River stands up, too. "Do you need a ride?" He tucks a strand of my sweaty hair behind my ear again in an affectionate way that makes me want to drop to my knees again and vomit some more. *Don't touch me,* I almost lose my voice again and growl at him, but manage to regain control and snap my jaw shut.

"No thanks. My car's outside," I manage to say politely, straining to ignore vertigo when it slaps me in the face. I feel like I'm slowly leaving my body and someone else is taking over my legs.

He follows me as I hurry from the bathroom, feeling hollow inside as I trudge down the hallway, desperately trying to summon up last night's memory of when I went down it and then locked myself in the freezer. Just like the first time I lost my memory, there's no spark of anything, only this time, there's no accident and I can still remember everything else, except for part of last night.

"Are you sure you're going to be okay?" River asks as I grab my bag from the cubby and head for the front door. The fresh air out front feels weird and my stomach still feels like it's on fire.

I turn around, hitching my bag over my shoulder. "Actually, do you know if anyone else was in here at all this morning? Or if you saw me with anyone wandering in the direction of the freezer?"

"No, not that I'm aware of..." His eyes skim the bar; chairs turned up onto the tables, floors swept, the air smelling of Clorox. Someone has cleaned up in here and closed up, which is usually Bella's and my job. And Bella would have a fit if she did it on her own. In fact, I once asked to get out of it, leave early, and she took off out the front door so I'd be the one to do it—and she barely helps out when she does stay. His attention lands back on me. "Why are you asking about the freezer?"

"It's where I woke up this morning." As soon as the words leave my lips, I want to retract them. *He shouldn't know that. It's weird. Crazy. I'm crazy. He's going to see the crazy in me.*

"You woke up in the freezer? Jesus. How long were you in it?" He scans my body as he continues to scratch at his arms.

It doesn't make any sense. Why I can't at least remember that part. I know I couldn't have gotten that drunk after I left his office, but I can't even remember going back up. I'm concerned that maybe all those thoughts about letting Lily take over finally might have made it happen. Perhaps that's why she's being so calm about this. Maybe when I blacked out, I turned into her. *God, what if I turned into her?*

"I'm not sure. Who cleaned up here last night?" I ask, hugging my arms around myself.

"Bella, I think... Leon was here pretty late, too," he says and I swear he flinches when he says Leon's name. "I think he might have a thing for her or something because I don't remember him being that motivated to help out before. But then again, it's been awhile."

"How long has it been since you've seen him?"

"Oh, I'd say about ten years or so," he says with a shrug. "But even so, he'd pretty much just stop by as he was driving through town. I think he's kind of a drifter or something. Never stays in one place too long."

I try to recollect meeting this Leon person, the alleged trafficker, but I'm drawing a blank; yet at the same time, it feels like I met him.

River crosses his arms, studying me. "Maddie, are you sure you're okay? You seem… I don't know…" He extends his arm toward me and brushes his finger down my cheekbone. "A little confused. Nervous. Lost."

"I'm fine. I promise. I just need to go home and get some rest," I assure him, moving away from his touch.

I swing around him and push out the front door before I can say anything more. The last thing I want to do is discuss in details what's going on inside my head right now. I just want to remember what I did and why the fuck I woke up in the freezer with blood all over my arms… Why I'm hearing voices outside of my head… more than just Lily's…

Swirling in my own confusion, I make my way across the parking lot. Fuck, it's bright out here. And my ears and head are ringing. Plus, the chilled air is stinging against my skin.

I'm rummaging in my bag for keys when I stumble across a white button shaped like a heart and an oval, bright red one. I shake my head. Even in a drunken stupor, the obsession still gets to me. I stuff the buttons in my pocket and then start digging around for my car keys again. I'm pulling out the contents—

lipstick, brush, a pack of cigarettes—when I notice red and blue flashing lights in the parking lot across the street at the One Stop Quickie Mart.

Cop cars are parked in it, an ambulance, people crowding around, gawking. I know that scene. Something bad has happened and I want—I need—to know what it is. I'm not even sure if it's an obsession this time. More like a need to find out if I'm connected to it at all. Lily grows extremely silent almost like she's left my body entirely.

Feeling even sicker to my stomach, I cross the road, wrapping my arms around myself as the cold air blows. Cars drive up and down the street slowly, people curious, wanting to know just as much as me what's going on; yet at the same time, I don't want to know, fear the answer and what it means about me. With each step, my heart slams harder in my chest. By the time I arrive at the curb, I'm barreling with adrenaline, my stomach burning. I know what lies on the other side of the crowd. God, do I know.

When I push through the crowd and reach the front, my hunch becomes painfully correct. A girl lies on the ground, a circle of dried blood pooled around her head, making her blond hair look red. She's wearing an apron, too, an apron from the *Devil & Angels Bar.* I know her. Sydney, the waitress I've been fighting with.

"Jesus," I mutter under my breath, unable to take my eyes off her.

*I know this girl and now she's dead. Just last night she was walking around in the bar and now she's here, lying on the ground. I got into a fight with this girl and now she's dead. I thought about killing this girl and now she's dead.*

"This is not good."

"I know. It's terrible, right?" some woman says from beside me, horror stricken as she gapes at the body, probably a first timer in the dead body department. She's probably in her forties, her black hair obviously dyed, and she's wearing too much pink blush that matches her shirt that says, *Jesus Rocks*! I actually think she's knocked on my door a few times to try and convert me to something or anotherism. It actually happens a lot and my mom always sends them away with a smile and a wave as if she's glad they stopped by even if she never goes to church. "Fairfield's such a good community... this stuff shouldn't happen here."

"And what? Stuff like this should happen in other places because they *aren't* good communities," I say in a low voice.

"That's not what I was saying at all," she gasps, offended.

"That's exactly what you were saying."

The woman shakes her head in revulsion and then she inches to the side, away from me.

I focus on the scene in front of me. Sydney looks so peaceful, like she's asleep, only the blood shatters the illusion, paints it red with the nightmare that this is a reality. That she's dead. Her shirt torn. Skin as pale as the snow. The white button down shirt, tied at the bottom, splattered with blood. *The white shirt that's missing a top button... a little heart button...*

I step back so suddenly that I bump into the person behind me. Muttering an apology, my eyes stay fixed on Sydney.

*It's just a coincidence. I must have found the button and picked it up before all this happened. I'm being set up.*

I wait for Lily to chime in with whatever she has to say on the matter, but she's still inside my mind. Everything's still. My body. My mind. It seems wrong, yet right. I seem empty, yet I seem whole at the same time.

Men in uniforms walk over to the body with a sheet in hand. They drape it over the body, covering it up from the wandering eyes. My heart slams against my rib cage as they start to scan the ground for evidence and I decide it's my cue to leave.

Turning away from the body, I squeeze my way to the back of the crowd and dash across the street to my car. Impatient to get away from here, I dump my purse out on the ground and search through the contents until I find my keys. Then I toss everything back into the bag and hop into my car, revving up the engine.

"This can't be happening. The button isn't real," I whisper as I push the car into drive, watching the lights across the street *flash, flash, flash. Feel the rain falling... let the building burn... help me... Don't leave me behind. Please don't let me die. I'm sorry. A loud bang and I walk up to the dead body, slowly pulling the buttons I've counted for years off his shirt, one by one. And with each one, I get a sick gratification from it.*

*"Good girl," she whispers. "I knew you'd eventually come around."*

With my foot on the brake, I stuff my hand inside my pocket and retrieve the heart shaped button, stained with a dot of blood. The red one, I'm not sure of who it belongs to, but I have a feeling that person might be lying somewhere in a parking lot, too.

I should throw both of them out the window, get rid of the evidence. The problem is, I can't. I attempt to several times, but my obsessive compulsive anxiety disorder is stopping me. I end up putting them back into my pocket and opening up the car door to throw up in the parking lot. My stomach is pretty much empty at this point and I mostly just dry heave.

When I finish, I shut the door, ignoring the tears streaming down my face and drive away, wondering what the hell I did last night. Wondering if maybe Lily got too out of control and finally went through with her dark thoughts.

Maybe the end of Maddie is nearing.

*Maybe she never existed at all.*

## Chapter 11
## Maddie

I think I'm paranoid. Insane. Joined the crazy train and there's no getting off. Not after what happened with Sydney. I can't stop thinking about it, no matter how much it makes me ill.

I've been trying to text Bella for the last day, hoping she could give me some insight to what I was up to, but she hasn't responded to my messages yet.

"Blood on my arms. Buttons. That doesn't mean anything. I could have been drunk, got into a fight or something, and simply passed out. Or maybe it was River's blood all over me," I say to myself as I pace my room, back and forth, back and forth, Lily chattering away in my head. She's growing stronger with each passing hour and Maddie is desperately trying to hang on to reality. "I didn't kill anyone. There's no way." Lily laughs and I let out a scream through my teeth in aggravation.

It's been a day since Sydney died. A day since I brought home that button like a psychopath collecting a souvenir. A day since I woke up in the freezer with blood all over my body. And about an hour since the news announced the murder of Sydney M. Ralwington, former daughter, friend, waitress, *soon to be worm food.*

"God, what the fuck is wrong with you?" There is no answer to that question, no resolution, no nothing. I never wanted to be crazy. Never wanted to fully act on my twisted impulses, the ones I've been fighting for the last six years. They were just supposed to be thoughts, but now...

Is it possible I've brought the madness out and made it reality? Did I kill Sydney? Or did something else happen? Was I set up by someone maybe? But who? Who knows me enough that they'd know putting a button in my pocket would mean something? There's only one person who knows about it and she lives inside me.

Walking over to the box of buttons opened up on my bed, I look at Sydney's, now part of the collection and the red, oval one that I have no idea who it belongs to.

Picking up the heart, I clutch it in my hand, feeling the slightest bit of a prickle in my mind. *Pick up the button, Maddie. What do you see?*

"I see a crazy obsession," I mumble, running my thumb across the front of the button. "All because of you."

*Don't pretend that this is all me. You think it, too, sometimes. And you see where the obsession started. You were just a kid.*

"So what. That still doesn't mean anything." I look around at the pictures of when I was a child, feeling like they can see and hear what's going on, feeling as if they're judging me. Finally, I can't take it anymore.

I start tearing them down, not caring that I rip some of them in half. I pull them all down because I don't want to see the past anymore—don't want to feel like I'm being haunted by a past that doesn't feel like it belongs to me. By the time I'm finished, I'm panting, there are photos all over the floor, and I feel strangely satisfied.

I pad over to the mirror and smooth my hands across my short, black hair that's nearly drenched in sweat. There's something in my eyes that I don't like, but that I do like at the same time. Untamed wildness, a specter of Lily.

"I really do hate you," I say quietly.

"No, you don't. You'd be lost without me." The reflection speaks and I jolt back, slamming my elbow into the wall. "That's why we're talking, isn't it? Because you need me? You created me because you needed me?"

I shake my head as I stare in horror at the mirror. This has never happened before, her appearing to me like this. She looks just like me only she has a streak of blond in her black hair and her eyes are a shade darker than mine.

"No, I hate talking to you. It's because of you that I'm going crazy." I touch where the streak would be in my own hair.

The reflection laughs at me. Actually throws her head back and laughs like this is all just a big joke. "Don't kid yourself. You're only going crazy because you're fighting the crazy inside you. If you'd just accept it—me—this would be a hell of a lot easier. I could take care of you, you know. Take care of all your problems." She sounds so much like Ryland for a moment that it throws me off. "Life would be so much easier if you'd just let me take over."

"Fuck you." I glare at her and she rolls her eyes. "And I know it was you that night. Somehow you took over."

"Maybe I did," she says with a shrug and a twinkle in her eyes. "But sorry to disappoint, it wasn't me that's making you forget. That was something else entirely. Perhaps you had too much to drink… I'm still trying to figure it out."

"I didn't have that much to drink. And you have to remember some things because I can remember you with River," I say.

"Yeah, but after, that I'm in the dark, too. I can honestly tell you I have no clue what we did that night, although, really, the possibilities are endless."

I don't believe her. "I know you killed Sydney that night and now you're getting some sick pleasure in the fact that you did."

"If I killed her, then you killed her. And if I find pleasure in killing, then you do," she responds dryly, coiling the blond strand of hair around her finger. "You and I are the same, Maddie, in so many ways, so think twice about the accusations you make."

My eyes burn with anger. "Fuck you."

Lily rolls her eyes, the anger simmering in the reflection. "Now, now, now, Maddie, don't let yourself get out of control. It's why you need me—for stability. I'm always taking care of you, all the time. And sometimes, it gets annoying how you repay me—with such hatred."

"Maddie, are you in there?" A knock on my door startles me and I drop the button onto the floor. I hesitate to respond to my mother. I've been keeping my distance from her for the last twenty-four hours, for her protection mainly, worried that Lily will take over again. That she'll hurt someone. I haven't even been able to shut my eyes, fearing what will happen the moment I go to sleep.

*Knock. Knock. Knock.* "Maddie, open up. This is important."

"Okay… just a second." I pick up the button, toss it back into the box, then put the lid on and hurry to the closet to tuck it safely away. I kick as many photos as I can underneath the bed before opening the door.

My mom's standing just outside it, looking more worried and more aged than normal. "Who were you talking to?"

I force my brows to knit. "No one."

She peers over my shoulder, her eyes enlarging as she takes in my bare walls. "And where did all your photos go?"

I shrug nonchalantly. "I got sick of looking at them, so I took them down."

She frowns at my attire "What are you wearing?"

Cutoffs, fishnet tights, and a torn t-shirt—I'm Rocker Girl today. The outfit was supposed to go underneath my work attire, but I never made it that far. "My lounge clothes." I sketch my fingers over a few studs in the collar of the shirt. "I was just about to change out of them."

She touches the hem of my shirt, her face draining of color. "Why were you wearing them at all?" She rubs the corner of the shirt between her finger and them, then withdraws her hand and looks at me. "I didn't even know you owned clothes like this. You look like..." She makes a face. "You look like a whore."

*You're a whore!*

*You're a whore!*

*You're a whore!*

My muscles spasm at her words, the deep voice thunders in my mind. My mouth opens and shuts. Opens and shuts. Lily is forcefully trying to push her way to the surface and it takes a lot to suppress her. I have no idea what I'm going to say to my mother. Cruel things. Hateful things. Terrifying things. Nevertheless, part of me just wants to keep my mouth closed.

"Did you need something?" I snap.

"There's someone here to see you," she says almost soundlessly, lifting her hand to point over her shoulder down the hallway. "A detective."

"What?" I can't conceal my shock, my voice coming out off pitch. *They know.* "Why?"

She shrugs, folding her arms around herself, looking very upset, near tears. "I'm not sure. I think he said it had to do with Sydney Ralwington's case." She doesn't sound surprised. I'm not surprised, but she should be, unless she knows more than she's letting on.

"Okay…" I feign confusion. "But why? I don't know her."

She stares at me for the longest time. "You should change first," she mutters with disappointment in her tone, eyeing up my outfit with disdain. "You look disgusting."

"I look fine for going out into the living room." I tug the hem of the shirt down and start to step by her.

She snags me by the elbow. "Maddie, please change—"

"I said, it'll be fine," I interrupt her, staring at her hand on my arm then lift my cold gaze to her. "Now let me go."

With her eyes pooling with tears, she withdraws back and grudgingly steps aside and lets me through so I can go down the hallway. As I step into the living room, I discreetly wipe the sweat off my damp hands as I spot the detective. He's fiddling with one of my mom's knick-knacks, a unicorn missing half its horn. There are actually a lot of knick-knacks in the living room, practically taking over the shelves, the tables, the windowsill. It overwhelmed me when I was first brought home from the hospital, feeling like I was being watched by the little glass figurines.

"Can I help you?" I ask, my guard up, an invisible wall around me. *I am unreachable. Untouchable. You need to be Lily if you want to get out of this. She's much stronger.*

*Never.*

My arrival must surprise him because he drops the figurine, but recovers it mid-fall before it can hit the hardwood floor and shatter. "Dammit," he curses under his breath then carefully sets the unicorn down before he stands up from the chair and crosses the living room with his hand outstretched.

"I'm detective Elliot Bennerly, from the Grove Police Department." He waits for me to shake his hand.

It takes me a moment to shake it, not to gather the courage, but to debate whether it's a good idea to touch him. Finally though, I decide it will make me look suspicious if I don't, so I gently connect my hand with his and shake it politely, a shiver moving down my spine.

*Do I know him?*

"I'm Maddie Asherford," I say.

"It's nice to meet you, Maddie." He pauses, his ice-blue eyes sweeping over me, either looking for evidence or checking me out. He looks familiar, but I can't figure out from where. Late twenties, smooth skin, short, brown hair, and nice facial features covered with a little bit of scruff. The only thing he doesn't have going for him is the suit, otherwise, he could be a Ken doll, too, although the brunette one. Even though he's good looking, I don't want him—or anyone else—looking at me so intently at the moment.

"Likewise." I causally slip my hand out of his and lower it to my side, unable to endure the touch of him any longer.

I wait for him to say something, but he just stares at me with a pucker at his brow. The longer it goes on, the greater the urge gets to pick up the unicorn he was messing with and bash him over the head. *Elimination.* This whole process would be a hell of a lot easier if he was unconscious and I just ran from it all.

*There you go. Now you're getting it. Survival.*

"So, my mother said you wanted to talk to me about something," I say, ignoring Lily's voice the best that I can.

"Oh yeah." He rips his attention away from me and then ruffles his hair with his hand before reaching for his jacket pocket. "I've come to ask you a few questions about Sydney Ralwington's murder."

"Okay..." Adrenaline is soaring through my body. Fear. Even Lily's afraid. I can feel her in me. Squirming. Restless. Worried.

*Just be me and you'll be okay. Be Lily.*

"It's strictly protocol," he explains, retrieving a miniature notepad out of his pocket and pen. "We're just questioning all the people who knew Sydney."

"I didn't really know her very well." I take a seat on the sofa and then motion for him to have a seat across from me.

He sinks into the chair, pen poised on the paper. "But if I'm correct, you worked with her." He fans through the pages of his notebook then squints at the paper as he reads over something. "At the *Devil & Angels Bar*?"

I nod. "I'm a waitress there and so was Sydney."

He glances up at me. "Are you a dancer like Sydney was?" he asks, his gaze flicking to my bouncing knee.

"Dancer. Bartender. Waitress." I place my hand on my knee to hold it still, attempting to keep my nerves under control. "You name it. I do it."

"Sounds like you can do just about anything." I'm not sure if he's flirting with me or accusing me of something, so I'm uncertain how to respond. Do I flirt back? Bat my eyelashes and show a little skin? Or is he hoping I'll do that so he can understand me better?

*Let me take over.*

I shut my eyes and open them, I swear I almost feel Lily slide under my skin and take over my body. I almost allow her to—let her handle the situation that she created—but right at the last second, I shove her away, not ready to accept that I can fully be her if I want to.

"When it comes to the bar, I do." I recline back in the sofa, my focus on Elliot, portraying that I'm steady, confident—innocent. That I'm not guilty. "In life though, not so much. I only do the things I want."

He gives me a cryptic look then jots down some notes. "Did you see Sydney at all the night of March 15th?"

I twirl a strand of my hair around my finger and for a moment, I swear it turns blond. "Yeah, at the bar when we were opening up."

"Was she with anyone? Or did she talk to anyone at all that seemed suspicious?" he asks. "A customer perhaps?"

I shake my head. "I barely saw her, for like, maybe ten minutes, so I'm not really a good person to ask."

The pen stops moving across the paper. "What about later that night? Did you see her at all after the bar closed up?"

"No, not that I can recollect," I answer as innocently as I can.

He assesses me again, his dark eyes drinking every detail of me in, from my messy hair to my bare feet. "What about the next morning?"

I feel like I've been cornered, walked straight into a trap. Either I can answer truthfully and have to explain why I was at the bar afterhours or lie and tell him that I wasn't. But so many people saw me yesterday morning, including River and everyone else standing around the crime scene.

"Yeah, I saw her the next morning." I let a slow, uneven breath escape my lips.

He puts the end of the pen in his mouth with his head angled to the side contemplatively. "When did you see her and where?"

"Around seven or so and I saw her… across the street from the bar." I pause, remembering what I saw that morning; the blood, the dead body, that stupid button that is practically screaming to be found from the box in my bedroom. "When the police and the ambulance were there."

He swiftly flips the page in his book then reads over something, his brows furrowing. "I have a note in here that the bar closes at three a.m., but the police and paramedics weren't there until after seven a.m., so why were you still at work?"

"I had an... incident that night with one of the coworkers." I feel like I'm failing a test.

He becomes very interested, even more than when I entered the room. "Incident?"

I wet my lips with my tongue and speak in the most sensual voice I can muster up, let myself pretend to be *Lily* for a brief moment. "Sexual incident with one of my coworkers. Completely welcomed and all, but we did end up falling asleep there." I wink at him, playing the part of Lily. Playful, fun, and composed. It almost feels like I'm watching myself in a mirror, instead of inside myself, actually doing it. "You know how that can go."

I think he might with the way he bites his lip, as if remembering some hot sex he had once and I seriously consider pinning him down on the sofa, tearing his shirt open and watching the buttons fly all over the place. Maybe that would get me out of this mess.

*Doubtful.*

"Yeah, I guess." He presses the pen against the notepad again, preparing to write I'm sure a big *F* for Fail. "Do you mind if I ask who the guy was?"

"River Everett, the manager of the bar." My hand twitches when I say it. I know I've made a huge mistake. I'm so screwed. He's going to talk to River and he's going to say that I didn't sleep with him. That I'm liar. And that I woke up in the freezer without any recollection of what occurred the previous night when Sydney disappeared.

After he scribbles a few more things down, along with River's name, he puts the pen and notepad back into his jacket pocket. I expect him to leave, but he just sits back in the chair. "Have you always lived here in Grove?" he wonders, mildly interested, tapping his foot on the floor as he looks around the room.

I shake my head, my eyes fastened on him as I slide my arms onto the armrests and curl my fingers around the edges, pressing all my energy there. "No, I used to live in Fairfield. We actually moved here when I was fifteen." I don't like the personal questions. "But what does this have to do with Sydney?"

"It doesn't have to do with Sydney." His blue eyes now look like steel as his mild interest turns to fully absorbed. "It has to do with me."

I'm hesitant to answer, but I don't think he'll drop it until I do, so I tell him the year I would have graduated if my mom hadn't made me change to home school after the accident. His eyes rise to the ceiling, recognition lighting up on his face. When he looks at me again, I can see in his eyes that he knows me. "Asherford… I knew you looked familiar. You were the girl who—"

"That lost her mind?" Bad choice of words. "Yep, that would be me." Bitterness seeps into my voice. I don't like that he knows me and perhaps even knows me before I lost my mind.

"Yeah, I remember when that happened," he says then scrutinizes me. "You look a lot different now."

I self-consciously run my hands over my hair and down the front of my shirt. "How did you know me exactly?"

"I was one of the cops that showed up the night you were hit," he says and it clicks in my head. *That's why he felt familiar.* "I wasn't on the case or anything. Just called to the scene that night for a little bit."

"Oh yeah," I say. He was there. The night when my life restarted. Suddenly, I'm the one interested in keeping this conversation going. "How did I look different?"

"Your hair was a lot longer and blond, and of course, you were a lot younger." He scans me over with perplexity. "I remember when I arrived at the crime scene, you were calling yourself Lily... and we had a hell of a time figuring out who you were because you had no identification on you at all."

There is no fear inside me anymore. I've gone beyond fear. My heart stops. Dies. I feel like I'm back lying in the street again. Speechless. Frozen in terror. *Lily?* I was calling myself that that night... How...? Why...? Was it because—

A door slams shut in my head. Hard. Causing me to flinch.

I stab my nails deep into my palms, channeling the terror inside me to my hands, to the pain. "Can I ask you a question?"

"That all depends on what it is," he treads cautiously.

"How did they figure out who I was?" I straight up ask him. "That night."

"I'm not sure. My partner and I got called out on another case before that happened." This strange look crosses his face and I can tell he's calculating his next words carefully. "It was really strange, you know. A girl in the road in the middle of the night with no identification on her. Some of the cops thought you were a runaway or a drug addict with how strange you were acting, but then your mother shows up out of the blue, like she knew you were there, but she said she didn't. And then there was that fire just a few miles down the road..." He scratches his cheek. "Very strange." The way he says it sounds like he doesn't think that it's strange, that it wasn't a coincidence, that he's accusing me of something.

"What fire?" I wonder.

He shrugs, lowering his hand to his lap. "Just a building. No one got hurt or anything, but still..."

I don't like the accusation in his voice at all. "Well, don't you have a file or something that says if I was involved in any of this?"

His gaze is unwavering. “Maybe, but that doesn’t really matter at the moment. I came here to question you about Sydney.”

“You brought it up.” *What the hell am I doing? Stop arguing with the detective.*

“I know.” His tone conveys speculation, his eyes lock on me as if he’s ready to turn bad cop and break me open. “Tell me, do you or have you ever gotten into trouble, Maddie? Or should I call you Lily?”

*Fucking asshole.* “No, I’m perfect. Just ask my mother,” I say wryly. “And it’s Maddie.” *Is it?*

His expression is indecipherable, but I have a feeling I’m in deep trouble. “What about that bar you work at? Does your mother know about what that turns into after hours? I’m guessing no.”

“If you know what it turns into afterhours, then why don’t you shut it down?” I question with a curve of my brow.

“I’m working on it.” There’s a silent warning in his eyes.

“Well, I’m not part of it,” I lie breezily. “My job title strictly sticks to during hours.”

I can tell he doesn’t believe me. I don’t know why I care, but I do. I’m about to insist he’s wrong about me, that I’m a good girl that never does anything wrong when his cellphone beeps inside his pocket.

He checks it and then quickly gets to his feet. “I have to go. I have a lot more rounds to make today. If you can think of anything else at all, feel free to call me." He rushes for the door and it takes a hell of a lot of restraint not to grab his collar, throw him to the ground, pin him down, and force him to tell me everything he knows, then eliminate him because he clearly knows something, or thinks he does anyway.

"Okay, but what's the number I can call you at?" I round the coffee table after him.

He hands me a card from his wallet. "My number is on the card. Feel free to call me day or night." He pulls open the door and I itch to slam it shut in his face, lock him in here, and torture everything out of him. "It was nice talking to you, *Maddie*." He pauses with the door cracked. "Why did you say you were Lily that night, if you don't mind me asking?"

"Maddie's my first name." I'm fighting really hard to keep it together as I lie my way out of this mess. "Lily's my middle name."

"Hmmm..." That's all he says and then he steps outside into the frosted air and sunlight, turning on his heels as he reaches the path in front of the house. "Take care Maddie Lily Asherford," he says, flashing a grin at me from over his shoulder. "I'm sure we'll be seeing each other again."

I have no clue what the grin is about—it seems more sinister than anything. Still, I give him a wave then close the door as he walks toward his car in the driveway. I slide the chain over, like I'm locking all the bad out, even though it's living inside me.

*Bravo. You really fucked that one up.*

"Oh, go to hell."

"Maddie, what was that all about?" my mother asks as she tentatively enters the room, rubbing her hands up and down the sides of her arms like she's cold. "You're not in trouble, are you?"

I'm leaning against the shut door, arms to my side, hands tremulous, palms bleeding from where my nails split open the flesh. "Why would I be in trouble?" I ask, watching her reaction. "If what you say is true, then I never get into trouble."

I detect a hint of a nervous fidget in her hands as she fiddles with the buttons on her shirt, her hair—anything she can get ahold of. "Maddie, please don't start with this," she says. "Just tell me what the detective wanted."

I don't know what comes over me. Or maybe I do and I don't want to admit that I'm allowing Lily to control me so much at the moment because I'm frazzled and irritated.

I stand up straight, calm as can be, embracing the darkness, the anger, instead of fearing it. "He wanted to see if I murdered Sydney Rawlington."

Her skin turns pale and I get a sick gratification over it. This is who I am and what I want to know is if my mother knows who I really am, too. If I've been this person my entire life and she's just trying to keep it hidden, hoping it will go away.

"Maddie Asherford, you will not take that that tone with me." She aims for a stern tone, but it comes out quivery.

"Don't you mean, Lily?" I observe the way she blinks, note the way she moves her hand to the bottom of her neck where her necklace rests, a nervous habit of hers.

Her jaw drops. "Maddie, what are you talking about?"

I move toward her, past the coffee table, the sofa, the pictures of me on the wall when I was younger, taking each step calculated. "That detective said he was there the night of the accident." I halt only a few, long steps away from her. "And that I was calling myself Lily and that somehow you knew about the accident before they even called you. Who's Lily, Mother? Because by the look on your face, I'm guessing you know something about it. And how did you know I'd been hit if no one called you?"

She shakes her head and I can see her pulse hammering in her neck. "I have no idea what you're talking about. The police called me and I've never heard you call yourself Lily before, so I can't help you with that one."

"Are you sure about that?" I ask skeptically. "You seem nervous."

"Yes, I'm sure," she says, lowering her hand to her side and shuffling away from me. "Now stop acting crazy, go change, and come eat dinner with me." With that, she turns on her heels and hurries out of the room.

I want to scream at her to tell me truth, but would there be a point, since I think I already know the answer. It's one that I've been burying inside me since the moment I woke up in the hospital.

That I am crazy.

That I am Lily.

And that I might be a killer.

*Maybe I started the fire that night.*

*Maybe I killed the man who hit me with his car.*

*Just like I probably did Sydney.*

## Chapter 12
## Maddie

I thought things couldn't get worse, but I was wrong. Bella won't return any of my messages or phone calls, so I still have no insight to what I was up to on March fifteenth, which leaves me over-thinking everything and coming up with the worst possible scenarios.

Then, came lockdown. Late one afternoon, my mother gets a phone call while we're having dinner. She instantly leaves the room, her face draining of color as she glances at the screen. I hear her muttering something and when she returns, she seems shaken up, but won't tell me why. The next day, she installs a security alarm, changes all the locks on the doors, and tells me that I need to stay in the house as much as possible and that it might be best for me to stay home from work until the murderer is caught.

"To keep us safe," my mother explains as she checks the locks on the front door and then crosses the room, me following at her heels.

"Safe from what exactly?" I ask, watching her mess around with the alarm system on the living room wall.

She sets the alarm and it beeps as it prepares for lockdown. No going in or out any of the doors or windows without the siren shrieking like the devil himself.

"Maddie, that poor girl was murdered only twenty minutes from here," she says. "We need to be safer with all the craziness that's out there."

"Out there?" I lean against the wall with my arms folded as I stare out the window at the frosted grass, the grey sky, the trees, the "out there" she's referring to. "You're the one being crazy. You can't just lock us in the house and expect us to stay here."

"I'm being crazy," she says unfathomably. She has dark circles under her eyes, her hair is pulled into a messy bun, and her clothes are wrinkled. She looks like a hot mess—a hot, stressed out mess. "You're the one laughing about this. This isn't funny, Maddie."

I shake my head, aggravated. It's not like I mind missing work—I'm worried about going there after the detective talks to River. But being locked up in the house, there's no way I'll survive. "Well, can I have the passcode in case I need to go somewhere?"

"No." She closes the lid to the security box. "If you need to turn it off, you can have me do it."

"Are you kidding me?" Anger burns venomously in my veins. This can't be happening.

*I can't be a prisoner again.*

"No, I'm not kidding you." She breezes by me quickly, striding toward the hallway, calling over her shoulder, "It's safer this way. I promise."

I think there's a hidden meaning in her words and I have to wonder whether she got the alarm to lock the bad out or to lock me inside—lock Lily inside.

***

Things only get progressively worse from there. My mom takes my car keys away while I'm getting something to eat one day. She actually goes into my room and gets them from my bag. While I'm looking for them, pretty much tearing my room apart, she walks into my room.

"What's wrong?" she asks, watching me dig through my dresser drawers.

"I can't find my car keys," I say, searching the pockets of a pair of jeans.

"That's because I took them," she replies, leaning against the doorframe. She has a pair of slacks on, a peach sweater that matches her shoes, and her posture is portraying confidence, yet there's a lack of it in her eyes.

"What the hell for?" I ask, tossing the jeans back onto the floor. I'm more testy than usual, but that's because I haven't slept in days; afraid once I shut my eyes, I'll relinquish control to Lily, handing it over to the killer side in me.

"Because I don't want you going anywhere," my mother says simply. "Not until things have blown over with this Sydney thing and you quit dressing like a whore."

*You're a whore!*

*You're a whore!*

I have to bury my instinct to slap her when she calls me that name. The good inside me tells me to respect her, but that part has been rapidly dying over the last few days, and the bad easily takes control over my mouth. "I'm twenty-one-years-old, Mother. I'll go wherever I want, whenever I want, and be a whore if I want to."

"You may be twenty-one," she replies curtly, "but you have the maturity of a fifteen-year-old, and so I'm going to treat you like a fifteen-year-old."

"You have no idea how mature I am." I kick some clothes out of the way and walk toward her. "Mom, please stop doing this. You can't just keep me locked up in the house. It's not right."

Her eyes skim up my short skirt and tight shirt that barely covers anything. "Maybe you should take a good, hard look at yourself before you say that." She backs out of my room, almost if she's afraid of me and I have to wonder if she knows what I am. Not Lily, but potentially a psychopath. "And I'm not giving you your keys back. Not until you can get your act together and be the daughter I used to know."

"And who exactly would that be? Because I honestly don't know." I reach the doorway, my voice rising and filling with a silent warning. I grip onto the doorframe, fighting to hold myself in my room because every muscle of mine is yanking me toward her. *If she keeps it up, I might have to teach her a lesson. Chase her down and make her give me the keys.*

My mother's expression snaps cold, yet there's a hint of nervousness beneath the surface. She hovers back, picking up her pace as she backs up the hallway. "This is for your own good. You'll thank me one day for it," she says before she turns around and goes into her bedroom, shutting the door.

As soon a she disappears, I calm down, like a fire simmering out. Prying my fingers away from the doorframe, I step back into my room and shut the door.

*You're going to get her back for this. You can't let her control you like this.*

"It might be for the better," I say. "It keeps me from doing anything bad if I'm trapped here."

*That's not entirely true. You're worse than you want to admit, Maddie Asherford. You're just afraid. And being bad isn't necessarily bad in certain situations. You need to stop fearing yourself so much.*

I don't argue with her because it feels too much like the truth.

I sit down on my bed and call Bella; still no response. I'm starting to worry that rumors are getting around that maybe I had something to do with Sydney's murder and that maybe Bella's afraid of me and that's why she won't answer. I also haven't heard from River and other than that, I haven't conversed with anyone for the last few days, besides my mother. My next appointment with Preston is in a couple of days, and I'm concerned what will happen if he tries to pick my brain about stuff—what might spill out.

Finally, I can't take it anymore. When my mom turns off the alarm to go outside and chat with the neighbor, I sneak out the backdoor and make a beeline for the bus stop at the end of the block. I need to go talk to Bella. Hopefully, she'll give me some answers.

Answers that tell me I'm not a killer.

## Chapter 13
## Maddie

Bella lives in an apartment complex on the more rundown side of town. It's still way too early for her to be at work, so I'm hoping that she'll be there. After knocking on the door for several minutes, I realize she's not. I think about just waiting on the steps until she comes home, even if it's tomorrow morning after she gets off work. However, there's a large Rottweiler barking at me from the window next door, a sketchy looking guy across the street smoking and drinking who hasn't taken his eyes off me this entire time, and two very large guys screaming at each other near the corner. It's making even the inside of me nervous.

I should leave; instead, I find myself wandering around the side of the complex and to the back door of Bella's place. At first, I just stand there, staring at the doorknob, wondering what I'm doing, but then I realize that I do know what I'm doing. I don't know how I know, but I just do.

Without thinking, I pluck a hairpin from my hair and pick the lock on the door. It takes only seconds, as if I'm a pro, and I'm guessing that somewhere in my past I've done this before. Many times.

I open the door and step inside Bella's home, noting that there's a sink full of dirty dishes, stacks of mail on the counters, and takeout boxes all over the kitchen. There's absolutely no kitchen table. No barstools. No furniture at all. And it's the same in the living room. The only thing in there is a sleeping bag on the floor. The curtains are drawn shut and the air is musty. It's as if she barely lives here.

I double check the address she gave me awhile ago that I punched into the phone just to make sure I came to the correct house. It matches, but still, I wonder if she gave it to me wrong or something. Or maybe she just lives like this.

Deciding maybe breaking in wasn't the best thing to do, I start to turn around to leave, but pause when I swear I hear a muffled cry coming from down the hallway. I'm not sure whether I should leave or run. Maddie wants to go. Lily wants to stay.

*You need to see what it is.*

"I'm afraid," I admit aloud and shudder at the truth. Not necessarily afraid of the danger the crying could lead to, but how much I like that it could. My thoughts drift to what the crying could be. Someone hurt? Someone upset? Someone locked up who I could hurt?

"What the fuck is wrong with me?" I ask as the last thought streams through my head.

I start to back away, tugging at my hair, but invisible strings tug me forward, toward the crying. At this moment, I'm a puppet and Lily is my puppeteer and suddenly she's in front of me, taking my hand and tugging me down the bare hallway. She leads me through the stale air until we reach the end where there's a single shut door. Light is slipping through the cracks underneath and cries are flowing from the outside. *Pain.* Whoever's in there is hurting.

"I don't want to see," I whisper in horror as my trembling hand reaches for the doorknob.

"You need to see," Lily insists.

My fingers brush the brass knob. A jolt of heat shoots up my arm as I turn it and push it open. Light spills over me. Screams pierce my ears. Something flies at me that's heavy and strong. Pain. Heat. Tears. Blood. My insides feel like they're ripping out of my body.

*Fire!*

*Fire!*

*Fire!*

*Burning!*

*Burning!*

*Burning!*

*Help me!*

*Help me!*

*Help me!*

"You killed me."

## Chapter 14
## Lily

I'm not sure where I am. Lost in Maddie's mind? Perhaps, but I'm not sure. All I'm certain of is that I can't see anything. I'm drowning in the yelling. The anguish. The darkness I'm accustomed to. So I think. A lot. Make up stories that feel more real than anything else in the world.

*There once was a little girl who lived in a fictional world, but the little girl didn't know it. What was hidden under the blindness, the incredibility was ugly, raw torment. What she couldn't see couldn't hurt her. What she couldn't feel, couldn't sting her. What she couldn't remember, she could make up. She could be anything she wanted to be, not what she was taught to be.*

*But over time, the girl forgot what was real and what was made up.*

*She became lost.*

*Hiding in the darkness of her own fears.*

*Letting the real girl be forgotten. The one that changed her. The one that trapped her. The one that created her.*

## Chapter 15
## Maddie

When I open my eyes again, I feel so cold. So empty. So disconnected. Nothing makes sense. Why am I waking up at all? How did I even fall asleep to begin with? Where am I?

My eyelids flutter open, half expecting to discover that I've fallen asleep in my room. That everything was a dream. That maybe I'm even still young. Then I remember everything. That I'm the good girl I've constantly been told that I was. But as the last thought crosses my mind, I don't feel as calm as I should. I feel gross. Disgusted.

The disgust only increases when I fully open my eyes and take a look at my surroundings. At first, I think that maybe this is a dream, or that the red splatters are merely paint. That in another world, in another life, I was a painter and this repulsive creation before me was simply an illusion. However, the longer I stare at it, the more I realize the red misshapen dots on the white wall, the lines running downward that look like crooked water, the large spots staining the carpet, are blood. Blood everywhere. There's so much around me that the air smells like pennies, so potent I can taste the vileness.

I immediately jump to my feet, trying to ignore how the carpet squishes beneath my fingers, the warmth of blood spills over the backs of my hands. Once I get upright, I nearly collapse to the floor as a spout of dizziness rushes through me. I refuse to buckle though, and fall back into the blood again.

"It's everywhere," I whisper to myself as I turn in a circle. The bed. The sheets. The walls. The window. The closet doors. Splattered like raindrops. Frayed ropes are fastened to the headboard and a blindfold lies on the blood soaked pillow. There's only one thing missing from the madness. A body. But the strange part is I can picture the body there, pallid skin, blood in her hair, her lips slightly apart, frozen from when she took her last breath. I'm not even sure who *she* is, but I think at some point in my life I've witnessed the scene before.

Swallowing the bile burning in the back of my throat, I make my way over to the closet door. There's bloody fingerprints smeared on the handle. I try to ignore how well they match up to my own as I turn the knob and pull the door open. It's empty inside. No body. No blood. I breathe in relief, although I don't know why. Blood like this had to come from death—I can practically smell it in the air.

It takes me a moment, but I manage to get down on my knees and check under the bed. It's the only place in the room where there could be a body. Again, it's clean. Except for a single, red button. Even though I know I shouldn't, I have to pick it up. Collect it. A tiny, little memory forgotten in the midst of sheer terror. My fingers clasp around it and I stand back up, trembling as I stare down at the oval shaped button that matches the one I have at home in my button collection. The mysterious one I found on me the day I found Sydney's as well.

"No." I shake my head, uncertain at what I'm even saying no to. The truth. *But what is the truth?*

I stand there for what seems like forever, trying to put the pieces together. What happened when I opened that door? I heard screaming, saw light, but that's it. There doesn't seem to be a bump on my head, just blood on my hands. Did I blackout and Lily took over? Did she kill someone? Did she kill Bella? If so, where's the body?

The longer I try to sift through my thoughts, the more confused I get. Something snaps within me and suddenly I lose it. I start tearing the room apart, throwing clothes out of the dresser and closet, scattering papers that are in the nightstand drawers. I tear the bloody sheets off the bed, leaving my fingerprints everywhere. If the cops had their suspicions about me being a killer before, I just gave them all the evidence to convict me. That is, if there's a body.

*Go. Before this gets worse.*

I start to turn to leave and step on a white shirt. The pressure of my weight makes it press against the carpet and stain the innocent fabric with blood, along with the red, oval buttons, two of which are missing. I don't even know why I do it. I've already left my fingerprints, DNA, and every other mark about me all over the place. Still, I pick up the shirt, letting my fingers stain with more blood as I examine it. It has to be Bella's, but then, why did I have the button in my pocket that night?

I drop the shirt to the floor, like it's made of coal. Then I take off, wanting to get the hell out of the house. It's still somewhat light outside and I'm covered in blood though, so instead of running out the front door, I hurry into the bathroom. It's the most sickening thing I've ever done. Well, maybe. Depending on what happens when I blackout. I still do it though—take a shower in Bella's bathroom and wash the blood that might be hers off my body. Then I put on some of her clean clothes that I find in the washroom. A black skirt and a white shirt, very similar to the one I left to be forgotten in blood on the bedroom floor. I leave my damp hair down and take it one step further, finding a tube of red lipstick and mascara in the medicine cabinet.

I stare at my reflection for a moment, looking for evidence that maybe the eyes staring back at me aren't my own anymore. Who is this girl in the mirror? A sinner? A good girl who's just gotten lost? A girl whose lost her identity?

Suddenly, I see a face appear behind me, a body of a girl that looks just like me only has long, blond hair and piercings covering her face. She smiles at me through the mirror and I whirl around, only to find that she's gone.

"Lily," I say with my hand pressed to my racing heart as I recollect seeing her take my hand and guide me down the hallway before I passed out. "Is that you?"

The only response I get is the quiet.

I hurry out of the bathroom and to the backdoor, ready to slip out of the house. As I'm rushing through the kitchen, I spot a piece of paper on the countertop. I'm not sure if it was there or not when I walked in, but what catches my attention is the bloody handprint on the front of it.

I pick it up and flip it over, my heart trying to escape my chest before I even see what's on the other side. It's like I already know what it is. When I see the picture of myself, I'm not even that surprised. I'm not even sure when it was taken; probably before the accident since in the picture my hair is blond and long like how the detective described it. I look rougher; piercings in my lips, darkness in my eyes, and an I-don't-give-a-shit smirk on my face as I flip the camera off. The real icing on the cake, though, is that scribbled in the corner is the name Lily Asherford.

"Why does Bella have this?" I mutter.

Someone over my shoulder whispers, *Go.*

I don't turn around to see if anyone's there; I just stuff the photo into my pocket and run away from the house, wishing I could run away from myself as well.

## Chapter 16
## Maddie

It was a project getting back into the house and I set off the alarm again, pissing my mother off even more.

She starts getting edgy, nervous, as if she's waiting for a killer to show up—or that she's living with one. She keeps her distance from me, glad when I spend a lot of time in my room, waiting for the police to show up like a vulture waits for death. It's all I think about; it consumes every inch of my mind.

I watch the news for a discovered body.

Hide the button. Throw Bella's clothes away when I get home. I call in sick for work for the next four days, worried what I'll find when I get there. The police. River had to have given up my alibi by now and if not, then someone had to have discovered the blood at Bella's apartment. Bella. I've tried to call her, tried to make sense of the blackout and the scene I woke up to, but her cellphone's been disconnected. Something's wrong. If I was a good person, I'd go to the police, risk myself to make sure Bella's safe; but I'm not a good person. I'm Lily. All her.

So instead, I stay home and lock myself in my room with my secrets. Nothing happens except for when I get a call from a concerned Glen asking if I'm okay on a voicemail. I've been sick for so long and he's worried about my health. I'm worried about my health, too—my mental health.

I don't sleep more than a few minutes a night, too afraid to shut my eyes. I can't take any risks. It's starting to affect me, though. I'm starting to see things that aren't real, like Lily standing in my mirror all the time. And I'm talking to her more and more. In fact, she's pretty much all I talk to.

To pass time, I do some research on fires nearby where my mother said I was hit, wondering if I put the pieces of my past together, perhaps somehow I can figure out the madness of the present. I find an article about a forest fire that happened in the general location. No casualties, but it did say an old building burned down. There's a picture of it in the article. It's faded, black and white, but it looks like an outdated hospital, one I know for a fact I've been to before.

*Flames ignite around me. Smoke smothers my lungs. My skin feels like melting wax.*

*"You did this," someone whispers, "so you might as well run."*

*Run? "I can't… not without her."*

*"She'll be fine. She did put you here after all."*

*They're right. She did put me here, made me take her place. And now it's time to run away from it. Let myself be forgotten instead of her. So I take off running into the scorching flames, letting room fourteen slip farther away from me, feeling lighter with each step. I can almost taste the freedom. Right there in the trees, but then I hear her call my name.*

*"Maddie, don't leave me. Please."*

*I hate her. I love her. I don't want to help her. But it's not about me. It never is. It's always about her. So instead of running away from the fire, I turn around and burn, burn, burn. All for her. Everything is.*

I jerk from the memory, trembling, my veins pulsating with adrenaline as I touch my finger to the scar on my hand, tracing the faint lines of the numbers. "Room fourteen." I look up at the picture of the old hospital. "Is this where I was? Was I locked up here once?"

"Does it really matter if you were?" Lily asks. "You already knew you were crazy."

"Yeah, but it's..." I trail off, looking at the computer screen. "It's terrifying to think about... being locked away."

"You're locked away now."

"Yeah, but this is different."

"How so?" she asks as I move away from the computer desk and study myself in the mirror. I can see her staring back at me, watching me through the looking glass; same face, same eyes, only the pupils look rounder, darker.

"Because it is," I reply, blinking quickly as my hair starts to shift from black to blond. By the time my eyes open again, the illusion is gone.

"You're afraid all the time," Lily says with a glimmer in her eyes, like she knows a secret. "But of what?"

"*You*," I reply then sigh. "Myself."

The reflection reaches up and touches her chin-length black hair, her fingers lingering on the blond streak, and then she traces her fingers along the dark circles under my bloodshot eyes. "Well, we are the same person."

I shake my head. "No, we're not."

"I think you've known all along that I am," she adds, the reflection lowering her hand to the side. "Maybe that's why we were at the hospital. Perhaps they kept you there because you were insane."

"But who's they?"

"Your mother probably." She says it like she knows it's true, like she understands what lies behind the veil blocking out my memories. Perhaps that's what Lily is. Maybe she has my memories and she's keeping them from me. Perhaps she knows that I was once locked away in a hospital because I was bad, because I talked to myself, was two different people. That the memories of the girl are really just memories of me. That my mother knows this, but doesn't tell me in the hopes that I won't become that person again.

That I'll turn into the good daughter she's always wanted.

"Yeah, but if that's true, you and I know that's not possible," Lily says. "We're not good—neither of us are good."

I want to argue, but as I look back at my bed at the box of buttons, the computer screen with the article, and then at my hands that only days ago were saturated with someone's blood, I can't deny the truth. I can blackout. I can forget. But in the end, whatever Lily does, I do, too, because she *is* me.

I created her.

## Chapter 17
## Maddie

It's going on five days since the detective showed up at my house and three days since the incident at Bella's. Thankfully, the days have been uneventful. At least, that's what I tell myself. But in the end, I start to go stir crazy. The endless hours get to me and the need to do... well, something works its way under my skin. So when the alarm suddenly goes off in the dead of night, I feel twistedly excited.

I'm fully wide awake when it happens, still suffering from insomnia. For a second, I think I'm hallucinating, but the longer the siren shrieks, the more I realize that it's reality and that something set it off. Moments later, my mom comes stumbling down the hallway and runs fearfully into my room, right as I'm walking out of my bedroom to see what's going on. We end up colliding into each other and she falls to the floor, landing on her ass while I brace myself by grabbing onto the door.

"What are you doing?" she hisses, fastening her robe as she scrambles to her feet. The house is dark, the only light coming from her room, so I can barely see her face, but can hear the annoyance in her voice. It's how she's been with me for days. Always annoyed, especially when I try to pry answers out of her. I'm starting to get to the point where I'm considering tying her up and forcing her to tell me what she's hiding.

I throw my hands over my ears and shout over the screeching, "Um, hello. The same thing as you are; turning that thing off."

She huffs and then stomps down the hallway. I hear a beep and the alarm silences then she's rushing down the hallway toward me with a stern look on her face.

"You didn't set that off?" she asks as she reaches me.

I lower my hands from my ear and fiddle with the drawstring on my pajama bottoms. "How could I if I'm standing here?"

She looks over my shoulder into my room. "You didn't open a window or anything?"

"Nope. I was just sitting here, reading." Lie. I was counting my buttons.

Reality seeps in as we both realize the truth and her hand instantly finds my arm, her fingers trembling as she grasps onto me for dear life, as if I'm as precious to her as the buttons are to me. "Maddie, there's someone in the house."

The hairs on the back of my neck stand on end as a crash comes from the kitchen. My mother shoves me backward and starts to race off in the direction of the noise, but I grab the back of her robe and pull her to me.

"Don't just walk out there," I hiss, taking control of the situation, "Call the police."

She nods erratically then veers toward her room with her gaze fixed on the end of the hallway. When she reaches her doorway, she looks over her shoulder at me and says, "Go back in your room and lock the door." Then she hurries into her room to get her phone.

I start to do as she says when I hear a voice mid-turn.

"Lily."

I freeze, muscles raveling as I slowly turn back around. Standing in the darkness at the end of the hall is a person about the same height as me. They're not moving, frozen, staring right back at me, unafraid. I don't know who it is, but I know they know who *I am* by the name they uttered.

I can hear my mom chattering in her room as I begin to inch backward away from the figure, but then they laugh under their breath and mutter something about me still being weak and a whore.

I know them.

That voice.

I've heard it before.

*You're a whore!*

"Shut up," I say through gritted teeth, my hands balling into fists. Emotions pour through me so potent I can barely control anything that I do.

*That voice. It belongs to a man. A man hurt you. Get our revenge.*

“I know we know him,” I whisper aloud to Lily. “But who is he?”

The man moves toward me and chills course through my body. “You don’t know me, Lily? I’m hurt.” He stops to press his hand to his heart, chuckling under his breath. It makes me feel like he’s making fun of me.

Abruptly all I see is red. Blinding. Powerful. Overtaking. Then comes the pain. A huge, massive wave of it that nearly sends me to the floor. God, it hurts. And all I want to do is kill him to make it go away.

*Then do it.*

## Chapter 18
## Lily

I know this person and Maddie knows this person, too. I don't know from where or how, but I know them—all I know is that I do. And I hate them with more passion than anything else in the world. This man has hurt us both, made us suffer, and created us, which makes me feel sick and vile. Loathe myself for the first time in a long time.

Maddie releases control to me quickly, just like that. Without a fight. And I know that she wants me to take care of it—act on her impulses, something she's always been too afraid to do. So I storm down the hallway, ready to attack. The man just stands there, fully welcoming it. I know this could end badly. I could get hurt. Die. That's not what I'm worried about—that's the point of me existing. To take care of the things that Maddie fears the most, to step up and deal with the pain when she can't. I'm the strong one and she's the weak. I'm what she could never be and wishes she always was.

I lunge when I near him and he still doesn't move back, allowing my head to ram into his gut. He smells like cigarette smoke, booze and ash. The three scents combined make me want to vomit.

I don't have time to brace myself as we crash to the floor and I land on top of him, my hands sliding up to his neck as I sit up, growling. I grip tightly, feeling his muscles tense beneath my touch, and his pulse throb just below my fingertips. I'm gasping for air, wild, mind racing more than it ever has before. I want this, more than anything.

At first, I think he's just going to let me kill him as he lies there in the shadows simply staring at me. Then suddenly, when he's getting to the point where he's struggling for air, he gathers his strength and in one swift motion, flips us over so he's lying on top of me. I bump my shoulder against the end table and a lamp falls off, crashing against my head, and glass flies, razor sharp shards that slice open my flesh, just like I want to do to his.

"Not now, my Lily," he says, pinning me to the ground by the shoulders. I try to kick him, knee him in the gut, but he's too heavy and the bump on the head is making my mind dance and my body go to sleep. "But soon."

It's the last thing I hear before he lifts his hand and presses it over my mouth, while gripping at my neck, choking and smothering me until I'm on the verge of passing out. I shut my eyes and wait to die. I'm surprised by how comfortable I am with my own death—or just death in general—like my warm blanket I used to carry around when I was a child.

Death. I know death. It makes me content.

Just as I'm about to give into the darkness and slip away forever, the hands release me. My eyes shoot open and my lips part. There's nothing there but an empty living room and the night.

He's gone.

Was he ever really there to begin with?

## Chapter 19
## Maddie

I'm not sure how I pass out this time, but as soon as I wake up, I know I've lost a lot of time. It makes me nauseous, knowing I can lose control like that, but at the same time, I'm glad I didn't have to deal with the man.

When I open my eyes, I'm in my bed. The sun is trickling through the window and my skull feels like it has been split open.

"Maddie, relax," my mother says from my bed-side. She's sitting in a chair, dressed in tan slacks and a blue blouse, her hair is in a bun, her makeup done, and a magazine is on her lap. "You're okay."

I press my hand to my aching head as I catch my breath. "What happened?"

I glance around my room, clean as can be, the computer shut down, and the buttons put away. She cleaned up my room while I was out, which means she saw the buttons, saw the article I had opened. "Did you clean up my room?"

"Yes, it was filthy." She sets the magazine down on the floor and leans forward in the chair, taking my hand in hers. "I did it while you were sleeping."

I yawn, trying to decide if that's what happened. Did I finally just fall asleep? "Sleeping? But what about the person that broke into the house? What happened to him?"

Her forehead creases. "Maddie, there wasn't anyone in the house. After I called the cops, I came out of the room and you were lying in the hallway like you fainted... You woke up and said something about there being a man, but the cops checked the house and there were no signs of a break in... They did a few tests on you and said you showed signs of exhaustion." She feels my forehead as if she's checking for a fever. "Why didn't you tell me you haven't been sleeping very well?"

"I've been sleeping fine," I lie, slanting away from her touch. "And if there was no man in the house, then why did the alarm go off? I was... there was..." I'm at a loss for words. It's difficult to defend myself when my mental stability is tottering from side to side and I can't quite remember what happened, yet it feels like I should.

"The cops said it happens sometimes," she explains, giving my hand a squeeze. "That even the slightest bump against a window can set it off."

I'm not buying it at all. I've hallucinated before and what happened last night was too real to be one. "But I saw someone... I know I did." I sift through my memories, through the haziness, to what I think I saw. "It was a man. He was tall and he... he called me a whore."

My mother winces at the word. “Maddie, you passed out. How long has it been since you’ve gotten a good night’s rest?”

I tilt my head away from her hand. “I already said I’ve been sleeping fine. And I know what I saw. There was someone in the house and he did something to me... Made me black out somehow.”

“I’m tired of arguing with you about this stuff.” She pulls her hand away from mine and touches the base of her neck. “Get some rest.” She gets to her feet. “I’ll come check on you in a while.”

“I know what I saw, Mom. And you just need to tell me—”

She walks out of the room and shuts the door behind her. She’s lying, but the question is why. What is she hiding from me that’s so terrible she can’t even speak of it? Is it about me being in the hospital? My insanity? Or is it something else? How much does she know about me?

I get up out of bed and go over to the closet. She didn’t say a word about the box of buttons either, which I find odd. Unless I put them in my closet. But I’m pretty sure I left them out on my bed.

When I get to the shelf, I know they’re gone before I even check. It’s like I can feel their absence. I check anyway and discover I’m right. I rummage through the rest of the shelves, under my bed, through my drawers. I start to panic and not because of the fact that I had Sydney's button in there and the oval ones as well. I panic because they're gone. They're gone and I realize just how much I need them. How much counting them has soothed me.

*"Count the buttons," he whispers. "Count the buttons and focus on that. Not the screaming."*

But they're gone and now I can hear the screaming, echoing inside my head. Over and over again.

*The pain. The blood. He tells me to do things I don't want to do. Lily does them so much better. She seems like a natural at this. Like nothing bothers her. She tells me I'm weak for not being able to do it.*

*"But I can't turn it off," I whisper. "The pain."*

*"Then you'll never make it," she replies with a tired smile. "That's life. Only the strong survive."*

*"I want to be strong," I say over the screams, the blood, the begging. "Just like you."*

*Her smile broadens as she tucks a strand of her blond hair behind her ear then sticks out her arm. "Then be strong like me." Her other hand moves toward me and she hands me a knife. "Make me bleed," she says. "And don't feel bad about it."*

*I shake my head in horror. "I can't."*

*She gives me this all-knowing smile. "I knew it." She starts to put the knife behind her. "And* he *knows it, too. That's why he always picks you to go up there. Because you never fight back."*

*"Don't listen to her," the boy says from behind me. He's sitting in the corner, in the shadows, tied up as usual. "You don't want to be like her."*

*I want to listen to him, but hearing Lily doubt me so much makes me want to hurt her, bleed the doubt right out of her. So even though it makes me feel sick to my stomach, I take the knife from her and with a trembling hand, I cut. For the briefest moment, if feels right, just like* he *always told me it would.*

*"Wow," Lily says, cupping her wrist with wonder on her face. "I really didn't think you had it in you."*

*"Me neither," I whisper, my voice faint as I watch the blood drip from her wrist to the floor and paint the concrete with dots. I wish I could erase them somehow, erase how easy it was to hurt her.*

The memory fades and I look down at my wrist for a scar, knowing that if I slit Lily's, I had to have done it to myself; but my skin is smooth and flawless. The only thing on it is a powerful vein carrying blood, the beat of it matching the screaming still streaming through my head over and over again.

"Mom," I shout as I sink onto my bed, trying to breathe through the noise. "Mom, get in here."

Moments later, the door flies open and she rushes in. Her eyes grow big as she takes in the sight of me, cupping my wrist, my skin damp, my eyelids wanting to close and shut out the noise. "Jesus, what's wrong? Are you sick?" she asks, examining me over.

I shake my head, my fingernails digging into my own skin. "No, I just need my buttons."

There's a pause. It's only the beat of my heart, but it seems like a lifetime passes. I've said my secret aloud, admitted how much I need those buttons. But the real shocking part is, she doesn't look the least bit shocked.

"I threw them away," she says in a firm voice then turns away without a second glance back, leaving me to drown in the screams.

## Chapter 20
## Maddie

The screaming never leaves my head, but starts to wear on me. Like a song you hate when you first hear it, but then after listening to it several times you start to understand the meaning. The screams have a meaning. They're my past. They represent a torturous time in my life, where I was hurt, where I hurt people.

Eventually, I become restless at the lack of movement in my life and fake conversations my mother tries to have with me. She pretends as if nothing happened, as if I didn't see a man in our house, as if the alarm never went off, as if her daughter doesn't need a box of buttons to make her feel better. To her, everything is perfect.

*She's fucking delusional. Always has been.*

The longer it goes on, the more Lily gets restless and starts whispering to me more and more. She tells me not to hide from the world. That hiding is for the weak and that I need to get the hell out of the house and away from my mother. She sounds an awful lot like the girl in the memory and even though there's no scar, I'm coming to the conclusion that it was her. That I talked to her then in front of a boy who seemed to know about us both. So who was the boy?

I want to find out. I want to find out everything. Lily tells me to do so then. That if I want to remember things, then find a way to remember, instead of running away from the truth. And if I really want to remember who I used to be, the girl the detective was talking about, the girl in my repressed memories, then figure out a way—do something about it.

Like it's that easy.

And what about the man I saw? And the broken lamp that's nowhere to be found? I'm not sure, but I know it had to be real. I even found bruise marks while I was taking a shower the next day and there was a bump on the back of my head, like I'd been hit hard by something.

One day, during one of my mother's rare trips out of the house to restock the cupboards, Lily gives me an idea to attempt to get some answers. I start searching the house. For what? I'm not sure. Photos and items that will show me what I already think I know. That behind the perfect daughter my mother has tried to convince me I am, I'm really a wild, confused girl who has no set identity.

I begin in the basement where my mother stores a lot of boxes. I don't find much there, other than old papers, her yearbooks and old clothes. So I work my way to the upper floor and search my mother's bedroom. I don't come across anything, until I'm snooping around on the top shelf of the closet. There's nothing there, but what I do notice is the entrance to the crawl space.

It takes me a moment to get up onto the shelf, the wood creaking beneath my weight. So I hurry and push open the entrance, and stick my head in quickly before the shelf gives out. I end up tumbling ungracefully onto the floor. It's dusty and dark, full of insulation that makes my skin itch as I feel around blindly for… something. I'm not even sure what I expect to find, but I do find something. An envelope that's sort of heavy. *I knew that fucking woman was hiding something.*

Clutching it in my hand, I duck out of the crawl space, shut it, and carefully climb down off the shelf. Then I go back into my room, lock the door and shut the curtains as paranoia sets in. I have something in my hand I'm not supposed to. I can feel it under my skin, deep inside my bones, and behind the veil that hides my memories.

*Why are you hesitating?*

"Because I'm afraid."

*Why, though? What exactly do you think is in there?* She knows just like I know. I don't even know how I know, but I do.

I stare down at my hand, clenched up, knuckles white as I grasp onto the bulky envelope. "Answers to my past."

*Don't be afraid. Open it and find out.*

I swallow the lump in my throat and then open up the envelope, dumping the contents out onto my unmade bed. It's stuffed with papers and photos and a few larger, heavier objects at the bottom—a hospital band, a few buttons, and a key. The papers are my social security card, passport, a small stack of photos and two birth certificates. The first one is for Maddie Asherford. My parents' names are listed: Madison May Asherford and Markels Wellfordton. I never knew my mother took her maiden name back.

I move to the next one, figuring it's my mother's, but it's not. Lily Asherford, born the same day only a year earlier by the same parents as my own, which would make her my sister.

"What the hell?" I pick up my birth certificate and examine it closely.

Lily is extremely quiet, as if she senses something bad is about to happen.

"What is this?" I turn both of them over and compare them from front to back. They both look exactly the same, but one of them has to be a fake. It has to be. Either that or I had a sister who no one ever bothered to tell me about.

*Keep going.*

I set the birth certificate down and pick up the hospital band, which has the name Maddie Asherford and the date of when I was in the hospital six years ago. Shaking my head, I set that down and pick up the buttons. They're all different sizes, shapes, colors. There's three total and I wonder if they're mine, and if my mom knows about my weird button obsession. I drop the buttons down on the bed. One by one they hit the mattress like little raindrops.

*One by one the buttons fall and each one makes me feel safe as I count them. They distract me, even though they belong to him. They're all I have in this world.*

*"I have no one."*

*"That's not true," the boy says, his voice so familiar, yet so far away. Distant.*

*I can smell the scent of flowers flowing from outside. Something so beautiful, yet I hate the smell because every time I smell them, it means I'm really with* him, *not matter how much I block it out.*

*"You have me. As long as you think of me, we can be whoever we want to be."*

*"I don't want to be me anymore." I can smell the scent of cigarettes as the boy fades from my view.*

*Hold onto him.*

*"Let him go." Sitting in the shadows of the small room, so confident, so content with all the screaming that seems to be echoing around us is a girl who looks so much like me. Long, blond hair and able to smile through all of this. I wish I was her. "Don't be weak, Maddie. Let him go and get through this yourself; otherwise, you're going to turn into that weak girl again."*

*I hesitate, deciding what I want. Good. Bad. Who am I? When I'm with Lily, I'm bad, but it feels okay. Yet, when I'm with the boy, I'm myself. I'm Maddie, and it feels right, but in the most painful way.*

*Finally I reach for him, refusing to let him fade away from me. I won't focus on the screaming, on the scent of the man, his voice, what he tells me to do, what he does to those girls, to me, to the boy. But it's so hard to keep reaching for him.*

*"I'm too tired… too broken."*

*He manages to get ahold of my hand and the warm contact of his skin makes me feel at peace with myself, not so cold and hollow. So dirty. So wrong. So Lily. "You're going to be okay."*

*I glance over at the girl in the corner, so confident, so strong. She doesn't fear the man as much as I do and I know she'd help me if she could.*

*"But I want to become her and that makes me crazy."*

*He shakes his head with a sad smile on his lips and I wish the sunlight would hit his face so I could see his eyes. "You're only crazy if you think you're crazy."*

I blink from the memory, the scent of lilies still lingering in the air. For a moment, I swear they surround me, white flowers growing from the grass, and I'm back in the place with the girl and the boy, fighting not to hold onto reality.

Soon it fades and I'm back in the moment. Taking a deep breath, I move to the photos and instantly discover why my mother hid them from me. They're of me when I was younger, early teens, and I look very similar to the girl in the photo I found in Bella's. Long, blond hair just like the detective said, just like in some of the memories, just like my Lily. Piercings in my nose, lips, eyebrows, and my ears are studded heavily. I'm dressed in black; a short skirt, boots, and a crop top that shows my ribcage. Right where my scar is now, there used to be a tattoo, cursive font that traced the name *Evan*.

I touch my side and whisper, "Evan." It rolls off my tongue, thick like honey and makes my stomach feel like it's igniting in flames. "I don't understand this." I want to cry, but Lily won't allow me to let tears fall. She's just like the girl in the memory, making me be stronger than I want to be.

"Who's Evan?" I wonder. "And why is there a scar where his name is now?"

*I don't know.*

"Is he the boy in my memories? Did I have his name tattooed on my side, but when I got in the accident it was ruined?"

*Go to the last item.*

I stare at the key sitting on the bed, engraved with the number fourteen, and I touch the scar on my palm absentmindedly.

*What are you waiting for? Pick it up.*

"I'm afraid." My voice is unsteady.

*Of what.*

"Of what it is... what it means... about me," I say.

Taking a deep breath, I slowly move my fingers for the key. The metal stings against my skin, icy cold. The sensation shoots up my arm and brands my mind. Scorching hot images come to me.

I've held the object in my hand before and it's not just the recollection that proves it. I know because it matches the shape of the scar on the palm of my hand. I clutched this very key that night in the road. That night six years ago when the rain poured down on me and the stranger who tried to take it from my hand. But it's more than that.

With my hand open, I hold the key in it. It's long and slender, silver with lines and diamonds fitting perfectly on top of the scar, the numbers matching up perfectly. It makes my skin tingle, makes my mind tingle... makes my whole body tingle... Room fourteen...

*Pitter-patter.... Pitter-patter... Pitter-patter... the rain crashes against the earth... Through it, there's a spark. I've seen it before. Heard the voice that follows me, calls out my name, shouts at me to stop!*

*As I look back, I see bright orange flames, scorching through the trees and toward the sky, so wild that even the rain can't even drown it out.*

*Don't be afraid... just run. We need to run! Now! Before they catch us and lock us back up again.*

*I pause in the trees, coming to a stop. "Us? But I wasn't locked up," I say to Lily, who is standing beside me, her long, blond hair wild, her eyes reckless as she scans the trees for a way out. "Just you."*

*She shakes her head and rolls her eyes. "That's always been your problem." She ducks under the trees and shouts out. "You listen to what everyone else tells you instead of seeing it for yourself."*

"What does it mean...? Why was I running with it that night...? And who was I running from?" I ask, tracing my finger across the jagged edge of the key. A solid steel door appears in my head with the number fourteen painted on it. "Does this go to the hospital room I was in?" As soon as I say it, I pause. In the memory, Lily told me that I was locked up, but I said I wasn't. She said I believed what everyone told me and never saw things for myself. "But how can I never see things for myself when I'm so blind...? I can't even remember anything."

*Because you repressed it yourself. Not because it was stolen from you.*

She's right, but still, at this point, I think if I could actually remember, I would. Just to have some answers.

"Do you know what I did that night when I got hit by the car?" I ask, enfolding my fingers tightly around the key. "Do you know what happened before all of that? How I escaped the hospital...? Why I was there?"

*I know as much as you. Your mind is my mind. If you don't want to remember, then neither do I.*

I feel my legs carrying me to the mirror of their own accord. "But I don't know anything." I study myself in the mirror, imagining myself as a blond like the detective said, imagining myself as someone else. "Other than these pieces that don't make any sense."

*You don't know anything because you chose to forget. Everything you do, you chose.*

She's right. If I was a better person, then I'd simply go talk to someone—go to Preston and confess what's going on. Tell him about Sydney. Bella. These horrifying memories and how I think I might be a killer. But I know I won't. I'm not sure if that makes me a bad person, for carrying those thoughts inside me, not speaking about them because I worry what they mean. Maybe if I'd spoken up sooner, lives could have been spared. Maybe Sydney would still be alive.

"Maybe," Lily says. "But maybe not."

## Chapter 21
## Maddie

"*Bartender Bella Anderfells Missing, Foul Play Suspected.*" This is the headline on the news the morning after I find the birth certificates and key. There aren't too many details, only that she was seen over a week ago on March fifteenth, on the day Sydney died. I don't know how to process this information, but every time I shut my eyes, I end up back at her place, surrounded by blood and no body.

As I'm struggling with whether I should be guilty or not, whether I killed her or not, I decide it's time to confront my mother about the birth certificate, convincing myself that maybe if I get more answers, somehow the mystery will be solved. Although, in the back of my mind, I think part of me secretly wishes to stay in the dark. What I don't know can't hurt me. If I'm a killer and I don't know it, then everything's still okay, right?

Wrong. But it's what I tell myself to keep moving and breathing.

I opt for a surprise attack, and catch my mother one day while she's eating a sandwich at the kitchen table. I simply walk into the kitchen and set the birth certificate down on the table in front of her.

She immediately drops her sandwich and her jaw drops as she stares at. "Where did you get that?"

"I think you know where I got it." I pull out a chair and take a seat across from her. "The spot where you were hiding it."

She shakes her head, staring at the piece of paper. Finally, she reaches out to touch it, her fingers trembling, but she quickly pulls back. "Maddie, you need to forget you ever saw this," she says, her gaze drifting up to me.

I cross my arms on the top of the table. "No. I've forgot enough during my lifetime. This is it for me."

She presses her lips together, so forcefully that they start to turn blue around the edges. "It was your sister's." Her voice is so soft, delicate, fragile.

"My sister's?" I act surprised, but I'm not. I had my suspicions. Still… "Why didn't you tell me about her before?"

She swallows hard, her hand clasps around the bottom of her neck as if she's trying to strangle herself. "Because the memory of her will only cause you pain."

"Try me." My tone is firm, demanding.

She shakes her head over and over again, tears dotting her eyes. "It's better if you don't remember her."

I grip the edge of the table, needing to hold onto something because I feel like I'm about to tumble into darkness, but I don't know why. "It's my decision whether I remember her or not and right now, I've decided that I want to remember her. Now tell me. Where is she?"

It takes her an eternity to answer. Cars drive by from outside, the wind blows, my mother battles to breathe evenly. "She died."

All noises fade away.

"When?" My voice cracks.

A single tear falls from her eye. "A long time ago."

"But why didn't you ever tell me about her?"

"Because she's better forgotten."

"What the hell does that mean?" I press my hands to the side of my face, struggling for oxygen. I keep thinking about the girl in my memories, the one with blond hair that told me to cut her wrist. She said she was Lily and I thought she was my Lily, but maybe she was my sister. But in the pictures... I look so much like her. Long, blond hair and the scar was there, so it had to be me.

"What the hell is going on?" The room is spinning, tumbling out of control, or maybe it's just me. "Nothing makes sense."

"Maddie, this is why I didn't want to tell you." She slides her arm across the table to take my hand. "It's better if you can't remember painful things like this. It's the bright side of your amnesia."

My hands drop to the table and I suck in a large mouthful of air. "Bright side? Are you fucking kidding me?" I jump out of the chair so abruptly it topples to the floor. "There is no bright side to this." I give an exaggerated gesture at myself. "Every day I feel like I'm losing my mind and you just add to that."

"I wanted to protect you," she says, slowly getting to her feet. "From the pain of having a sister."

"Pain of having a sister. Are you fucking crazy?" I grasp at my head. This isn't how a conversation should go. She should be talking about the pain of losing a sister.

I lower my hand to the side. "What happened to me, Mother? In my past? With Lily? Were we locked up once?" I pause. "Did you lock us up?" As soon as I say it, I know it's not true.

"How dare you." Her entire body is quivering, not with fear, but with rage. She grips onto the back of the chair for support. "I would never do anything to hurt you or your sister."

"I don't believe you," I say and I partially mean it. I don't know my mother enough to know whether she would hurt me or not. All I know is that in my past, I've been hurt by someone.

"How can you ever say that?" she asks. "I would never, ever do anything but protect you. Even if it means causing pain to myself."

The last part is a little strange. Why would protecting me cause pain to herself? "What do you mean by that exactly?"

She shakes her head, releasing the table and squaring her shoulders. “I’m not talking about this anymore. There was a reason I never talked about it.”

“Because it caused you pain?”

“Enough,” she snaps harshly. “No more of this. I’m done.”

And with that, she runs out of the room and I’m left unsure what to believe. Who to trust.

*You can always trust me.*

## Chapter 22
## Maddie

I'm moving out of the house. I haven't told my mom yet, but I can't do it anymore. Crazy or not, being cooped up in the house with her lies, locks and alarms is making my situation worse. I'll get my own place. Go to work and spend the rest of the time by myself, trying to piece together my past—who I was, why I was locked up, and what happened to my sister. That I can do—I'm better at being alone anyway.

Although I'm never really alone. I always have Lily. Part of me wonders if maybe I created her out of my sister. Perhaps when I lost my sister Lily, my Lily arose. But the idea is kind of frightening because my Lily is frightening, which makes me wonder what my sister was like.

Over the next couple of days, I start looking for places to live and a new job, one that will satisfy my darker cravings, one where I can start over and get some help from someone who isn't my mother.

I'm looking through the classifieds in the newspaper, trying to ignore the best that I can the picture of Bella on page nine, when my phone rings.

River's name flashes on the screen and I freeze. He never calls me, not outside of work, which makes me wonder why he is now. I think I know and even though part of me doesn't want to know, the other part has to know whether I need to be worried or not.

He starts off by asking me how I am, acting casual—too casual. I know something's up and I think I know it before he even asks it—the real reason he's calling me. He continues casually asking me why I haven't been to work.

"Is it because of Sydney's death? Or because Bella's gone missing?" he questions. "I know it must be hard for you, losing people you know." The fact that he says it, tells me just how little he knows about me.

Sometimes, I think I'm numb to almost everything going on around me. I hardly feel any emotions except toward Lily. And fear when I'm put in a panicking situation.

"Yes and no," I respond evasively, wondering if the police have talked to him yet. Perhaps that's where the casualness is stemming from.

"Well, I hope you won't stay away from work forever," he says then gives an elongated pause. "I kind of miss you… I know the place seems kind of cursed. At least, that's what people are saying right now, but I assure you the bar had nothing to do with either of their disappearances."

I want to ask him how he can be so sure, but I bite my tongue.

"How could you possibly miss me, River? You barely know me." *I* barely know me.

"That's not true..." He struggles for an answer. "I miss spending time with you. You should really come in today, even if it's to talk. And your job's still waiting for you, whenever you're ready to come back."

"I can't do that," I say, lying down on my bed and staring at the key on my nightstand, the one I found in my mother's room. "Besides, I'm moving."

"Where?"

"I'm not sure yet, but I'm figuring it out."

He pauses, his breathing heavy on the other end. "Maddie, I don't think you should go anywhere right now."

"Why not?" I put the key in my pocket. I don't even know why or if I'm the one who did it.

River pauses for the third time. "Maddie, we really need to talk," he says as I roll over on my back and stare up at the ceiling. "It's important."

I tense. The way his voice deepens carries a warning and sends goose bumps erupting across my skin. I uncontrollably shiver. *He knows something.*

"About what?" My voice is rickety just like my pulse.

"Come to the bar and talk," he says, his tone lightening. "I'll be at my office in about ten minutes."

"I can't do that," I repeat as I sit up on the bed. "Trust me, River; this is for your own good."

"Maddie, this is important," he stresses. "Just get down here as soon as you can."

I grind my teeth in frustration, more with myself than anything. I should have been better with the detective, given him a better answer to why I was at Sydney's crime scene that morning because that has to be what this is about. Either that or it could be about Bella. Have the police gone to her apartment and found the bloody mess? Have they linked me to that somehow? But why would they go to River about that? I need to find out just how much they—River—knows.

"Fine." I get up from my bed, cross the room, and peek out the curtain at the sound of thunder.

What will happen when I go back into the real world again? Around people. Around River. What if I lose control? What if I get arrested? Locked up again? What if the police show up?

"I'll be there in like an hour."

*You're making a big mistake.*

"Drive safe," he says casually, his voice shifting to its normal, friendly tone. Like he didn't just make things weird between us.

I don't say anything, just hang up. I put the phone in my pocket, not bothering to cover up the short, black skirt, knee-high socks, and tight t-shirt I'm wearing. My mom's not home to see me, but quite honestly, it doesn't really matter anymore if she sees me dressed like this. I'm not even sure what I'm supposed to be today. A mixture of someone? Perhaps Lily and Maddie.

I pull on a jacket as I prepare to head out because it looks like it's going to rain, heavy clouds rolling in, a grumble of lightning in the distance. *I hate the rain.*

I go over to the security box and try to unset the alarm, even though I don't know the code. After several failed attempts, Lily gets irritated and pretty much forces me to walk out the door, setting off the alarm before sprinting out into the rain.

I take the bus because it's the only form of transportation I have at the moment. On my way there, I debate getting off and taking another bus that goes up to the foothills, taking a detour up to the cabin and just blowing off River completely. I haven't seen Ryland since the night Sydney was killed. I want to talk to him about it because he's the only one I can talk to openly; but at the same time, I fear that even he might think twice about being near me if I divulged I think I might have killed someone. What is his limit? How much is too much? Do I trust him? *No. I don't trust anyone.*

I need to go see River, though, and find out what he knows, whether I want to or not. So I head to the bar.

By the time I get there, raindrops are splattering against the window and the ground like the blood I see in my memories. I can hardly see through it, it's coming down so hard. I can make out the building across the street as the bus slows to a stop; the parking lot where I saw Sydney splattered in her own blood. I try to picture myself luring her over there. What would I have said that would make her go with me? Maybe we were fighting and she tried to run away from me. Maybe I chased her down and then, just at the right moment, I stabbed her multiple times. But where would I get the knife? And what about Bella? Why would I hurt her? I liked her, well, more than I liked anyone else.

"I think I really did it," I say as I get off the bus and once again, Lily has nothing to say. "It seems so easy to picture—someone dying because of me. And what happened at Bella's…? I can't deny the blood."

I stand on the sidewalk, staring at the bar, afraid of going inside. I listen to the rain drown the world. The thunder boom. The lightning crash. I remain there until a memory of me wrapping my fingers around a woman's neck starts to slither into me, a venomous snake slipping its fangs into my skin. Until I can feel the rain drenching my body, the cold concrete against my flesh, hear the deep voice calling me a *whore* and that I *deserve to be punished*, see the flames ignite through the storm, her voice that sounds just like mine telling me not to be weak, to do whatever it takes to be strong. *Be the darkness within you. It's so much easier.* Once it gets to that place, I jog inside, trying to outrun the images; but they're always behind me, chasing at my heels.

The bar is empty as I stumble in, drenched in rain from head to toe. The place doesn't open for another half of an hour. The faint smell of sweat and tequila is in the air, the lights are low, the chairs turned up. I think about the last time I was here. The chill of the freezer. The voice. The blood. I try to remember the rest. Connect the dots, but everything is still hazy.

I find River in his office, just like he said, talking on the phone.

Lily is screaming inside me. *Don't do it!* And then suddenly she's out, walking around in River's now clean office—he must have had someone clean up in here.

"No, Leon, I don't think this is a good idea." He shakes his head as I stand in the doorway and wait quietly while he talks on the phone. "I don't want to be a part of it anymore." A pause. "Look, I don't fucking care if I owe you. This is wrong... not to mention ille-gal."

"Hmmm... interesting..." Lily says, watching him have the heated conversation. "He's doing things with Leon, the drug trafficker."

I want to ask what she's implying, but that would require talking aloud and making me look as insane as I am. So instead I stand there, listening to River argue with Glen while Lily wanders over to a shelf, glances at a stack of papers, then grins at me and says, "Well, well, well, what do we have here?"

I'm about to go over there when River sees me and his face drains of color. "I have to go. I'll call you later." He quickly hangs up and then stares at me for a moment or two before he casually says, "We seriously need to get a bell on you so I know when you're coming."

I don't respond, trying to measure him up before I go any further into the office. He looks the same as he always does; faded jeans, a dark grey shirt, a hint of scruff on his jawline, and he has a beanie on his head. He doesn't seem afraid, like he thinks I'm a killer.

*But then why did he need to talk to me*?

*Don't trust him. No matter what.* Lily is now just back in my head, where she belongs. Not a visual representation of my sister.

"You look tired," he notes, taking in my appearance as I inch closer to his desk. "And wet. Is it raining outside?"

"It is... and I haven't been sleeping well." Deciding I should sit down, I cross the room, combing my fingers through my wet locks of hair. "So what did you want to talk to me about?" I take a seat across from the desk.

He reclines back in the chair, crossing his arms, studying me with his head cocked to the side. *Always watching you.* "The police came to talk to me this morning," he says. "They wanted to ask me a couple of questions about Sydney."

"Oh yeah." I pick at my nail polish, pretending to be blasé, even though I'm a nervous wreck. "Do they have any leads yet on who they think did it?"

"I don't think they do yet." He pauses, making heavy eye contact with me. I know what's coming even before he says it. "They wanted to ask me a couple of questions about you, too."

I drop my hand to my lap, refusing to look away from his penetrating gaze. No eye contact shows a guilty conscience. "Oh, yeah? What about?"

"About how you said you were here that morning because apparently we spent the night together."

I twist a strand of my hair around my finger. "Technically, we did."

He tugs off his beanie and rakes his fingers through his hair, making it stick up in all directions. "Are you in some kind of trouble? The detective seemed really interested in you and if I'd spent the entire night with you or if that was a lie... He seemed convinced that it was."

I unravel the strand of hair from my finger and put my hands on my lap, stabbing my nails into my legs to channel my anxious energy there. "What did you tell him when he asked?"

He smashes his lips together. One. Two. Three seconds go by. "That you were with me all night."

I sit up straight in the chair, freeing a trapped breath I was holding in my chest. "You lied for me? Why?"

"Because I care about you." He gives a shrug, like it's no big deal, when it is. He leans forward and rests his arms on the desk. "It's not that big of a deal."

"I'm not buying it," I tell him with skepticism. "You can't care about someone you hardly know."

"I know you better than you think," he says, his tone carrying an underlying meaning that sends a chill up my spine. "You just don't want to believe I do. You want to be mysterious. Want people not to see who you really are."

I don't like where he's going with this. I slouch back in the chair, keeping eye contact even though I desperately want to look away. "You might think so, but you're wrong."

"Am I?" he mumbles to himself without taking his focus off me. He seems so undecided, so confused. "I have to ask you something and I need you to answer me truthfully."

"What makes you think I'd lie to begin with?" Maybe he does know me better than I thought.

*You might want to prepare yourself.*

*What does that mean?*

"Because I know you do a lot," he says straightforwardly. "But I need you not to lie this time. I need you to give me this for lying to the police to you."

"I didn't ask you to do that," I remind him. I know I should be being more cooperative, but he's troubling me with his persistence for the truth. It worries me what he's going to ask.

"I know you didn't," he replies. "But like I said, I did it because—"

"Because you care for me," I finish for him. Is he being genuine? It seems like it, but I don't think I'm the best judge to come to this conclusion. I can barely understand myself, let alone another person.

I place my arms on the armrests, knowing I have no choice but to let him ask his question. Whether or not I answer truthfully is an entirely different story. "What do you want to know and I'll try my best to give you a real answer."

*You better be ready.*

He seems undecided, taking a deep breath and exhaling. "I want to know whether I'm talking to Maddie right now… or Lily."

## Chapter 23
## Maddie

It takes a moment for my mind to catch up with what he said. Quite honestly, I think I'm having one of my hallucinations. But as River stares at me from across the desk, waiting eagerly for a response, I realize that this is reality. That he did ask me if I was Lily. That somehow he's discovered my alter ego that might be named after my dead sister. Perhaps he's even met her. I can't help but think of the man that broke into the house. He called me Lily… It didn't sound like River, but still…

"Who's Lily?" I play dumb, coiling a strand of my hair around my finger.

"Maddie, please don't do that," he says in a soft, soothing voice, which seems out of character for someone who knows about the other part of me that has killer tendencies. "Don't go back to where we started."

"Where we started? What start? We never had a start, River. We fooled around sometimes. That's it."

*Wow, you're just as cruel as me. I didn't think you had it in you. Bravo.*

I can't help but think of the memory of me cutting Lily and how she seemed proud of me when I did it. *Why do you like when I'm bad?*

*Because it's who you are, yet you fight it so hard. You let fear own you, so afraid of being what you are.*

River blows out a frustrated breath. Seconds tick by and I veer toward hyperventilation. I need fresh air. Need to get out of here. I glance at the door, just over my shoulder, wondering if he'd chase me if I bailed. If he did, I could fight him. Hurt him. Maybe even get rid of him. It might be necessary now that he knows.

Before I can budge, he scoots back his chair to get to his feet. "That's not true. We had a start," he says, rounding the desk and coming up in front of me, in an intimidating manner. "The start of where you told me who you really were."

I tip my chin up, eyes narrowed as I slant forward instead of leaning back. I won't be afraid of him, even if he knows my dirty, little secret. "I'm Maddie. That's it. No one else."

The corner of his lip tips up and he gives me a half smile, reaching forward and cupping my cheek. "I know that."

"I'm not this Lily person." I move from his touch, working to take slow, even breaths. My chest is heaving though, like a volcano ready to erupt, and he notices, his attention sliding downward to my breasts. "That would make me crazy."

He tears his gaze away from my chest, his hand following me, his finger tracing a line back and forth across my cheekbone. His sleeves are rolled up and I can see faint lines of healing wounds up his arms, probably from where I clawed him a week ago. He notices me staring at the marks and pulls his hand away from my cheek to touch them.

"That night, when you came up to my office and gave me these," he begins, "you were calling yourself Lily."

My breath catches and I quickly clear my throat. "That's my nickname. Sometimes I like to go by it."

He shakes his head then drops to his knees in front of me, so we're at eyelevel. "You told me everything. About Lily. About Maddie. How you two coexist together." He glances down at his arms then back at me, then places his hands on top of my thighs. "This was, of course, after you attacked me."

"Attacked you? I thought you said things got kinky and I got rough."

"They did. But it started when you burst into the office, strolled up to me, and... wrapped your fingers around my neck."

*Oh my God, Lily. What the fuck did you do?*

*I was trying to protect us. He sees too much, but things didn't work out how I planned.*

*Great job. Now he sees everything.*

*It was an accident.*

*How?*

She doesn't respond and I flick my eyes to the door again, which is wide open. All I need to do is distract him and make a run for it.

"Don't worry," River says, his hands clamping down on my knee, securing me in place, as if he senses my desire to flee. "You didn't hurt me. You let go as soon as I asked you to, almost like you didn't even realize you were doing it. Then, after I got you calmed down, you told me... about whom you were... about Lily."

He's met Lily? Actually talked to her?

My lips part then shut again. Part then shut. "I don't even know what to say." I'm racking my brain for a way out of this. Usually Lily takes care of this, but she's silent, probably enjoying my uneasiness. "Why didn't you tell me before? Why didn't you tell me that morning when I couldn't remember what happened the night before?" It seems suspicious that he didn't. Most people in his situation would have—most would have reported me to the police or the nearest insane asylum. Maybe he has. Perhaps this is why he wanted me to come here. Maybe at any moment, the police are going to bust in here, handcuff me, and take me away. Lock me up.

*Speaking of handcuffs. He has a pair in his top desk drawer, just in case you want to go that route,* Lily whispers.

*And there you are... Wait, how do you know about the handcuffs?*

*He brought them out that night.*

*That doesn't seem like River at all.*

*Well, maybe you don't know him as well as you think, which is why you shouldn't trust him.*

*He's not... the man that broke into the house, is he?*

*How the hell would I know? You think I know more than I do?*

"Because I could tell you weren't her that morning," he answers my question and I tear my concentration from Lily and direct it on him. "And I could tell you were pretty fucking scared as it was that you couldn't remember anything, so I didn't want to add fuel to the fire by telling you I knew about her. Multiple personalities can be tricky, especially if you don't know about it already." He searches my eyes, maybe for her. "But I'm guessing you do."

I grip the edge of the seat, pierce my nails into the wood, fight not to hurt him—fight not to protect myself. "Please get out of my way so I can leave."

He shakes his head, only getting closer to me, his warm breath caressing my flushed cheeks. "Maddie, I want to help you." His voice conveys fervidness as he gently puts a hand on my cheek again. "There's no need to be afraid. These kinds of things can be helped... I want to help you."

"What are you? Some kind of psychology expert now?" I sit up straight, put my hands to his chest, and force him to move back and give me breathing room. "This isn't a sociology study, River. I don't want your help. I can handle it."

"That's not what it looks like to me." He brushes his fingers through my damp hair and tucks a few strands behind my ear. "You look like you haven't been sleeping very well."

"I already told you I haven't. But it's normal for people to have trouble sleeping."

"Is it..." He chews on his bottom lip, thinking. "Is it because of her?" he asks and I find myself shrugging. "Or is it because of the police? And how you are handling the thing with Bella?"

"It's nothing. I just get restless sometimes." I bite down on my lip until I draw blood to distract myself from the pain of thinking what I might have done to Bella and how River's sitting here worried about me over something I may have caused.

For the last six years, I've pretty much lived in solitude with only Lily as my company and Ryland, who doesn't ask me questions unless I offer openings. I don't like sharing my personal life with anyone and there are reasons for that—because it's fucking insane. Now though, well, Lily's taken it upon herself to give River an opening to ask questions. I hate her for it. And I don't really understand why she would do it.

*Why did you do it?*

*Accidental slip up.*

"So, if you were with me—Lily—that night, then maybe I did have an alibi." I look for the silver lining in this mess.

He shakes his head, pulling his hand away from my face. "What I told you about losing track of you was the truth." He tugs his fingers through his hair and sits back on his heels, frustrated. "I mean, one minute you were there and the next you were gone. But don't worry, like I said, I told the police you were with me, so it doesn't really matter."

"Yeah, but I still don't get why. You could get into a lot of trouble if they catch you."

"I know that, but I want to help you. I really, really do. And it seems like you might need my help. You're just afraid to take it for some reason."

"You keep saying that you want to help me, but it doesn't make sense. No one ever wants to help." I say it with no true meaning behind it, yet it feels like I meant it. I can't help but think about the dreams I keep having, the times I zone off, where I've been locked up before for whatever reason. Maybe no one helped me when I was locked away once, but if that's the case, then why am I free now? Who freed me? Was it Lily? Did she help me escape? But then why would my mother act like she was bad?

"I like you, Maddie, even if you don't believe so." River's gaze sweeps across my body, my clothes wet and clinging to my curves. "I've liked you from the day I ran into you outside of my AA meeting."

I'm not sure if I'm buying what he says or not, but I want to pick his mind some more because he seems to be my only lead to what I did that night.

"So, you don't remember me talking to anyone?" I ask as he puts his hands back on my legs again, seeming really determined to keep me in the chair. "That night, I mean... anyone that might could give me a legit alibi, or at least help me put the pieces together."

"Bella. Me. You talked to some of the regulars."

I shut my eyes, take in a deep inhale, and let it out slowly. "I'm not sure it's going to look good if I was talking to Bella." I open my eyes and try to decipher his reaction.

He seems far too calm in this particular situation. "You didn't do anything to Bella." He considers something with his brows furrowed, fingers massaging my legs. "She talked to a ton of people that night. And so did you." He gestures at the window. "I watched you guys for quite awhile and you talked with each other, costumers, Leon."

"Why would I talk to Leon?" I ask curiously. "I don't know him."

He shrugs, his hands sliding up to the tops of my legs, making my body betray me and shiver with need. “Bella was with you. Maybe she was introducing you to him.”

“Bella was with Leon that night?” It feels vaguely familiar, but maybe I’m searching for an answer to avoid the truth. Because no matter what, I did go to Bella’s apartment. Did black out. Did wake up in a room stained with someone’s blood.

“Yeah, they talked for a little while. I saw it through the window and then they parted ways and she spent most of the night with either you or clients.” He pauses. “From what I saw, no one seemed suspicious. Including you.”

“You were watching me through the window?” I ask, looking over his shoulder at the window that gives me a great view of the room below.

*Get out of here. Now.*

He shrugs again, but something in his demeanor changes—grows anxious. “You told me I could watch you that night, so when I wasn’t near you, I studied you from up here.”

*I don’t trust him,* Lily says.

*Neither do I… I want to, but I can’t.*

*We need a plan. To get you out of here and away from him for a while, at least until you figure some stuff out.*

*Yes... I guess we do… but how?*

*Handcuffs,* she entices.

Even though it makes me feel sick to my stomach, I decide that it's time to get the out of here and away from River without him being able to follow me and insist he's helping me. I need to figure some stuff out before I can go around trusting people. And the route I'm going to take is definitely stemming from my bad girl side—from Lily. I think about the knife and how she convinced me to slit her wrist. Deep down, a small part of me wanted to give into her so easily, just like I'm going to do right now.

"Are you watching me now?" I ask River, gliding my hands up the front of his chest and almost smiling when he shudders under my touch.

"What do you mean?" His voice is raspy as desire blazes in his eyes. "Of course I am. You're right in front of me."

"Clever." I slant toward him and he doesn't move back.

His eyes flick to my lips. "I know."

"I'm sure you do," I say in my most seductive voice then move closer to him. "You sure you want to help me?"

"Positive." He wets his lips with his tongue.

"Okay then." I press my lips to his and give him a soft kiss.

*I'm not a good girl. I don't care what they say. This is me. This is all I can be. I can't fight who I am anymore. I'm a bad girl. I do whatever it takes to protect myself. Be a whore. Be whatever you need to be to survive; otherwise, you won't.*

River kisses me for a moment, slipping his tongue deep inside my mouth. He tastes like cherries and smells like rain. It's delicious and intoxicating, but ends too quickly. He pulls back, his lips leaving mine. "Maddie, just relax." He holds me back by the shoulders. "We could go to my place and talk for a little while, if you want."

That's the last thing I want to do, go somewhere alone with him. So instead of responding, I slant forward again and taste him deliberately.

"Maddie... we should... talk..." He's reluctant at first, but then gives in, letting his arms bend and allowing my body closer to his. I kiss him and run my fingers through his hair, while his hands travel all over my body. It feels mind-numbingly good, makes me feel alive at the moment, makes it easier to push away the dirt inside me, the voice that shouts at me I'm being the whore the unknown man always told me I was. I wish it were that easy. That I could kiss him and just enjoy it, instead of worrying if I'm going to snap and kill him.

So that's what I tell myself to get through this. That I'm doing him a favor by what I'm going to do to him. Protecting him from me.

Getting to my feet, I guide him with me, making sure to keep our lips sealed as I back us around the desk, bumping into the corner and knocking over a picture on his desk. I bite at his lip then gently push him into the chair. He gazes up at me, eyes glossy, lips parting to say something, but I silence him by tugging his shirt off and discarding it to the side. My movements are reckless, rough, almost violent, and it frightens me so much how I feel inside that I'm shaking.

I trace my fingers up his lean muscles covered in tattoos, allowing them to slowly wander to the base of his neck, my fingertips quivering when I feel his erratic pulse. I feel him stiffen and wonder if he's afraid of me. But as if answering my silent question, he grabs me by the hips and jerks me forward so I land on his lap then he crashes his lips against mine.

I slide my hands around his shoulders and to his back, scratching at his flesh, feeling something unravel inside me. I'm not Maddie at the moment. Nor Lily. I'm just a confused person who's trying to survive the madness. Maybe that's why I take it as far as I do. I could have just stolen the handcuffs before our clothes came off, but I don't want to. I want to go further. I want to unfold, shed my skin, and just feel something other than fear for one goddamn moment. I want to become the person that I'm always fighting not to be. So I let him rip my clothes off and I do the same to him. Then he touches me, inside and out, his fingers wander over my nipples, my thighs, in me, while he devours my lips. It feels so wrong, yet right at the same time.

After I explore him, a condom goes on and before I know it, he's sinking deep inside me. I try not to think about if Lily went this far with him. It's so fucked up and I don't want to think about it—I don't want to think.

So I don't.

We rock together in rhythm, driving each other to the edge, fingers delving into each other's flesh, crying out each other's names, begging for more. River is as equally rough as me and I start to understand a little, why he might have not cared when Lily hurt him. I think he might like the pain as much as I do. It makes me wonder why. But not for very long because then we're coming. Together. Nails scratching his skin apart, panting, breathless, covered in sweat. It takes me a little while to return to reality and realize what I did. How rough I was. How sickened I am because I liked it. How alarmed and subdued I feel at the moment.

*I knew you had it in you. You're becoming so much like me. Soon, you'll only be me.*

She's right. I do have it in me. The bad. I can admit that now. And it's terrifying and enthralling. As River's trying to settle down, I climb off his lap and reach for the drawer, ready to push my bad out some more.

"What are you doing?" he asks, breathless as I pick up a set of handcuffs and the key to them.

His brows knit and his lips part in protest, but before he can do anything, I clip one to a handle on a filing cabinet right by the chair and one to his wrist. At first, I think he thinks I want a kinky round two, but when I pick up my skirt and put the keys into my pocket, his amusement turns to alarm.

"What are you doing?" he asks as I collect my bra and panties from the floor and put them on.

"I'm leaving," I say, slipping on my shirt and skirt, noting there's music playing downstairs. The bar must have opened.

He glances down at his wrist and then jiggles it, causing one of the drawers to the filing cabinet to jerk open. "Why did you handcuff me then?"

I shrug, picking up his pants and chucking them to him. "You might want to put those on, so when you're found, it'll make the situation a little less awkward."

He glares at me. "Maddie, unlock me now."

I shake my head, flipping my hair out of the collar of my shirt. "I'm sorry, but I have to go."

"Where the fuck could you possibly be going that you would have to cuff me up?" He wrenches his arm, the metal making a loud bang. I can tell that he'll probably break the handle before too long.

I back toward the door, picking up my shoes from the floor. "Somewhere."

"Please let me go," he begs, tugging on the handcuff again and nearly tipping the cabinet over. "I'm worried about you and I want to help… just let me go and I'll help."

I slip on one of my boots as I keep walking backward, my eyes fastened on him. "I can take care of myself."

"No, you can't," he says firmly, struggling to get to his feet, but manages to, the filing leaning forward. "And locking me up isn't going to stop me from wanting to help you."

"I don't take help from anyone," I say, putting my other boot on, but I trip in the process and stumble into another filing cabinet in the corner, causing a huge stack of papers to fall to the floor. "And I think you'll get the picture after this," I say, starting to kick some of the papers out of the way, but freeze when I see my name on a lot of them.

*This is what you were looking at, weren't you?*

*Pick it up and see.*

I bend down and pick one up. River's handwriting is scrawled over it, lines and lines of rushed notes.

"Maddie, don't touch that," River pleads, pulling hard on the handcuff and the cabinet shifts again, almost toppling over. "Please, it's for your own good."

I read the paper that's in my hand. "Maddie Asherford is an interesting girl. One I'd like to get to know and crack open, and that's why I'm choosing to do my thesis on her." I stare at the paper, not even glancing up when I hear a loud thud from in front of me. "She doesn't quite fit into society and the other day, when I was talking to her, she zoned out for a very long time and started whispering something about hearing voices. When she came to, she couldn't remember doing it and carried on the conversation as if nothing happened."

"Maddie, please don't—"

"She referred to herself the other day in the third person and there was a moment where it seemed like she'd turned into someone else. Her posture changed. Her voice did as well. She looked at me different, too, but then she must have snapped out of it. I did a little research on her and her past is very interesting—very scarred and dark.

"She's done some time in an institution. I'm not even sure if she knows half the stuff she's been through, but I want to find out if she does."

River calls my name, but it's faint, barely existent as I turn the page over. "I found out last night that Maddie has multiple personality disorder. I met her alter ego who goes by the name of Lily. She was only out for a little while, but she seemed very different from Maddie. More cold and uncaring. Darker, probably created because of her horrible past. In fact, I was a little bit afraid of her. I'd really like to study her, too, and see how she acts in society compared to Maddie herself. I just need to get close to her, but it's complicated when she's so guarded. I have a few experiments I'm going to try with her, too see how Lily comes out, who she is and how she differs from Maddie. I'm also getting some outside help and if this all works out, I should have a fairly good paper in the end.

"This is why you want to help me?" I look up at him, gripping the paper tightly in my hand. "Because I'm insane and you want to study me and do experiments on me." My voice burns with anger and I'm tremulous, not with fear, but with wrath.

He's managed to drag the filing cabinet over far enough that he's close enough to me I can see the horror in his eyes. "You're not insane. I don't believe that for one minute; otherwise, I wouldn't be in here with you."

"Why are you in here with me?" I ball up the paper and chuck it to the floor. "To study me some more?" I step forward, ready to hurt him. Make him pay in ways I didn't even know were possible. I discover in this moment, just how sickening my mind is. Pain, it can come from more ways than my mind can grasp. "Did you even tell the police what you said you did or was that a lie? Were you hoping to get me here so I'd confess that I killed Sydney or something and you could write it in your paper?" My eyes widen. "Did you break into my house the other night, hoping to see her?" Was that what happened? Was it him?

"Break into your house…? What the hell are you talking about?" He looks baffled, but River might be just as good as a liar as I am.

*Told you.*

*You did. I should have listened to you.*

River shakes his head as he moves toward me, reducing the space between us, dragging the filing cabinet with him. His wrist is starting to bleed from the cuff, but he seems unbothered by it. "I don't think for one second you did anything to Sydney. It's not in your nature."

"And what about Lily?" I challenge, stepping back toward the doorway or else I was going to go toward him and do something I'll regret.

His brows dip together. "What about her?"

I reach the doorway. "Is it in her nature?"

He doesn't answer, staring at me as if he's trying to unravel my thoughts. "I'm not sure yet, but I want to help you find out. You know it's not your fault—what she does. You're two different people, just stuck in the same body. And the things that happened to you in your past… it's totally understandable."

"You know nothing about my past!" I shout, surprising the both of us.

"Yes I do," he insists, giving the cuff another tug. "And if you'll just uncuff me, I'll tell you everything I know."

"You really think I'm stupid enough to believe you?" I shake my head, turning my back on him and rushing out the doorway before I can act out on my need to hurt him. Or worse, trust him.

He calls out my name a few times, but I don't look back. I jog down the stairs, ready to get the hell out of here. I just want to run away. From everything. And what did he even mean about my past? What does he know that I don't?

I pause at the bottom of the stairway. Should I go back and press him for more?

*No, you can't trust him.*

*I can't trust myself.*

I step out of the stairway and into the bar. It's not peaking hour, so it's only about half full, a few guys getting lap dances, soft music playing from the stereo. There's a waitress at the counter. I'm not even sure what her name is, but it hurts me to see someone else there besides Bella. She's counting out some one dollar bills, stacking them on the counter.

She glances up at me, giving me a dirty look. "Why are you here?"

"I'm not sure," I say, checking the stairway to make sure River hasn't escaped yet.

She gives me another nasty look. "You know, River may think it's okay for you to be here, but no one else wants you around." She puts the stack of ones in the register and shuts it. "Hopefully, Leon will fire you soon."

"Leon fire me?" I question. "He can't do that. Only Glen can."

"Yeah, he can. He's in charge of the bar now," she says haughtily. "Has been for the last couple of weeks while Glen's been gone on vacation."

I glance around the bar, looking for him. Maybe seeing his face will spark a memory. "Is he here now?"

"Nope." She pauses. "And aren't you supposed to be sick or something? That's why you haven't been to work, right? Or are you hiding from what you did to Sydney?"

So word has gotten around. Vomit burns at the back of my throat, but I force myself to remain strong. "Yeah, I was just stopping by to pick up my paycheck."

"Sure you were," she says snidely.

There's a bang from the stairway and when I turn around, I expect to see River there. Instead, there's a guy with dark hair that matches his eyes, wearing a black shirt and stone washed jeans. His arms are covered in tattoos. One is of a dragon breathing flames across his flesh that I'm pretty sure I've seen before… I think I've seen more of him before.

His gaze is on the dance floor, but it shifts to me and a small smile touches his face. "Maddie?"

I'm speechless and thankfully the waitress speaks first. "Hey, Leon," she says, reaching for a cup. "We're running low on chicken wings."

Leon. That's Leon. And I've met him before… more than once, but where?

His gaze remains on me and I can't help but think how Bella told me about how he used to be into drug trafficking. "I'll get some more ordered," he says, still staring at me. I tell myself that it's because he's going to fire me, right here, right now, but when he gives me a friendly nod and then heads off for the stage area, I'm left scratching my head.

I decide it's time to bail and hurry out from behind the counter, bursting out the front door outside and into the rain. I start across the parking lot, wrapping my jacket tighter around me as rain soaks through my clothes. I have my head tucked down, determined to get the hell out of there without being seen by anyone else, when I hear my name being called out.

"Maddie."

"God, what now?" I keep walking away, puddles splashing all over my legs, hair soaked. Maybe if I move quickly enough, I can outrun him.

"Lily."

I stop dead in my tracks. Fuck.

Grinding my teeth, I turn around. Detective Bennerly is standing near a black car, smoking a cigarette and holding an umbrella. He has a long trench coat on, the collar pulled up, like he's desperately trying to play the part of detective. I'm hesitant to go over to him, but at the same time, it'll probably look bad if I don't, so I amble over to his car, stopping just short of him.

"It's Maddie," I remind him. "I don't go by Lily anymore."

He takes a long drag of his cigarette then ashes it, eyes fixated on me. "Sorry, but you weren't answering to Maddie, so I thought I'd give it a try."

"I didn't hear you," I say as he stands up straight and steps toward me, moving the umbrella with him and positioning it over both of our heads. I wipe the water from my forehead and cheeks, chattering from the cold. "Did you need something?"

It takes him a second to answer and the whole time, his eyes are on me. "Do you want a ride?" he asks, throwing me off guard.

I quickly shake my head and begin to step back. "No thanks. I can take the bus."

"Let me give you a ride," he insists. It's not a request, but an order.

I reluctantly nod and he gestures for me to get in. I climb into the passenger seat while he gets into the driver's, putting away his umbrella before he closes the door. He starts up the engine and then cranks up the heat.

"Where are you headed?" he asks, ruffling his hand through his hair in an attempt to dry it.

I was planning on going to see Ryland, get a break from this, and maybe hide out for a while, but now I have no choice but to go to one place. "Home."

He nods and then backs out of the parking space. "You know the police were called out to your place today," he says as he cranes the wheel and turns onto the road with the windshield wipers on high as the rain pours down from the cloudy sky.

I buckle my seatbelt. "Huh? Why?"

He glances at me. "You don't know?" he asks and I shake my head. "Oh, your mother said it was because of you... that you set the alarm off." He slows to stop at a stoplight. "She seemed a little upset about it."

"That's just how she is," I explain, getting the feeling that this is more than just a ride home. "She worries about me all the time."

"I wonder why that is?" he asks, pressing on the gas when the light turns green.

I shrug. "I don't know. Probably because I got hit by a car and lost my memory," I suggest. "That can make a person worry."

"How old are you, though?" he asks, but I can tell he already knows. He just wants to hear me say it.

I answer anyway. "Twenty-one."

"That's a little old for your mother to still be worrying about you so much. Don't you think?" He flips his headlights on.

"I completely agree with you." I rotate in my seat to face him. I think about telling him I'm moving out, to show some maturity, but that also would probably make him a little suspicious. "Detective, what's this really about?"

"What do you mean?" he asks, his expression guarded, making it impossible to read him.

"I mean, you showing up at the bar when I'm there and then offering to give me a ride home," I say. "I'm guessing that it's not a coincidence."

"It's not," he replies, steering the car down the side road that leads to my house. "I was there because your mother said you went to work—that's why the alarm went off." He pauses. "But by the amount of time you were in the bar, I don't think that was why you were there."

"Have you been following me?" I ask. *Calm down.*

He shrugs, reaching to adjust the heat. "I happened to show up just as you were going inside," he says. "So I waited to see how long you were in there."

"I was picking up my paycheck," I lie without missing a beat.

"Can I see it?"

I pretend to check my pockets then frown. "Shit. I must have left it back at the bar."

"Well, that sucks," he says, not buying it. "You want me to turn around so you can go pick it up? Besides, I've actually been meaning to talk to River about your alibi, not just about Sydney but about Bella Anderfells. I'm not sure if you've heard, but she's been reported missing, strangely the same day as Sydney was killed."

"I have heard," I tell him, facing forward in the seat again, watching the raindrops river down the windshield. I wonder if they found her bloody apartment yet. "It was on the news."

"Yeah, weren't you guys close?"

"Sort of."

He continues toward my house, making a left on Cherry Lane Road. "I'm guessing your alibi's still the same for Bella, too. That you were with River on the night and morning of March fifteenth."

I nod, thinking about how if I did kill her, it was days later, so technically, I'm not lying. "I already told you I was."

"Yeah, but I was just double checking." He gives me a sidelong glance. "Sometimes people change their minds about stuff like that."

"Well, I don't have to change my mind because it's the truth."

"All right."

He doesn't believe me and quite honestly, I'm not even sure I believe me.

"Oh, I forgot to mention that I went through your file." He's making it sound like a casual mention, but it's clearly been planned. He wants me to hear whatever it is he found.

I look at him, puzzled. "File?"

He glances at me again, getting a good look at my face, and I hope it portrays that I'm calm, casual, and completely cool, instead of the erratic instability I'm feeling inside. "Yeah, the one filled out for the accident six years ago."

"Oh yeah?" I ask smoothly. "Find anything interesting?"

"Should I have found anything interesting?"

I make steady eye contact with him. "You tell me, since you've gone through it. I, on the other hand, have no idea what it says."

His eyes land on me and the intensity flowing from them almost causes me to melt back in the seat. "Did you know that you had a high dose of flinitrazepam in your system the night you were hit?"

I shake my head, baffled. "I don't even know what that is."

"The street name for it is Rufi." He watches me closely.

"You mean, the date rape drug…? What? How?"

"Yeah, I'm not sure why. I don't think it was ever looked into." He presses on the brake and I realize we're at my house and turning into my driveway. "You know, it's strange." He puts the car in park, parking it right in front of the garage. "A girl in the middle of the street gets hit by a car, the driver takes off, and you have drugs in your system. Yet her mother doesn't want the investigation looked into further. Especially one that worries so much."

I want to ask him what else he read, but in doing so, I feel like I'm putting myself at risk. For whatever reason, he seems to think I have some kind of connection to Sydney's murder and asking him questions will probably make him question me more.

"Thanks for the ride," I say, pushing open the door and hopping out into the rain before he can say anything else.

"Any time," he says with a trace of a pleased grin on his face.

I shut the door and run inside the house with every intention of confronting my mother about the drugs, the fire, the hospital, but to my shock, she's gone. I'd left my phone in my room and find about a dozen missed calls from her and a text.

**Mom: Went looking for you. If you get home before I do, don't leave. Do you understand me? You weren't supposed to leave the house and the cops came today. I'm serious, Maddie...**

I stop reading it because it doesn't matter.

My life is one big lie.

*You can trust me. I tell the truth, no matter how painful it is.*

I sink down on my bed and watch the rain shift from a downpour to a drizzle, listening for the front door to open, for my mom to walk in. The longer I wait, the more frustrated I get.

I was drugged that night and she didn't want it investigated. *Drugged*? Why wouldn't she have it looked into? Why is she always lying to me about everything? To protect me? Because what I'm going through now is anything but protection.

"I wonder what she'd do if you were here," I say to Lily. "If you showed up and spoke to her… she has to know you exist?"

*Maybe we should find out.*

I remain sitting on my bed and consider that for about an hour. The more time passes by, the more I just want to get away. I know I'm moving, but that can't happen overnight. I need to just take a day off. Away from my mother. Detective Bennerly. I don't want to be somewhere where River can find me and confront me after he gets the cuffs off. I just want to be alone, where I don't have to worry about anything, just for a little while. I want to be able to breathe again. I miss breathing.

Without much deliberating, I grab a blanket and pillow from my closet, grab a heavy coat and fill up a bag with snacks. Even if it's only for a day, I need a break from all this madness and there's only one place I can go to get just that.

## Chapter 24
## Maddie

I rip the house apart until I find my car keys. She's hidden them in the freezer of all places, pretty coincidental considering I woke up in a freezer the morning Sydney was found. I get in my car and drive up to the foothills, stopping near the turnout. I text my mother that I won't be coming home tonight then turn off my cell phone before she can flip out on me and stop me from bailing out for the night.

I know I'm running away from my problems. Know it's probably the chicken's way out of this. But it's hard to live life when nothing makes sense around you or inside your head. There's no downtime. No quiet. No peace because even when the detective and my mother aren't accusing me of being someone else, I am. I know what I am. Fear what I am. Yet, at the same time, part of me likes it and the like makes me sick, makes me feel wrong inside.

The closest stop near the cabin still leaves me a couple of miles of walking distance. Thankfully, the rain has ceased, but it's still cloudy and the ground is a murky mess. By the time I arrive at Ryland's, it's late. The sun is lowering behind the mountains and pastel colors glow from underneath the clouds, making the sky look like a watercolor painting. I'm exhausted, hungry, and out of breath. My boots and the bottoms of my jeans are coated in mud. And I am more mentally drained than I've ever been in my entire life. But as soon as I see Ryland standing inside the cabin, watching me from out the window trudging through the field, my panic silences. Air enters my lungs easier. My steps become lighter—life becomes lighter.

*I'm free for the moment.*

"You've been gone for a while. I was beginning to think you had finally decided not to come up here anymore," Ryland says, sounding disappointed that I'm here as he opens the door to let me in. He's wearing old jeans and a stained white shirt, his sandy hair is its usual mess, and everything about him screams comfort. Safe. Home.

"I've been on lock down," I divulge as he moves back and lets me enter the cabin, closing the door behind me. I drop the bag and blanket onto the living room floor, noting that he has a few leaks in the roof, rain slipping in from a handful of different areas. The fireplace is burning bright, making flashes of memories surface in my mind, but I don't feel a thing because I'm here.

*Safe.*

"My mother pretty much had me trapped in the house," I admit, turning away from the fire and facing him with my hands on my hips.

"And why's that?" He tentatively walks up to me with his hands tucked into his pockets.

I shrug, not wanting to get into any of the crazy stuff. "I don't know yet, but I need to find out."

We stare at each other briefly, a silent exchange. I swear he can read my thoughts, sees through me and sees that I don't want to talk about why I'm here, that I just want to be here and not think about my life away from him.

He gives me a soft, but depressed smile as I sit down on the floor in front of the fire and lay my blanket over me. He follows my lead without questioning me and then we lie down, side by side, with our arms stretched out. Rain trickles in through the holes in the roof. The smell of rain usually provokes fear, but not this time—not up here. It could downpour and I could drown in it and be completely and utterly okay with it at the moment because Ryland is here with me and somehow, I know that with him everything will be okay. At least, until I leave the cabin.

"I wish I could stay here forever," I admit, lying motionless as I close my eyes. "Life would be so much easier if I just stayed up here and lived with you."

"I think you'd think differently if you did live up here," he replies. "I think you'd realize how lonely it can get being by yourself all the time."

"I already feel like that most of the time. Even when I'm around people, it feels like I'm alone. But with you… I feel like I exist. Me… Maddie…"

It takes him a while to respond, so quiet I worry he's vanished. "I think I'm becoming your crutch whenever things get bad," he conclusively says. "And I'm not sure if it's healthy anymore."

"That's not such a bad thing," I say, refusing to open my eyes and see the heartbreaking look on his face that he always wears. "You and me and the cabin. Nothing else. What's so wrong about that?"

"Because it's wrong," he whispers. "You and I and this thing we have is wrong. You shouldn't be up here with me."

It hurts me to hear him say it. Silence stretches between us. Thunder booms in the distance. The wind starts to howl and rattle the walls, but I swear I can hear voices in it, telling me he's right.

"I didn't mean for that to sound so bad," Ryland says softly. "Please, tell me what you're thinking."

I breathe in the fresh air that smells like rain and fresh grass. "I think I might be in trouble… I think Lily might have done something really bad."

"Like what?"

I suck in a deep breath and let it out slowly. *No fear with him.* "Like killed someone… people." I discreetly attempt to reach over to him and touch him, but he's too far away.

"No, there's no way you're a killer," he says, "if that's what you're thinking."

"How do you know that for sure…? Some of the things I think about sometimes… Lily makes me think… see…" I shudder, hugging my arms around myself. "I could very easily be one. Even the cops think so."

"You need to stop thinking you're a bad person," he says in a firmer voice than I've ever heard him use. "I've told you before that we all have a little bit of crazy in us. You just fixate too much on yours. And the moment you realize that it's okay to be yourself, is the moment it'll be easier for you to live."

"I'm pretty much two people and I found out that my alter ego, my bad side, is named after my… sister," I tell him as I feel the first couple of raindrops splatter across my face. "A sister that my mother seems to think is bad."

"What? How did you find that out?"

"I found her birth certificate and my mother told me about her, so I'm not sure if it's the truth or not. But it definitely would make me crazy. An alter ego named after my dead sister."

"I've already told you we're all crazy in one way or another," he reminds me once again. "And we're all two people in a way... The one we show to everyone else and the one we keep hidden to ourselves. I think your other side just gets out sometimes because you try to hide it so much and it becomes exhausting for you. You need to just focus on being yourself."

"But which one is truly me?"

"That's for you to find out."

"I don't know how, though," I say, thinking about the multiple times I felt conflicted over being good and being bad. Being Maddie and being Lily. "The only time I really feel like myself is when I'm here. That good girl that my mother swears exists, only exists here. But she's still not even completely good. She's just... well, she's just me."

I'm not even sure if I'm making sense, but it feels so good to say it aloud. Feels so good to not be the girl lying all the time, the girl handcuffing people up to protect themselves, the girl who does anything to hide who she really is. Not with Ryland. With him, I'm just me, good or bad. I feel like he really understands me on a level no one else can.

I wish I could just finally get the courage to touch him. God, I could only imagine how amazing it would be. I should just open my eyes and do it. Lean over and press my lips to his, like I did with River just a little while ago. Only this time, I would just be me and maybe, just maybe, it'd finally mean something—I'd finally feel something.

It grows silent again. I can hear my heart beating steadily in my chest. Thunder rumbling. Birds chirping from somewhere. The fire crackling in the fireplace. I wish I could die right now and sink into the earth and never come back. Death would be so peaceful. So renewing.

"Maddie, open your eyes." His voice is so soft, so breakable.

My eyelids flutter open and I blink against the raindrops, my body magnetized, tingles kissing my skin, my heart dancing. River is leaning over me. One eye blue, one green, taking in every inch of me. Wisps of his sandy hair dangle across his forehead and his full lips are only inches away. His arms are next to my head, close, but still not touching me.

He doesn't say a word. Simply leans down like he's going to rest his forehead against mine, but leaves a sliver of space between our skin. "I want to kiss you, but I'm afraid..." He shuts his eyes, his hand coming up beside my cheek, but again, not completely touching me, yet I find myself shivering in anticipation. He lets out this soft groan as if this is the most human contact he's had in ages and I shiver more, moaning.

His body leans over me and I nearly stop breathing from his closeness. All I would have to do is lift my body up an inch and we would finally, physically connect with each other after all these years. That's all it would take, but I don't do it, fearing the moment we do, all this peace will shatter, that everything I have with him will be ruined—changed forever.

"I want to kiss you, too," I say so quietly the sound of the rain sweeps it away. I close my eyes and lie there as the rain seeps down on us and dots my clothes and hair. Any craziness in me stills.

We remain that way until it stops raining outside, until the sun goes completely down, then he takes a deep breath and rolls to his side, lying next to me again. It's dark, except for the fading fire. Night surrounds us and my insomnia wants to surrender. I try to let it, but even next to Ryland I can't get my mind to a state where it's okay to go to sleep. So we end up lying there for the entire night, underneath my blanket, not touching.

If I was smart, I'd let things stay that way forever. I'd never move until time really did standstill. But I can't do it. When the sun comes up, I know it's time to go home. Something's telling me to go back there. To get some answers. To face what I ran from. Plus, there's also a voice inside my head saying I can't stay here forever, that I need to let it go—let Ryland go. I think it might be Lily, but it's so faded that it's hard to tell for sure.

"I have to go," I finally say with a sigh as the sun shines down on us through the window. The rain has saturated the wooden floor and my clothes. I'm dirty and smelly, but I've never been so content in my own body.

Ryland doesn't argue, getting to his feet with me and brushing the dirt from his damp jeans. He walks me to the door without saying a word, but as I'm getting ready to duck out, he whispers, "I don't think you should come here anymore."

I turn to face him, hitching my thumb under the handle of my bag and hugging my blanket to my chest. "Why not?"

He swipes his fingers through his hair, slicking his hair back out of his eyes. "Because... I..." He lets out a frustrated sigh. "Because I just don't think it's healthy for you to come up here anymore—I'm not healthy for you."

I get that Ryland must have his own problems, otherwise he wouldn't be living up here, secluded from society, but I still need him.

"But I don't want to stop," I say, wringing out my wet hair. "I like it up here with you; good for me or not."

"If you want to keep coming up here, then you can," he says miserably. "But I just don't think it's good."

I explore his eyes for signs he's gotten sick of me, but all I see is the comfort and tranquility. "What do you want me to do?"

He gives me a torn look. "You know it's not about what I want. It's about what you want."

"I'll see you in a few days," I tell him, stepping out of the cabin and into the dewy grass.

The sadness in his eyes deepens as he watches me walk away. "If that's what you want."

"That's what I want," I say then hurry away through the grass, feeling my peace slip away with every step I take.

## Chapter 25
## Maddie

My mom about loses it when I get home, especially when I won't tell her where I was. I let her get her anger out and when she tells me to go to my room, I confront her about what the detective said about me being drugged that night.

"I have no idea why he'd say that," she says in shock with her hand pressed to her heart. We're in the living room, the alarm light blinking red, telling me it's set and I'm trapped once again. "I would never, ever just let someone hurt you and get away with it. I already told you that I want to protect you."

"So you didn't know I was drugged?" I ask, letting my backpack fall to floor as I drop down into a chair, tired to the point that I might collapse. "And you've been trying to track down the person that hit me, right?"

She doesn't miss a beat. "Of course. I'm your mother. I want that man caught as much as anyone else."

"Who said it was a man?" I dig my fingers into the armrest until my knuckles turn white. "I never said anything about a man and from what I understand, the driver was gone before anyone showed up." I pause. "But I think what I really want to know is why I was out in the road to begin with. What was I running away from, Mother? A hospital maybe?" She has to know that I know since she had to have seen the article on my computer that day.

Her eyes narrow as she lowers herself into the chair across from me and folds her arms. "Why would I ever put you in a hospital? You were in the hospital afterward, but that's it."

"Then why was I out in the middle of nowhere?"

She shrugs, rolling her tongue in her mouth and examining her nails. I can nearly envision lunging out of my chair and tackling her to the ground, wrapping my fingers around her neck, making her tell me her secrets.

"That's what no one really knows."

"Except me," I say. "If I could remember."

"Well, you can't. Trust me. Preston's tried a lot and you know as well as anyone that you can't," she says then glances over my muddy, filthy clothes and hair. "Now go change. You look like you crawled out of a dumpster. And tomorrow, you're going to see Preston. It's been too long and I'm not going to let you skip anymore appointments. I'm not going to let you regress back to the girl who woke up confused in the hospital."

"I don't want to see him anymore."

"Well, you are."

"I'm an adult, Mother. I can make my own choices."

"No, you can't." She rises to her feet and adjusts her floral dress. "Trust me, you cannot make your own choices—you never have been able to. And when you try, you end up in the middle of the road, half dead." It's the last thing she says before she walks out of the room.

*You need to get some answers,* Lily whispers. *Stop being such a pushover and make her tell you. Or let me do it. Just make her tell you. Think about the girl in the hospital and how you made her bleed. Either be that girl or be me.*

*Aren't we sort of the same?*

*Not at this moment.*

I start to picture ways to make this possible. Tie my mother up, handcuff her, and torture her. And just like that, the craziness is back. And the peace I found with Ryland is gone.

***

Late that night, the screaming in my head starts up again. It's more powerful and deafening than it ever has been. After lying in bed for what seems like forever, staring at my ceiling, I make a choice, on my own. I tear off all the buttons on my clothes. Every single one. Then I put them in a box. When I'm done, I have my very own button collection again. And even though it's not quite the same, it still helps me calm down and silence the screaming, something it's done in the past when I was locked up.

*"For each person I kill," he says as he cuts a button off the blouse. "I keep one of these. It helps me keep track."*

*I feel like I'm dying in the corner, hugging myself so tightly I swear I'm going to crush my own bones. "Why do you do it?" I whisper in horror, pretending like there isn't blood all around me, death, pain. That I didn't see the worst side of life moments ago.*

*He tosses the knife aside and it lands beside my feet. Then he holds up the button between his fingers, examining it in the light, his dark eyes filling with elation. "Because these people are wicked, Maddie. Bad. Just like you."*

*"Yes, she is," a woman whispers from somewhere. "And it's time to make her pay, too."*

I jolt from the memory and fall out of bed, landing on my back. It knocks the wind out of me, but the pain is small in comparison to the pain I felt in the memory. I was locked up once, by a killer, someone who killed bad people and who thought I was bad, too. And there was a woman there… her voice… I've heard it before.

I try to put some of the stuff I've figured out together as I run my fingers through the buttons, scooping up handfuls and letting them go. I was locked up once, not counting in the hospital, my memories tell me it could not have been a hospital, not all the time, if that theory is true. Once with a boy who I'm guessing is Evan and a girl, that's either my Lily or my sister. Evan and I counted buttons to distract ourselves, hence the button collection now and the calming effect it has over me. But in the memories, the buttons came from something dark and morbid. And the fire I keep seeing... that had to be the fire the detective was talking about.

The real question is, if I have been locked up, once, twice, however many times, why is my mother refusing to tell me? Does she really think that ignoring the problem will allow me to forget? Does she really think it'll help me never remember the horrible memories I can feel about to come forward?

"Is that why I created you?" I wonder. "To help me deal with whatever happened to me? Is that when you surfaced?"

"Who said you created me?" Lily replies in my mirror.

I sigh, scooping up a handful of buttons. "Who else could?"

"Life. Your environment. Things done to you. Lily."

I freeze. "My sister? Do you remember her?"

"No, but you seem to."

I drop the buttons in the box. "I think I was locked up once because I was crazy, but that was when I was older... the younger memories, the ones with the girl and the boy... I'm not sure what was going on there... or who the man was, the one I'm so afraid of in the memories. The one that calls me a whore. The one that was in my house... the one I hallucinate sometimes..."

I'm trying to push my brain further, to put the pieces together when I see a face appear in my window and the sound of something scratching on the glass.

"Shit." I jump, but then hesitate, wondering if it was the man who broke in that night, who knows about Lily, who maybe had once locked me up and killed people in front of me. Perhaps he tried to kill me once, too, and now he's doing it again. Maybe that's what I was running away from that night.

Gathering up enough courage, I cautiously tiptoe over to the window and peer out into the front yard. I see a figure standing in the middle of the road, just out of the light of the lamppost, with their arms crossed, watching the house. I hear the words *you're a whore! Bad! You're just like all of them!* I almost bang my head on the glass just to get it to stop. My breathing quickens as I rub my eyes and by the time I lower my hands, the figure is gone and the voice has dissipated into the night.

As I turn away from the window, fearing the possibilities of who could be stalking me, I notice that my breath has created fog on the window. The words *I know* are traced in it. At first, I think it's on the outside of the window, but I'm able to wipe them away from the inside with the sleeve of my shirt, which means two things: 1) I zoned out and wrote them, or 2) someone was in my room.

But I'm not one-hundred percent sure which one it is. It's hard to see the reality when there's so much craziness inside me.

## Chapter 26
## Maddie

I quickly discover that the longer my insomnia goes on, the more insane I get. It makes me fear my mind less because there's so much scattered non-sense in it that Lily's voice has even become incoherent. But the longer it goes on, I do start to get paranoid about allowing myself to sleep. I start waiting by the window for the figure to show up and another message to appear every night, but it never does.

Every time I shut my eyes, I slip into the night-mare full of rain and cold concrete, where I'm afraid and imprisoned by a man who loves to kill and who always threatens to kill me. The woman's voice al-ways appears, but I can never see her. I'm forced out of my nightmare by the worry of what I'll do when I close my eyes. I get jittery, unsettled, twitchy, not a good combination for a girl with a split personality.

Lily and I both are desperate to rest, but I won't cave and give in. My mom starts to notice, too, and when she catches me one day in my room, talking to myself, she loses it and tells me no more skipping out on therapy anymore. I'm too exhausted to argue and tell myself that in a few weeks I'll have my own place—my own life—and none of this will matter an-ymore.

Preston notices right away how tired I look and starts probing me with questions about my sleep schedule the moment I enter his office. Then he brings up my behavior at home.

"Your mother called me today before you came here," he says with a pencil tucked behind his ear, like he's a shop teacher ready to build something. I wonder if that's how he sees me. If I'm a project he's trying to put together. "Your mother said you've been having a hard time the last few days and that you've been very uncooperative."

"I'm too old to be living with her," I state, tapping my foot restlessly against the floor.

His desk is a mess today, papers in a chaotic order, folders everywhere, and his shirt looks wrinkly, the smell of cigarettes more potent than ever, a real hot mess just like me.

"I'm an adult for God's sake. I think it's time for me to move out. I'm too old to deal with this anymore, no matter what she wants to believe. Besides, it might be good for me to get some space from her… she makes me worse instead of helping me. Always lying."

It takes him a second to answer, as if he's calculating the right thing to say. "Maddie, I know you don't want to hear this, but I think it might be for the best if you continue to live with your mother." He fidgets, taking the pencil out from behind his ear and tossing it onto the desk. "I know in age you're old enough to live on your own, but I think your confusion with your identity sometimes makes you act younger than you are. And the lying part… I can assure you that everything your mother does is in your best interest."

I stare out the window at the grey sky and beads of water rolling down the glass. Out in the parking lot is a blue Camry that belongs to my mother—she refused to leave me here alone.

"You sound like you're on her side."

"On whose side?"

I meet his gaze, wondering if he knows the stuff my mother refuses to tell me. Maybe he's in on whatever it is, too. "My mother."

He swiftly shakes his head. "I'm on no one's side, Maddie. All I'm here for is to help you."

"But you talk to her all the time, right? About me? Which isn't allowed."

"Yeah, I do, but for a good reason."

"You know that doesn't help with the trust factor, Preston," I point out, crossing my legs. "You say everything here is confidential, but you talk to my mother about me, which is wrong." I wonder if he knows about the accident and that I was doped up when it happened. I wonder if he knows about Lily, my supposed sister. I wonder if he knows about my entrapment with the crazy man.

"I'm not breaking any trust by talking to your mother. You signed a release form so I could," he says evenly, collecting a stack of papers and shoving them out of the way so he can rest his elbows on the desk. "I would never do anything behind your back or against you."

"I never signed a release form," I argue, shaking my head in protest. "I would remember if I did."

"Yes, you did," he says, reeling his chair around. He opens up the filing cabinet that's behind his desk and retrieves a folder with my name on it. Dropping it on the desk, he opens it up and takes out a paper. "Back when we started these sessions." He slides the paper across the desk at me.

I stare down at the paper that definitely has my signature, yet I can't remember signing it. There's no date on it either to remind me. I drag my fingers down my face. "Well, I didn't know what I was signing."

"I explained it to you and you understood it then," he explains. "You even agreed it was a good idea."

"If that's the case, then why is this the first time I can remember hearing anything about this?" I skim read over the paper that specifically explains he's allowed to talk to my mother about the things that go on in here with me. I clutch the paper in my hand, crinkling the corners. "I would never sign this. I know I wouldn't."

"It was for your own benefit," Preston explains as if he truly believes it. "Back when we started these sessions, you were really struggling with simple tasks, like picking out outfits for yourself or writing your name down. It was for the best that you and your mother could talk about your progress so she could help you while you were at home."

Shaking my head, I tear up the paper, not once, not twice, but into tiny pieces then drop them to the floor like confetti. He stares down at the shreds of paper scattered all over his desk and the floor. I expect him to get cross and call me out on my temper tantrum, but instead he says, in a very composed voice, "How about we get started with our session for today?"

I don't answer, but I don't leave the office either, so he takes that as a yes.

"Do you want to tell me why you haven't been sleeping very well?" he asks, folding his arms and resting them on top of the folder. It makes me wonder what else he has in there. What else I've signed without knowing.

"Who says I haven't been sleeping very well?" My eyes are fixated on the folder.

"You look exhausted, Maddie," he states, sliding the folder off to the side, out of my line of vision.

*I need to get a hold of it.*

Suddenly, out of nowhere, Lily appears behind Preston. She's grinning, in her blond form, piercings, happy. God, I'd forgotten what happy looked like. She puts her finger to her lips then traces her fingers through his blond hair, Preston completely oblivious to the factor.

"You need to get a hold of that folder, Maddie." She leans over Preston's shoulder, her hands wandering to the front of his neck. "Even I'm curious what the Ken doll has in there." She's almost strangling him, her hands resting just at the base of his neck, eyes sparkling with need. "You know, you could always hit him over the head, knock him unconscious, and then search his office. God knows what you'd find." She cocks her head to the side, her fingertips digging into his skin. "Or you could just let me strangle him. Either way works for me."

I consider what she said. Me, Maddie, hurting Preston… it feels easier to do than it did a few weeks ago.

"Maddie, did you hear me?" Preston's giving me that look that lets me know I've dazed off.

I shake my head, blinking my eyes several times in order to focus on him. Lily is still behind him, giggling and watching me with amusement. "No, not really."

He releases an exhausted breath, leaning forward in his chair, causing Lily's fingers to fall from his neck.

"I asked you if you wanted to tell me why you haven't been sleeping very well."

"I've already told you that I've been sleeping just fine." I deliberate my next words as Lily wanders around his office. "But can I ask you a question?"

"You know you can ask me anything," he says seriously.

Lily rolls her eyes as she skims through folders. "Wow, I'm beginning to prefer even River over this idiot," she says, tipping her head to the side as she stares at the filing cabinet, putting her finger to her lips.

"When someone isn't sleeping very well is it normal for them to... I don't know... see things that aren't there?" I ask Preston, my gaze skimming back and forth between Lily and him.

"Have you been seeing things?" he asks interestedly, overlapping his fingers and resting his hands on the desk.

"No... but I'm wondering if it's possible."

He sighs. "I can't help you if you don't tell me the truth."

I'm trying to figure out where to go from here. I don't trust him, yet I want answers. "Sometimes I do, but it's nothing major," I say and Lily smiles at me, laughing under her breath. "And I've been really tired lately."

He picks up a pen to jot some notes down on his legal pad. "What sort of things have you been seeing?"

I press my lips together and shake my head. "No details. I've said enough."

"Maddie, I can't—"

"Preston, it's all I can give you right now," I say as Lily waves and then fades away into the sunlight. "So if you want to answer me, then go head. If not, then drop it."

He taps the pen on the desk, thinking over what I said carefully. "Insomnia can cause hallucinations, but other things can, too, as well."

"Like what?"

"Lots of things. There are a ton of mental disorders that can cause people to see things that don't exist." He pauses and his penetrating gaze makes me squirm. "If you aren't sleeping well, then I can give you some sleeping pills to help with it."

"No," I practically shout and then quickly lower my voice. "No pills. I hate pills."

He sets the pen on the desk. "Since when?"

"Since now," I say then add, "Since I found out that I had rufi's in my system that night of the accident."

He stares at me quizzically. "Where did you hear that?"

"Not from you or my mother," I say bitterly. "But I'm guessing you both knew about it."

"I honestly have no idea what you're talking about." He shakes his head, baffled. "Maybe if you told me where you heard it from, I could figure out what you are talking about."

"A cop told me."

Either Preston really doesn't know what I'm talking about or he's a damn good liar because he maintains his sheer perplexity. "I'm shocked. This is the first time that I'm hearing about this... but if what you say's true, then I need to look into it."

I'm not buying it. "Sure you will."

He frowns and then we fall right back into our rhythm. The one where we play cat and mouse, although I'm not exactly sure who's the cat and who's the mouse anymore. The game goes on and on—me being evasive and him desperately trying to crack me open. And when he eventually gets tired of it, he suggests we jump in to some more hypnotherapy.

"I'm really not in the mood," I say after he suggests it, but still get up and wander over to the chair because, deep down, I'm curious what I'll see. All these memories are resurfacing and maybe if I see enough, I can figure out the entire thing—my entire past.

"You've said that a lot today," Preston says, slipping his suit jacket off then hanging it on the back of the chair. "Maybe we could talk about why. Or perhaps how you're feeling about the thing with the detectives." He puts the file back into the cabinet, locks it, and then drops the keys in the desk drawer. "I didn't know you knew Sydney Ralwington and your mother thought it'd be a good idea to talk about it with you. Maybe you could talk about your feelings... about being questioned by the police over it."

"My feelings?" I rest my arms on my stomach and arch a brow at him. "Really, Preston? I thought you knew me better than that."

"I know that it's hard for you to talk about them, especially when you're so confused by them," he says, pulling up a chair next to mine. He lights the candles with his matches then sits down and rests his foot on his knee. "But it might help to get some things off your mind and talk to me about it."

I fix my eyes on the ceiling, trying to get off the Sydney subject as quickly as possible. "Look, if we're going to do this, can we get it over with? I have somewhere I have to be soon."

A sea of confusion fills his eyes. "Where?"

"Somewhere." I squeeze my eyes and wish I had the superpower to disappear. I'd vanish up to the cabin with Ryland again. *I never should have left.*

Seconds later, the sound of rain flows from the speakers as he clicks on the iPod. *Pitter patter... pitter patter...*

"Just relax."

*Pitter… patter… pitter… patter… The rain is falling… my cheek is pressed against the cold concrete. My hair is wet, my bones aching. I don't want to be a prisoner anymore. I want to be free…*

*Please, someone help me.*

*The rain gets quieter and is replaced by an eerie calm. I can smell smoke, feel the heat of flames. My skin feels like it's melting. I can't breathe. I need to help them, but I can't see them. I can only hear* him. *I don't want to hear him. I want him to die in the flames.*

*"Wake up. Open your eyes. Now."*

*"I can't… I don't want to…"*

*"Maddie, wake up. We need to get out." It's a girl's voice, pleading with me as she tugs on my arm. "We have to go. I started the place on fire."*

*"Lily?" I try to lift my eyelids. Try to see and breathe through the smoke, but it's blinding me, searing at my skin. Metal scorches my body. The building is caving in around me. Boards land on my body, tear at my side, rip flesh from my body.*

*Where is Evan? I need to see Evan. Help him. But she's saying run, leave him behind. He's going to die. And I'm going to let him.*

"Maddie, wake up. Open your eyes."

*Fire. Blazing. Flames. Smoldering Smoke. Smothering. I'm going to die. He's going to die. Watch him burn. Feel his pain. The pain you inflicted on him. I didn't save him. I just ran and left Evan with* him. *The man who hates us. Tortures us. Does God awful things. The man I could kill and not care.* He *says I'm bad all the time and maybe I am.*

"Jesus, Maddie. Open your eyes."

*Evan is gone and* he's *chasing us, through the flames and the smoke as we race through the house, Lily pulling me along with her, my feet fighting to keep up with her. She's faster than me, stronger than me. She is everything I want to be. And* he *wants to hurt both of us. Wants to punish us for trying to escape. For being bad. Like* he *punished all of those people that used to own the buttons scattered all over the basement floor. I wonder if* he *catches us, if he'll scatter mine along with them.*

*"He'll kill us if he catches us," I call out to Lily as we head for the front door of the house, coughing against the smoke.*

*She pauses, fumbling around through the smoke for the doorknob. "You go," she says and suddenly she has something in her other hand… something silver… a gun? "I'll take care of him. I'm better at this stuff anyway."*

*It makes something deep inside me twinge and I find myself shaking my head, my eyes skimming the flames and the smoke. "No. Not this time."*

*Her grip on my arm tightens, her nails piercing into my skin, splitting open my flesh. "Just go. You'll never be able to do it."*

*Her words are painfully right. "But what about Evan—"*

*There's a thud and before I even know what I'm doing, I snatch the gun from her hand. I'm not even sure what comes over me. If I really am bad or if her words have finally gotten to me, but at the moment, I don't feel like myself. I feel like Lily.*

*When I see* him *walking through the fire and smoke toward me, I aim it at him. Flames engulf the wood, beams crash to the floor. Ashes spill all over my skin, singe my clothes, grey smoke swirls around, but even through it I can see* him *smiling at me.*

*"Do it!" Lily cries as the man grows closer and closer*

*I start to squeeze the trigger, but when I see* his *eyes,* his *face,* his *life, I can't do it. I may hate him, but at the same time, I love him. I may want to kill him, but at the same time, I'm not a killer.*

*Flames ignite, roaring brightly and smothering everything with smoke. I can't breathe and I fall to the ground on my knees, choking for air. "I can't do it."*

"Maddie."

*"Well, I sure as hell can." Lily points the gun at him, smiling as she pulls the trigger. And when his blood splatters, it feels like it's on my hands, too. Like we're one and the same.*

*"Maybe we are," she whispers. "Then again, you might be too weak to be me."*

*I look up at her and for the briefest moment, I think about taking the gun and aiming it at her, but then the fire ignites, a gun fires, and then everything smothers in flames*

*The fire shifts… fades… sucks us both away. I'm being carried... moved somewhere else. I can't move… I claw at the ground. My flesh.*

*Four white walls surround me… the number fourteen brands in my mind, just on the other side. I have to get out. The smoke and rain is gone and all I can see is the florescent lighting and feel the cold air.*

*I'm alone.*

No you're not. We're in this together.

*They tell me I'm crazy.*

*But I'm not!*

*I see her.*

*She's real.*

*She didn't leave me to die.*

*"I'm not crazy! Let me out!" I pound on the door, scream at the top of my lungs, but no one hears me.*

*My fingernails dig into the door and I scrape at the metal until my fingers bleed, until some of my fingernails rip off.*

Calm down. Everything's going to be okay. I'll take care of you. I always do. After all, you're too weak without me.

*"You keep saying that," I say, continuing to bang at the door, panting and trembling with fear. I haven't seen sunlight in days. Haven't breathed fresh air in ages. I need out. "But it's never okay. My weakness has won."*

It will, though. But you need to calm down. Panicking's not going to get us anywhere.

*"But I want out. I want to breathe the fresh air again. Want to be out of this place."*

*"You will be," she promises.*

*I turn around and sit down on the cement floor with my head resting against the door, tucking my damp, blond hair behind my ears. I stare at the scribbling on the wall. The sentence that I wrote over and over again:* I'm not a killer. I'm not a killer. I'm not a killer.

*"Just trust me. I know a way to get us out, but it's going to have to be me."*

*"Why?"*

*"Because you don't have it in you to escape—you never have. Remember what happened last time?" As she says it, she shows me images of the things she*

*could do to get us out. They make me sick. Disgust me. But a lot of the things I've done here make me feel the same way.*

*So I make a choice, but it doesn't even feel like a choice. It feels like it's the only thing left to do. So I shut my eyes and let her take control over me. Seconds later, the place is on fire and I'm running through the forest, barefoot, cold, but finally free.*

## Chapter 27
## Maddie

Someone stabs me in the arm and I'm jerked awake, my eyelids shooting open. I quickly sit up, backing away from Preston, like a cornered cat hovering against the wall. My hair stands on end and my pulse is racing as the room spins round and round in magical colors.

"Don't touch me," I snap, aware that my face is covered in tears. I've been crying. I'm shaking. I'm terrified. "Don't you fucking dare touch me!" My voice sounds like an echo that bounces off the walls and slams back against me.

Preston's eyes are wide and full of concern as he tosses something aside. I squint and try to see what it is, but my vision is blurry. He elevates his hands in front of him. "I'm sorry, but you were screaming and crying and I couldn't wake you up. What happened? Please, tell me what you saw."

He's too close. I can't breathe. Can't process if I'm in reality now or if I was just a minute ago.

It takes me a minute to catch my breath. Takes me a minute to realize I'm not locked behind that door or shooting someone or running in the woods. In a burning building, letting Lily shoot a man... or me shoot a man and blaming it on Lily.

"I have to go," I slur as I attempt to climb off the lounge chair, but end up stumbling and Preston has to catch me in his arms. We crash into the wall and his framed degree falls to the floor, the glass breaking. "I need to go… get out of here..."

"Maddie, please just wait a minute." Preston holds me in his arms as I blink and blink and blink, trying to get the room to stop twirling like a merry-go-round on crack. "We need to talk about what just happened."

"Nothing… happened." I wiggle out of his hold and stumble over to the chair. I pick up my bag and sling it over my shoulder before staggering over to the door.

"Maddie, would you please—"

I stumble into the hallway and slam the door closed before he can say anything else. Then I take off, but only make it a few steps before I have to brace my hand on the wall. I hear Preston coming up behind me and he says something in my ear.

"What did you do to me?" I mutter, my skin dripping with sweat as I reach the exit door and burst through it, out beneath the clouds and the trees. My mother's already rushing toward me with her phone in her hand. Preston probably already called her.

I fall to my knees on the sidewalk, feel the skin split open, feel blood gush out, saturating my skin, like so much other blood has.

"What did you do to her?' My mom asks furiously as she storms across the parking lot toward us.

"She had an episode," Preston says, his shadow casting over me. "I had to give her a sedative to calm her down."

"No..." I fight to keep my eyes open as I put my hand on the concrete and hunch over. "Sedative... was it... you?"

They exchange words, but I can barely comprehend anything they say. Then, somehow they get me to my feet and into the car. My mother buckles me in, gently pushing me down while I try to get out. She then shuts the door and talks to Preston for a while in front of the car as my surroundings fade in and out.

By the time she gets in, I can hardly keep my eyes open. "Mother... who's... Evan..." I turn my head toward her, examining her reaction the best that I can.

Her eyes widen as she stops pressing on the gas and the car gradually keeps rolling forward toward the curb. She shakes her head about a hundred times. "I have no idea."

I touch my side where the scar is and try to say something about the tattoo, but I can't find my voice. My head slumps back and I'm jerked back into dreamland, unsure who I'll be when I open my eyes again.

## Chapter 28
## Lily

Her eyes shut for only a few minutes, exhausted from fighting the crap that they injected into her veins, along with the shit she saw while she was under. She never was good at the emotional stuff and that's why she had me to help her out. I've always been there for her—I'm slowly remembering now. She's growing weaker, but maybe that's because she's seeing the truth more and letting the strength within her rise. The strength being me. It's why she chose to create me, after her sister, the stronger of the two.

It takes me awhile to shake off the drugs, but I'm stronger and wake up sooner. The second I get control, I get to my feet. I need to get out of here. Now. I can't take being imprisoned again by anyone. It's time for me to take matters into my own hands and figure out some stuff. Like what Preston and her mother are hiding from her. Who Evan is. Why there's so much fire in our memories. Why I was running through the trees that night and in front of a car. Whatever it was, has something to do with the driver. He knew me, knew me enough to know my protective instincts are to kill. But somehow, he knew I wouldn't kill him, even though I was acting like it.

I get up from the floor and make my way out of the room, picking up the key Maddie found in her mother's room on my way out, and then slipping it into my pocket. It's dark, only a few lights on in the house. I can hear the television on in my mother's room. She's awake. Good.

I rap my hand on the door, deciding how to go about this. Should I just pretend? Or fuck with her head? I've never liked her much and am pretty sure she knows about my existence. I'm not really sure why she won't admit it. I wish I could find out what she doesn't want me to find out. And hey, maybe one day I'll torture it out of her. It could be therapeutic.

The television turns down and moments later my mother opens the door, tying her robe. Her hair is up in a messy bun and without any makeup on she looks aged.

"Are you okay?" she asks with concern in her eyes. "I'm sorry Preston had to use a sedative on you today, but he's just worried about you and so am I. You haven't been sleeping very well and he said you had a little episode when he put you under hypnotherapy today." She squints at my face. "You look like you feel a lot better, though."

"Oh, I am," I assure her.

"Good." She seems thrown off by my indifference.

"I need to leave the house," I say calmly with my arms resting at my side. "And need you to come unlock the alarm so we don't draw the police here."

She shakes her head, her face reddening with anger. "You're not allowed out when it's so late, especially when you were so upset earlier and you're probably still going to feel a little groggy from the sedative."

*Patience,* I tell myself. "There's somewhere I need to be."

She steps forward to intimidate me, but she's scared of what I'll do to her. Maddie doesn't see it clearly, but I do. She's afraid I'll hurt her and I'm guessing I have once in the past. I'm guessing that's why she kept who I used to be hidden. The blond in the photo, the girl who was once me, not her sister. I understand that; can see past the blindness, unlike Maddie sometimes.

She raises her chin, appearing confident. "Maddie Asherford, you aren't going out and that's final."

My patience vanishes. "Oh, dear *Madison*, how ridiculous you are," I say and her face drains of color. I think she knows who I am. I've suspected all along that she might have; the obsession to make her daughter good based on the fact that she knows me and what I'm like. "You better be ready."

"F-for what?" she stammers, her knees wobbly and she almost falls to the floor. She has to grab on to the sides of the doorframe for support.

I let a slow grin expand across my face then turn away toward the front door. She follows me, demanding for me to stop, but I disregard her, walking out of the house. The alarm screams and she starts shouting at me over the loudness. I shrug her off and go outside into the cold air and walk away beneath the stars and the crescent moon.

By the time I reach the end of the driveway, the alarm has silenced. I pause, waiting to see if she comes out of the house, but she doesn't. She just stares at me from the window and I can picture how relieved she looks that *I'm* out of the house.

Smiling at her, I give her a little wave and then stroll out into the night, breathing freely.

## Chapter 29
## Maddie

As soon as I realize I've fallen asleep, I jump up in a panic. They drugged me. Preston drugged me and I fell asleep and I... no... My anxiety goes up a notch when I realize I'm lying on the floor on my side in front of my mirror, surrounded by mud tracks. There's also mud on my skin, my clothes, my hair. My shirt is torn and I have a cut on my finger. And the worst part is, my hair is blond, like in the pictures. I've transformed overnight into someone else.

*Into Lily.*

"You dyed my hair." I shake my head in denial as I touch strands of it. "No... I didn't... This is just a dream."

"More like a nightmare," my reflection says from the mirror, looking just as wrecked as me, yet in more control. "Calm the fuck down, would you? It's not as bad as it seems."

I narrow my eyes as I let go of my hair. "What did you do?" I ask, sitting up and tucking my legs under me. "While I was out?"

She rolls her eyes. "I didn't do anything, except..." She pauses and it's the longest pause ever. "Well, your mother might be a little upset with you today, more than she already was."

I clamber to my feet. "What did you do to her?"

She shrugs, but there's a wicked glint in her eyes, "Honestly, do you really care?"

I briefly pause, deciding. The good rises in me and I dash out of the room and down the hallway. "Mom," I call out. "Mom, are you here!" I reach her door and try to turn the doorknob, but it's locked. "Mom, are you okay?" I ask with a desperate knock.

It takes three more knocks before I hear her moving toward the door. She doesn't open it, just says, "I'm fine. Now go back to bed."

"Okay, but..." I scratch my head, wondering why she won't unlock the door. "You're okay, right?"

There's a pause. "Yeah, I'm fine."

It gets quiet, but I think she's still standing on the other side of the door. I wait for her to say something about the sedative, thinking maybe I should say something, but Lily tells me not to worry. That she already took care of it.

*I always take care of you.*

I wander back to my room and shut the door. "What did you do?" I ask aloud, noticing that my window's wet. It's been raining outside, the grass is muddy and the streets are puddled. Lily's been outside somewhere doing God knows what.

Of course, she decides to play the silent treatment and doesn't respond. I check the time—four thirty in the morning. I've been out for twelve hours.

She could do so much in twelve hours. I have to check—have to know.

Reaching into my pocket, I hold my breath, waiting to see if I feel a button. I exhale loudly when I don't feel anything and move my hand to the other one. There is something in this one, but not a button. A piece of paper. I pull it out. No, not paper. A photo of a man. In the picture he's just sitting there, staring at the camera. Brown hair. Dark eyes. Maybe in his thirties. Not smiling. Not frowning. Not anything. He looks hollow. Empty. Yet he makes me feel full of emotions I never knew existed inside me and with no control of my own, tears flood from my eyes. I cry for what seems like forever, my shoulders shaking, my body frozen in fear, my heart beating a million miles a minute. *Fear. Fear. Fear.*

*I know this man well.*

*This is the man who kept me a prisoner.*

*This is the man that hurt me.*

*Beat me.*

*Hurt others.*

*I'm afraid of him.*

"Where did you find this?" I ask, shutting my eyes tightly, willing myself to forget the man. But he's there in every one of my memories. Killing people. Making me watch. Trying to teach me about wickedness. Evil. When the evil is him.

"From your file in Preston's office," she says in the gentlest voice I've ever heard her use. "There were a lot of interesting things in there."

"Like what?" I whisper, but deep down I think I already know. Pain. There's a lot of pain. Caused by this man, who I know as well as I know my own mother.

"You really want to see?" she asks cautiously. "Because you really need to make sure you're ready. It's worse than looking at that photo."

I hesitate, opening my eyes and looking down at the photo. Do I really want to know? Pain. My chest aches. Vomit burns at the back of my throat. It's just a man. Just a man. But I know it's not. Deep down, I think I know who he is, not just the man who kept me prisoner, but I'm not ready to admit it to myself anymore. The things he did to me… to all those people… to Evan. *You're the one who hurt Evan.*

"I don't want to look at it anymore," I whisper through my tears as I clutch the photo.

"Then get rid of it."

"I can't," I sob, so afraid of the picture I can barely move.

Lily sighs exhaustedly. "Oh, fine. I'll do it. It's always been me anyway. I'm your out when you don't want to do things."

Without warning, my feet move toward my bedside and my fingers move toward my nightstand drawer. I'm not in control anymore and I'm gratefully handing it over because I want to stop crying, want to stop staring at the photo that instills fear in me.

I open the drawer and take out the lighter. Then with a flick, I ignite the flame and watch the photo burn.

*Burn.*

*Burn.*

*Burn.*

And only when it's nothing but ash—gone, dead, burned—do I feel content again.

"Now, show me what else you found," I say, feeling better that it's gone. Like I can breathe again. Like I'm not a child cowering in the corner.

"Not yet," she says. "Not until you're ready."

"And when will that be?"

"When you can't feel anything anymore," she says cryptically. "When you become me. Otherwise, you won't be able to handle it."

## Chapter 30
## Maddie

I'm not sure what Lily means by until I become her. Become insane—accept the insane. Maybe she just means become tougher, more capable of handling things the way she does, with such indifference. I want to believe that I can't get to that place, but with each passing day, it feels like I'm getting closer to it.

It's been two days since Preston gave me a sedative, almost a week since I last talked to River, almost two weeks since Sydney died and I woke up in Bella's apartment with blood everywhere. I haven't heard anything from the cops since Detective Bennerly dropped me off at my house a few days ago, but I don't think I'm in the clear yet.

It's late, the moon shining through my window, and I have my lamp on. As I sit on my bed, going through my new button collection, it seems like each button holds a memory, but the memory is hidden. What I really would like to know is if the ones my mother got rid of belonged to any murder victims. Was Sydney my first one or have I done this before? In my memory of the hospital I'd wrote I wasn't a killer on the wall. But it feels like I am and with everything I'm seeing in the memories, all the death and murder by the man, maybe I somehow turned into him.

*Don't make yourself guilty when you don't even know if you did it for sure yet. And you could find out if you—*

"I know. I know. Become you, but that's not going to happen. And besides, I'm pretty sure I've done a lot of bad things, without you having to tell me about them," I mumble, scooping up the buttons and letting them slip through my fingers into the box. They sound like heavy raindrops when they land. "I saw it… in hypnotherapy… I think… I took the gun from that girl to shoot that man… but I couldn't… but it felt like I did shoot him… I think…"

*Pitter-patter… pitter-patter… I can hear the rain falling… Hear someone yelling out in anger. It makes me feel sick. Makes me fear what's going to happen to me in just a few moments.*

*"Maddie, count the buttons with me. Count the buttons we've collected and don't listen to the screams," someone says in a gentle voice. "Count the buttons and pretend you're someone else."*

*"You always take good care of me, Evan," I say, sitting up and scooting forward.*

*One by one, I start counting the buttons. With each one, I feel better because the buttons are the only things that belong to me anymore. And when he comes to get me, it's easier to walk up the stairs, even when I know the pain is coming because Lily is stronger and handles it so much better. She knows how to turn it off. She knows how to not feel anything and is okay with it.*

My hand starts to shake as the voice starts to echo in my head over and over again.

*You're a whore!*

*You're a whore!*

*You're a whore!*

*"This is all your fault," he says as he pins me down. "You make me like this. You and that other whore. You're evil and so you're going to have to be punished. The bad must be punished, Maddie." He touches my hair and the smell of cigarettes, booze and sweat make me want to puke. I'm holding my breath and I can hear the voice of a woman in the background, the one I've heard but never see, like she's afraid to come in here—see the truth. "This is all your fault, for being such a bad girl. And now you're going to have to pay for it by watching her suffer and die. But don't worry, Maddie; she's been a bad girl, too."*

*I shake my head. "No." Then I fight with all my strength to get out from under him and somehow I manage to kick him off me. He's surprised by my strength. He always thought I was the weaker one. But not this time.*

*I hurry to the nightstand and pick up a lighter while scooping up his bottle of booze and smashing the bottle to the floor. Liquid and glass spill everywhere as I flick the flame on.*

*He rushes at me, screaming at me, that we'll all die. But I don't care anymore. About me. Him. Her. Anyone. I feel nothing but hollowness inside as I drop the flame and let the place burn.*

My phone starts ringing from my nightstand and the memory fizzles away like dying smoke. It's eleven o'clock and no one ever calls me, so I'm confused. But I get up and check the screen. It's from an unknown number. *Weird.*

"Hello," I answer, sitting down on my bed. There's music playing in the background and I can barely hear anything at first.

"Maddie, I need your help."

My entire body goes rigid. My heart stills. Time stops.

"Bella… is that you?" Oh my God, she's alive. Oh my God, I didn't kill her. Oh my God, then who the hell's blood was splattered all over her apartment?

"Yes!" she shouts over the music. "And I…" I hear someone else in the background. "Look, I need you to come down here right now. It's an emergency."

"Where the hell are you?" I get up and start pacing my room, biting my nails. Is this real? Or another one of my hallucinations? "You know everyone thinks you're missing. The cops are looking for you and everything."

"I know," she says warily. "Look, I'm in some really big trouble and I just need you to come down here and pick me up."

"From where?"

"The bar."

"I can't do that." I struggle with what to say to her that will make sense without having to tell the truth. "Can't we meet somewhere else? Or maybe you could call the police if there's something bad going on."

"I can't call the cops… I did something… Look, this is really important," she pleads and it sounds like she's crying. "You know that guy that I've been dating? The one I met from AA?"

"I remember you vaguely talking about him."

"Well, he and I… well, we've been hooking up a lot and I thought I was falling in love with him and everything… but he wasn't what I thought he was and he got me into some trouble. And I… Look, I really just need you to come get me. I'm hiding out in the back room and I need you to drive me to my place so I can get some stuff and then go to the bus station. I have to get the hell out of town now."

"What about River?" I ask. "Is he there?"

"No, he never showed up for work tonight," she tells me and then starts sobbing so hysterically I can barely understand her. "And I don't dare walk into the bar anyway. I need to lay low... make sure as few people see me as possible."

"Where's your car?" I ask, glancing at the clock. "How did you even get to the bar?"

"My car's home. He dropped me off here... or more like kicked me out," she says sniffling. "Maddie, I really need you right now. Please?"

I want to tell her just to take the bus, but it makes me feel like an asshole when clearly she's upset. I knew I should have never made friends with anyone. There's this unfamiliar sense of obligation to help her out, even if it means getting into trouble. Besides, maybe if I go to her, I can convince her to talk to the police and help eliminate *that* suspicion toward me. Although, it still won't explain my fingerprints in whoever's blood is painting Bella's house.

"Fine, give me like twenty minutes and I'll be there," I say, grabbing my leather jacket from my closet.

"Okay," she says, her voice hoarse. "Thank you so much, Maddie. It means a lot to me."

"You're welcome," I say and hang up, only realizing the alarm is going to go off like a firecracker on the Fourth of July the moment I open the door.

"Now, what?" I ask my reflection as I pull my hair back into a ponytail and put some eyeliner on.

"I'm not the one who told her I'd come get her," my reflection replies as I apply some red lipstick. "And honestly, the whole thing seems sketchy to me."

"Yeah, me, too." I shake my head as I pick up my keys. "But I still think I should go down there, even if it is to check on her. It's important... I need to see... to know if she's real for myself."

"Then go," Lily says with a shrug. "Your mother's not going to do anything when the alarm goes off—she never does."

I consider it, but not for very long, then I slip on a pair of boots and I head out of my room. At the front door, I take a deep breath and hesitate before I turn the doorknob. The alarm sounds off and I throw my hands over my ears, running out of the house and to my car parked at the end of the driveway.

By the time I have the engine started, my mother's looking at me from the front doorway. She's wearing her pajamas, her hair undone, and beneath the light of the porch she looks exhausted. I wait for her to run out and yell at me, but she just scrutinizes me with a look like I just shattered her heart into a thousand pieces. Like I'm about to vanish from her life, like I did six years ago. Like she's given up on something, perhaps protecting me.

"She could call the cops," I say, buckling my seatbelt with my eyes glued on my mother. "Technically, she owns this car."

*She won't.*

"I hope so," I say, putting it in reverse and backing down the driveway. "I really do."

I drive to the bar in fear, constantly checking my rearview mirror for flashing lights and listening for sirens, but they never come. Maybe Lily does know what she's talking about.

When I reach the bar, it's around two o'clock, nearing closing time, yet there's still a lot of people loitering around outside and crammed in the inside. The place is packed, lights low and flashing, and the air smells like musk and beer. The music is throbbing, and there are people dancing everywhere. The pole on the stage is empty. The dancers are by the tables instead.

As I squeeze my way in deeper, my eyes instantly go to the office window above and I breathe freely when I see that the lights are off. I focus on heading for the back room to get Bella when I get intervened by the waitress who was giving me dirty looks the last time I was here.

"Hey," she says, rushing over to me like we're friends. "I need your help."

"I'm just dropping by," I say, my gaze skimming the thick crowd. "Nothing more."

She ignores me, grabbing my arm and tugging me to the bar area where men are crowded around waiting for their drinks. She grabs a few shot glasses and turns them right side up.

"It's been so busy here," she explains, getting a bottle of tequila from the shelf behind the bar. "I'm so glad you showed up." She starts filling the glasses with the golden liquid. "I really need help tonight."

Shaking my head, I start to back away, ignoring a few perverted remarks from some of the men sitting in the barstools. *Nice ass, let me see those tits*—I've heard it all. "I said I didn't come here to work. I just need to check in the back room for something."

I notice her hands are shaking as she pours the drinks and she ends up spilling as much tequila on the counter as she gets into the glasses. "Good, then you can take one of the many guys who've been requesting to go back there with you," she says, taking some money from a tall man with a beard for the shots. "I can't keep up with all the madness."

I pause, arching my brow. "And why is that my problem?" I ask as she strides to the back wall to put the tequila back on the shelf with the rest of the hard alcohol.

She shakes her head, looking frazzled as she wipes her hands on the sides of her skin tight jeans and releases an unsteady breath. "Maddie, I'm so sorry for being such a bitch the other day. Please just help me out with this and I'll owe you a huge, epic favor."

I can't even remember her name, so why the hell would I want to help her out. Besides, I only came here for Bella.

She points her finger at a guy sitting at the end of the bar. He's younger than a lot of people who come here, with blond hair that has a slight wave to it. He looks pretty innocent in his polo shirt, but when he sees me looking at him, his smile is nothing but innocent. "He's been requesting you all night."

I rack my brain for an idea of where I've seen him, but I'm drawing a blank. "I have to go," I say to her and her expression instantly sinks.

"Bitch," she says.

"Yep," I reply, turning around and grabbing one of the drinks off the countertop. I throw it back, the alcohol burning my throat as I set the glass back down.

As I'm wiping my lips with my hand, my gaze travels up to the window above where I notice someone standing in front of it, staring down in my direction. I snag the waitress's arm as she's breezing by me.

"I thought River wasn't here." I discreetly nod my head in the direction of the window.

She looks up and her brows furrow. "No, he is. Why would you think he wasn't?" She looks at me momentarily, slipping her arm from my death grip.

*Why would Bella tell me he wasn't here?* I walk away and breeze by the guy who wanted a private dance, hurrying out from behind the bar and to the dance floor.

"Hey baby," he says as I rush by him.

Disregarding him, I make my way through the crowd, each step getting heavier and heavier. The lights are flashing and my head's swimming by the time I reach the door to the private area. No one else is in there and I fumble around to turn the lights on, my fingers really struggling to work, which is very unlike me. Finally, I get it and step inside then frown when I realize Bella's not there. I'm about to back out when I feel someone come up behind me and put their hands on my hips.

"Don't touch me," I warn, slipping out of their touch and turning around to see Mr. Polo Shirt standing behind me. I ungracefully stumble over my feet and almost fall to the floor, but catch myself on one of the chairs. "What the hell do you want?" I say as I stand upright, trying to compose myself. *Bella, where the hell are you?*

I'm getting a little woozy. The world is dancing, neon colors, lots of light. I see flashes of images. *A woman tied to the bed at Bella's apartment. A blond haired girl hovering over her with a knife, ready to cut. The girl screams and the walls are painted red with her blood.*

The guy has got a shit eating grin on his face as he moves for me again, reaching to grab me. "I want you."

I try to walk around him, taking crooked steps and my struggle seems to be making him happy as he blocks my path. He puts his fucking hands back on my hips again and I try to shove him off, but my movements are lethargic, slow motion. Everything is slow motion.

He gets rough, his nails digging into my skin as he sits down in the chair and forces me to straddle his lap. "Quit fighting it and be the fucking whore that you are."

*You're a whore!*

*You're a whore!*

*You're a whore!*

"I'm going to fucking kill you." I see red. I don't know what's happening, but I can feel myself falling into the darkness, not sure I want to come back out.

## Chapter 31
## Lily

She releases control easily this time, but that might be because she's been drugged. I'm not sure who did it to her, but I recognize the over-drunk state I've been thrown into with just one shot. I'd think it might have been the waitress since she poured the shot, but I can't be certain since the glass sat on the counter for a few moments. Really, anyone could have done it. Besides, I'm starting to think the random call from Bella wasn't random, but a set up. And I don't think this is the first time it's happened.

I'm a hell of a lot tougher than Maddie though, and this fucker is about to pay for his assault on me. I slowly lift my slumped head up and meet his dark eyes that I'm sure match mine. He's got his hand up my shirt, cupping one of my breasts, his other hand down my pants and inside me as he watches in lust as he violates a woman he clearly knows is out of it.

Maddie would flip if she found herself in this condition and maybe that's why she turned everything over to me without a battle. She did it a lot back when she first started creating me; at least, from what I read in the files she seemed to embrace me more back then. Probably a defense mechanism from all the shit she'd been through. The pain. The things she said. The guilt she felt for the things she'd done. The choices she made. The pain she caused. But it wasn't just her fault. There's so much more to it than she can even begin to understand.

I get ready to clean up this mess the only way I know how and even though Maddie will never admit it, she'll be grateful for it.

"Do you fucking like that?" I say to the pervert, having to work real hard to make my voice even, the anger subdued.

"God, yes," he moans, shoving his fingers inside me.

"Good, I'm glad you like it," I say numbly, leaning forward and putting my lips up to his ear. "It's going to make this a hell of a lot easier."

He chuckles against my neck. "Oh yeah, what are you going to do to me?"

I lean back and let a slow grin expand across my face. It throws him off a little, but then he smiles back.

"Suck my dick," he commands.

I shake my head. "Oh, I'm going to do a hell of a lot more to your dick than suck it," I tell him then shift my knee, slamming it into his balls and bulging cock without any warning. His face twists in pain and now I'm the one getting sick pleasure off vulnerability.

I knee him again and again until he finally gets enough energy to slap me across the face. It stings and my ears ring, but I'm an expert at being hit. I jump off his lap, almost losing my balance but manage to keep my feet under me as I pick up an empty beer glass on the floor near one of the chairs. By the time I stand up straight, he's running at me, growling.

"This wasn't part of the deal, God dammit," he shouts, his head down, veins bulging. "Fuck them for lying to me!"

I freeze. "What deal?"

"Fuck you," he says, ignoring my question. "You're going to pay for this."

When he gets close enough, I take swing at him and bash the glass against his head. A fire explodes inside me. I want to hurt him like he hurt me. Make him pay. The glass doesn't break, but it makes a weird noise against his head. He collapses to the floor and I hit him over and over again, not sure when I'll stop, the fire burning brighter and brighter with every swing.

From the midst of the bashing, I hear someone move up behind me. Hands touch me. A whisper fills my head from a voice I've heard before. The only voice in the world that can instill fear in me and make me curl within myself.

"I thought you were dead," I whisper before I crumple to the ground.

## Chapter 32
## Maddie

I wake up with my face pressed against a moist surface, cold, sick to my stomach, and disoriented. I think I'm in the freezer again, but when I push up, I'm blinded by the sunlight. My body groans in protest and I instantly collapse back onto the muddy ground covered in dead leaves. I just lie there, refusing to believe what's around me. Trees, the sky, the sound of a river flowing.

I'm dreaming. I have to be dreaming.

"A forest. How…?" I trail off with my eyes shut. "I can't… I don't even…" I try to let my mind travel back to last night, but all I can remember is going into the back room, the guy coming in after me, then blacking out as if I were wasted. It makes no sense since I only had one shot of tequila. I have a way higher tolerance for alcohol than that, which makes me instantly want to point my finger at the one thing that has made me blackout before.

"You're getting stronger," I say to Lily. "You took over when I was awake."

I don't move for a very long time, waiting for Lily to say something to me, but she doesn't. Finally, I sit up; relieved to see that at least this time I don't have blood on me. Although, I do have a few bruises forming on my hips and scratches on my arm. For a minute, I wonder if maybe the guy raped me then dumped me out here to die. The thought makes my mind race, my adrenaline soar, but from somewhere inside me, there's a sense of peace, telling me not to worry. I try to remember what happened, but all I can see is darkness and once again, I'm left trying to conjure up a reason on my own as to what happened during my lost time.

After sitting for a while, I manage to get to my feet and check my pocket for my phone, but it's gone, so I stagger through the trees and mud. I don't even know where I'm going, what woods I'm in, or how deep I am in the trees. I could walk for miles and be going in a circle and never know it, but I'm not worried about that. There's a spark of recognition in my mind and it feels like my feet are following an invisible path, like they're my compass, guiding me toward wherever it is I need to go. Maybe I subconsciously remember hiking out here last night. And I luck out.

After walking for about five minutes, I hear the sounds of cars. There's a road nearby. Even though it hurts, I pick up my pace, tripping over my feet and bumping into trees. I'm getting closer, the sound of the cars becoming more defined, when suddenly it happens. A split second before it occurs, my mind registers that it's going to happen; but before I can respond, I trip over something solid and fly to the ground, face first in the dirt, my nose slamming against a rock. Blood drips out of my nostrils and runs down my chin as I roll over, terrified to look, because I know what it is

A dead body.

Lying in the dirt. Face up. Eyes open. Wavy hair matted with dirt and smothered with blood, along with his polo shirt missing the top button. The man from the bar that got rough with me is dead by my feet. And I can't remember last night. Again. I can't do anything, but check. Putting my hand into my pocket, my fingers brush a small, smooth object. I don't take it out, already knowing what it is. Tears burn at my eyes, my heart thuds violently.

*Run!*

I get up with zero hesitation and run like hell through the forest, but moments later, I stumble over something unexpected. Another body. *Oh God, no*. I know him, too, by the tattoo of the dragon breathing fire on his wrist.

Don't look back. Don't scream. I let my legs carry me through the trees until I stumble out of them and into the street. The sight of it sends a chill up my spine, a jolt of recollection up my body, as cars zoom up and down the street and I almost run straight into traffic. There's a water tower in the distance and I can almost feel the key in my hand.

*Pitter-patter… pitter-patter… I can feel the rain falling… If I don't get up and run fast, I'll never escape it, the place hidden in the trees.*

I walk like a zombie in a trance across the street, step by step, my eyes fixed on the water tower that I've seen before when I was lying in the street six years ago. A couple of cars honk their horn, but I don't so much as flinch, stepping into forest on the other side. I let my subconscious be my guide, hiking through trees and bushes for what feels like hours, robotically, my mind and feet numb. Finally, the trees open up, then I stop and look up at the white building shielded by half-dead trees, the roof caved in, some of the siding charred, just like the cabin where Ryland lives.

Only this isn't a cabin.

This is the Beleview's Mental Institution. Or it used to be anyway. Until I burned it down. The memory comes to me, hot and fiery like the flames that burned half the building down. I lit a match.

*I lit a match.*

"You did it because I let you—because I wanted to escape this place," I say, stepping out of the shelter of the trees and crossing the open, toward the building. I can see some of the images in my mind. The screams. The shouting. The way the ground burned my bare feet and how I ran through the forest, trying to escape the doctor who chased me down... the blond haired doctor wearing a white coat.

*I ran for hours until I reached the road. Then the car hit me. I lay in the road, the man leaning over me, unafraid, even though I was trying to hurt him, like he understood what I needed, what I was on the inside. How he struck a match to light his cigarette… just like Preston does every time he lights candles…*

"Jesus, he was there." I pause at the entrance of the building. It's boarded up with a *No Trespassing* sign on it, which I disregard, stepping inside. There's debris on the floor, papers sticking to everything, several doors lining the walls. The last one was mine… I can remember… yet I can…

"I was here." I walk down the entrance, tracing my hand on the walls, remembering. "I was locked up here… and I found a way out. I got a hold of a match… from my therapist… Preston… he was my therapist back then."

The memories move over me in waves. Lily's silent, giving me time to put it all together. I burned this place down with Preston's matches because he was my therapist back then, had me locked up in here, and it was the only way to get out. I let Lily do it—let her take control and escape because I was too afraid to.

Preston was the one in the road. I can almost see his face. The way he lit a match, smoked his cigarette, let me strangle him.

"Why, though? Why was I here to begin with? And why are they trying to keep all of this hidden?"

*That is the million dollar question.*

"You know why," I say, stopping in front of a door, my fingers brushing the pocket of my pants where I keep the key I found. Thankfully, it's still there. Room fourteen. My Room fourteen, where I lived, day to day, for two years. God, I can practically hear the screams… smell the tranquilizers… feel the pain…

"This wasn't a normal mental institution, was it?" I ask, pressing my hand to the door as I take out the key. As my mind flashes back, I swear the steel burns my hand and I jerk back. "This was something different."

*Do you really want to know what they did to you? What you are?*

My hand trembles as I turn the key and it unlocks. With a deep breath, I push it open and a wave of emotions hit me. Written all over the charred walls are *Lily, Maddie, Lily, Maddie. Help me. Help me. Help me get out of here.* Over and over again. God, how I hated this door, when it was shut and when it was opened, too.

"Yes, I do. I want to know now. I'm ready."

*Then let me show you.*

## Chapter 33
## Maddie

Finding out the truth is painful, but not as painful as it probably would be if I didn't let Lily be a part of it, let her show me instead of discovering for myself. As I read over the papers she had shoved under the bed the night she dyed my hair, I let her partially control me—half in control over my emotions so it's not quite as excruciating. I think I've done this many times before—let her take some of my emotional pain like this.

I haven't showered since I left the forest. I'm tired and filthy. I had to hitchhike home which ended up being over two hours away. I should clean myself up, get rid of the evidence that will link me to the bodies, but there's worse evidence right in front of me. Preston's files.

Lily stole the file the night I passed out, after Preston tranquilized me. Apparently, he did that a lot in my past; at least, according to my notes. It's why I had the rufi's in my system that night. He'd given them to me during a "session" to try and subdue the rage inside me and then made a note about it.

His notes are actually pretty straight forward. I was admitted to the hospital when I was fourteen because I beat up my mother during a very heated argument in a fit of rage, which apparently happened a lot due to childhood trauma. It was my mother who had me admitted, not wanting to get the cops involved. So she took me to the institution, which I'm still not sure was a legal place of practice. Guessing by the methods, I'd say no.

Shock treatment. Questionable medication. There's some note about some sort of torture treatment Preston did because he believed that when I felt like I was being bad or around bad, I'd run to Lily, my alter ego.

Being her was a mechanism I established during my traumatized childhood of being locked up in a basement for three and a half years, from the ages of around nine to thirteen. But there was more to it than that.

Whenever I did anything bad, I would become her because apparently, I couldn't bear to think of myself as bad. Preston had believed that this had something to do with what happened to me while I was kidnapped, that my captors were on some sort of mission to rid the bad from the world and that they were trying to teach me and so I created Lily to carry the guilt and put blame on her for whenever I did something bad. The worst part, my captor was Markels Wellfordton. My father.

Lily told me the picture that I burned was him. It was a picture from the file. I think I knew who he was even then. The man who beat me, made me watch horrible things, told me I was bad, who gave me buttons to play with while I was locked up. And the man who I hallucinate about all the time whenever I hear the word whore, something my mom and Preston know about and are still trying to cure with hypnotherapy.

I'm about to read another page, but freeze when I hear a door open from inside the house, footsteps, then comes a knock on my door. "Maddie, are you in there?"

The alarm was off when I came back. I could hear the television on so I knew she was home. She didn't even leave her room when I walked into the house earlier. I was kind of hoping she'd stay in there while I read over all these papers and got as much information as I can.

"Go away," I say.

I hear her try the doorknob, but I locked the door. "Listen, we really need to talk. I thought maybe we could go to Preston's office and have sort of a group meeting."

"Why? So he can drug me again?" I call back, reaching for another paper.

Silence.

I don't think she left though, but I ignore her, going back to the papers. Evidently, my mother knew of my alter ego even before she admitted me. In one of the papers she filled out, she stated that I had blackouts for a year where I would become someone else, who I referred to as Lily. That when I was her, I was difficult to deal with and that I reminded her so much of my sister that it frightened her.

The longer I read, the angrier I get. Why would my mother let them do some of the stuff they did to me? Why not tell me now about my past? Why am I not in a mental institution anymore if she clearly still thinks I need help?

*Why?*

*Why?*

*Why?*

“I'm going to make her tell me,” I say, getting to my feet. There are papers everywhere, some that are so professional and with medical terminology that I have no idea what they really say. “I'm not going to let her lie to me anymore.”

*You really think she's going to tell you?* Lily laughs at the absurdity. *Have you learned nothing?*

“I'm going to make her.” I march toward the door, hearing the floorboards squeak on the other side, my mother retreating I'm sure. “Maybe I'll just be you.” I pull open the door.

My mother is heading back to her room, but turns around as I exit my room. She starts to say something, but then sees something in my eyes and stops herself. Her eyes take a good look at my blond hair and dirty clothes.

"What did you do to her?" she finally manages to ask, backing away from me toward the living room.

"With who?" I match her steps. Could I hurt my own mother if she pushes me that far? Could I hurt her like I did Sydney and the guys in the woods? All the evidence says yes, but the idea of actually doing it makes me feel sick to my stomach.

"With my daughter?" my mother stammers as she bumps into the chair. "With my Maddie."

"Oh, you think I'm Lily," I say and her face whitens like she's seen a ghost. I stop just short of her, arms folded, head tipped to the side. "Nope. No Lily here. Just your daughter Maddie. Although, technically, Lily was your daughter once, too, for quite a few years." I lean the slightest bit forward to get in her face. "But who I'd really like to talk about right now is my father."

She instantly shakes her head, hurrying around the chair so it's between us. "No, you don't, Maddie. It's for your own good that you never remember *him*."

"How about Beleview Mental Institution? Should I remember that?" I ask. She's silent, taking in raspy breaths as I continue. "No? Okay then. How about my traumatized childhood? Because Preston kept a lot of notes about that." I cross my arms and watch her closely. "I'm guessing it has to do with my father and what he did to me."

We stand there in the living room for what feels like an eternity, but I'm guessing it's only a few minutes. The clock on the wall ticks and ticks and ticks and finally she says, "How long have you been able to remember?" She sounds choked.

"A while," I lie. If she thinks I know, then she's less likely to lie herself. I hope.

The images of being forced to do things against my will by my father flood my head. How he believed the bad needed to punished, how he told me I was bad, how he told my sister and the boy in the basement the same thing. Then there's the voice of the woman in the background and I can only pray that it wasn't my mother—that she didn't know what was going on…

I feel like I'm going to throw up.

"Why have you been keeping so much from me?"

"Because." She shakes her head several times, growing frustrated. "You forgetting… it was like a clean slate for you. An opportunity to start over. You were such a wreck when you came out of the cabin. Even though you were alive, it was like you died. And then you took on the identity of Lily and it made things even worse. I thought with the amnesia that you could start over and be Maddie again… and I think part of you wanted to, too—that maybe that's why you got amnesia in the first place."

"That's not what happened." But I'm not so sure about that. Part of me right now would love to forget that Lily exists inside me and where she came from.

I point my finger at myself. “Do you really think that losing some of my memories would heal me? That it’d make everything that happened not exist anymore?”

Tears dot the corners of her eyes as she stares out the window. “It seemed to be working for a while... you forgetting... and you were finally my Maddie again. The good daughter you were before all this stuff happened. You were always the good one.” She sinks down on the arm of the chair, still not looking at me, and I wonder what the fuck she’s talking about. I was the good one? Then who was the bad one? My sister?

“When Preston found you in the road that night... after you escaped the mental institution, he thought maybe we could look at it as a clean slate for you. Thought if you forgot the timeframe when... when all the stuff happened and just remember the good parts, like when you were a little girl... like in those photos I put up all over your wall...” She twists a strand of her hair around her finger, dazing off. “That maybe you could just be the little girl who used to play and have fun and smile. Who didn’t talk to herself, who didn’t have to remember all that horrible stuff that happened in that place, who had violent outbursts like *her*. God, you acted so much like her toward the end. So we... we did things that were... questionable.” She can’t even look at me.

"Who's her?" I step in her line of vision and make her look at me. "And what do you mean questionable?"

She swallows hard, still not looking at me. "Starting fires. Getting into fights." She's avoiding my first question and I want to press her about it, but she keeps rambling. "You would get so violent every time anyone tried to make you do something you didn't want to do. And then there was Evan." She shakes her head and sighs with remorse. "You wouldn't let him go either. And the hallucinations all the time..."

I absentmindedly touch the scar on my side and say softly, "Evan... Evan Ryan Wellings." I'm starting to remember something, a lost memory perhaps. The boy in the cabin that I counted buttons with, buttons that belonged to the man upstairs who kept us trapped. The boy who told me to pretend to be someone else. The boy who made me feel safe when everything else felt so wrong.

"You refused to let him go, Maddie. It wasn't healthy talking to a person who wasn't there like that. Who didn't exist, but that you wanted to exist because you were afraid to accept what really happened."

"I don't understand?" I ask. "I thought I talked to Lily."

"And Evan." She pauses. "You don't remember Evan at all?"

"Evan Ryan Wellings..." I say his name again. It sounds so familiar. "Tell me about him," I demand, inching closer to her, feeling Lily scratch her way to the surface. I think she might remember him and she doesn't like it.

"I don't want to," she whispers, her fingers going to the base of her neck. "It's good you can't remember him. I wish you couldn't remember Lily either."

"My sister?" I ask in horror and she nods, sobbing. "Why?"

She shakes her head. "Because she wasn't good."

Again, I think of the woman upstairs and wonder if it was her.

I want to run, yet at the same time, Lily forces me forward, making me stay strong and get answers. I get in my mother's face, ready to do whatever it takes to get her to tell me. "Tell. Me. Who. Evan. Is," I demand.

She flinches back and almost falls out of the chair. I see the fear in her eyes. She probably thinks I'm Lily at the moment and maybe I am. "Evan's the little boy that was in the cabin with you and Lily," she says.

"And where were we exactly, Mother?" I pause. "Did my father... did he do something to me, Lily, and this boy?"

She touches the base of her neck, tears slipping down her cheeks. "Your father... he was such a nice man when I met him. A little wild, but he seemed nice... but sometimes people aren't what they seem. And he... well, he ended up having all these crazy beliefs about right and wrong, good and bad, and then he started hanging around these people who sort of pushed out these beliefs, but to an extreme extent." She chokes back a sob. "I should have never let it go on for as long as it did. I should have left him sooner... maybe then he wouldn't have taken you and Lily and that boy."

"Evan."

"He was the next door neighbor's son." More tears pour out of her eyes. "Your father had something going on with his mother and they took off with all of you... hid out in the forest..." She starts to sob. "Hid out in a cabin in the woods for years. I thought I'd never see you two again, but then you burnt it down. But Evan... he didn't make it out and you blamed yourself for that."

*Pitter-patter... I can hear the rain falling.*

*"Maddie, please wake up. You need to get out of here. Go get help."*

*Fire. Blazing. Flames. Smoldering Smoke. Smothering. I'm going to die. He's going to die. Watch him burn. Feel his pain. The pain you inflicted on him.*

*I didn't save him. I just ran and left Evan with* him, *trapped in the cabin to die.*

We *left him trapped in the cabin to die.*

"*No!*" I trip back, slamming my elbow against the wall. Hard. Tears well into my eyes, but not from the pain. "No. No. No. No. No."

"Maddie, I'm sorry." My mother stands up and reaches for me, but I step away from her. "See, this is why we didn't want you to remember. The pain in your eyes—it nearly killed me to look at every day."

"I have to go," I say, my voice sounding hollow as I stare at the wall in front of me. All this time and I think I always knew. "I have to go," I repeat then go to my room to grab my jacket and wallet.

"Where are you going?" she demands as I pick up her car keys. "Maddie, you're not going anywhere until we talk about this. We need to go see Preston."

"You and Preston have done enough," I snap, my voice so angry, so dark. But I know I'll hurt her if she tries to take the keys from me, so hopefully the anger in my voice will scare her off.

She calls out to me, this time chasing me down the driveway, shouting for me to stop. The neighbors outside stand there, watching in horror; but I don't stop, hopping in the car and locking the doors.

She bangs on the window. "Maddie Asherford, you will open this door. Now!" She wiggles the handle as I start up the engine. "I won't let you drive off when you're this upset."

I buckle my seatbelt and put the car into reverse, feeling like I'm going to puke. The one thing in my life that made me feel whole wasn't even real. It was more false than Lily. And as soon as I drive down that road, I'm choosing to let all that go. What do I want? False peace? Or the painful truth?

I take a deep breath and give my mother one last look, thinking about how much she's lied to me over the years, and how I hated every moment of it. Then I back away, heading to my secret spot, heading to Ryland.

To Evan.

## Chapter 34
## Maddie

I sit in the car for quite a while, knowing that the moment I get out is the moment that I'll be admitting the truth. That Ryland is nothing but a ghost. A memory of Evan Ryan Wellings, the boy I lost a while ago and who I can't let go. The boy I counted buttons with, who told me to be someone else, who I left to burn in this very cabin after he kept me sane all those years. I'm slowly remembering, yet forgetting at the same time, memories so distant, slipping away like pieces of sand in the wind.

It's not raining, yet it feels like it's raining as I get out of the car. Hours feel like they pass as I walk through the field toward the cabin I burned down so many years ago. And when I approach it, it somehow looks faded, more nonexistent, as if it's just a shadow of a memory sitting out in the middle of nowhere, hidden by the grass and the trees.

I enter without saying a word and walk around the place that used to be my solitude. I can remember now; how he kept us here, chained up in the basement below, hidden beneath the floorboards. Lily, Evan and I. The things they did to us for years until Lily got a hold of a match, struck it, and the whole place started to burn.

"I was so happy when I first saw the fire," Ryland says from behind me, close but so far away. "All I could think was, either I was going to get away or burn to death, and I was happy with either way because I knew I'd be free."

I swallow the lump in my throat, staring at what was once the trap door that led to where he kept us hidden. "I let you burn... You told me to run and I did... I just left you."

I don't hear him step up, but I feel him right behind me, the coldness that brings me warmth. "There was no way for you to get me out." I swear I feel him touch me, trace a finger up my back, but it might just be me remembering another place and another time that doesn't exist anymore, even though I'm trying to hold onto it. "I was locked up with chains. All you could do was run and get help."

"If I wouldn't have tried to shoot him." I struggle for air as I recollect pulling the trigger, missing the shot, the man coming at me, but Lily stepped in the way and took the gun from my hand. After that, there were only flames and the feeling of melting. "Then maybe I would have had enough time to get help before the place burned down."

"You know that's not true," he says. "You knew the moment the place started on fire that I wasn't going to make it out."

I shut my eyes, remembering how he kept Evan chained up, wanting nothing to do with him, but wanting everything to do with me and Lily. "I'm sorry."

"You don't need to be sorry," he says quietly. "What's done is done. You need to stop blaming yourself and let me go."

I shake my head. "I don't want to… You're the only person that makes me feel like everything is going to be okay when clearly it's not."

"Everything *is* going to be okay," he promises as I open my eyes and face him. His hair is in his eyes that look brighter, not as sad as they usually do, like he can sense that he's about to be free from the place. *Free*. "Once you admit the truth, it'll all get better from there. You just need to accept what is."

"I don't even know what is or what was," I say, reaching for him, wanting to touch him just one time. *Just once.*

"That's life, Maddie," he says. My hand moves toward him, so close, just a little more and I finally feel him. J*ust once.* "No one knows much of anything, whether they have amnesia or not, but they keep on living, just like you need to. It would be a tragedy if the fire ended up destroying all three of us."

I stand on my tiptoes and lean in toward him, our lips so close. "And what about you?" My hand hovers right beside his cheek, a sliver of space between us, just another inch and I'll touch him.

"That's up to you," he says, his eyes drifting to my mouth. "I already told you that as long as you wanted me here, I'd always be here."

"But you don't want to be here?"

"I just want you to be happy. That's all I've ever wanted for you."

I want to ask him what will make him happy, but I think I already know. Being trapped is something no one wants. I'm the thing keeping Ryland—I mean, Evan—a prisoner here, simply because I'm selfish. And it's not Lily who's doing it. This is solely me. Maddie Asherford. I'm selfish and it's time to stop.

"Thank you for everything," I say, tears stinging my eyes. "And I'm so sorry for what happened to you."

Before I can back out, I move my mouth toward his quickly, bringing my hand against his cheek. The contact sends a surge of heat through my body, so sweltering I feel like I'm back in the cabin again when it was on fire.

And then the heat goes cold—I go cold. And I know he's gone.

I stand there for a while, unmoving with my eyes shut, knowing the second I lift my eyelids, it'll all officially be over. It'll all be gone. If I could, I'd probably stay that way forever, holding on for just another second, another moment, just one more. But eventually, I have to move forward and open my eyes.

And when I do, I'm not standing in a cabin, just a field that once held one.

All alone.

## Chapter 35
## Maddie

The entire drive home, I try to figure out what to do with my mother. She spent so much time lying to me, thinking it was for my own good. I don't think she's necessarily a bad person, just delusional and perhaps insane. But I know it's time for her to let me go so I can move on and try to live life on my own, either with or without Lily—I haven't decided yet.

Never once does it cross my mind that there's so much more to this than Evan being a memory or simply remembering my past. Quite honestly, I'd forgotten about a lot of the stuff that had happened over the last couple of weeks, like the murders and how I'd never even figured out if I was doing them or not.

But then I enter the house and see *her* sitting on the sofa in the living room.

At first, I think I'm hallucinating again, seeing her outside my head. But there's something different about her this time. More life in her eyes. More confidence. More darkness.

"Lily?" I whisper in astonishment and horror. The door blows shut behind me and I whirl around in surprise. It's quiet except for the wind howling outside as I press my hand to my heart and rotate back around to face her.

Her lips turn upward like she's going to smile, but it looks warped and wrong, like it's melting off her face and her mouth instantly sinks. Her blond hair matches my freshly dyed hair, only hers looks longer and shinier—better. Her eyes are even darker than they were in my hallucinations, her cheekbones more defined. She looks less like me and appears more in control of her surroundings, which is very unlike me, except for when I'm Lily—or her, I guess.

"Hello, my dear Maddie," she says, uncrossing her legs and getting to her feet. She's wearing a red dress that hugs her body, knee high-boots, and fishnet tights. "How have you been?"

"Are you... are you real?" I haven't budged from the foyer, too afraid to get close to her, too afraid she's like the Maddie inside my head. But what if she's not? What if she's alive? But then, why am I just meeting her for the first time now? No, she has to be a hallucination.

"About as real as you," she says, skimming me from head to toe. I haven't showered since I woke up in the woods and my clothes are caked with dry mud, so I look like shit.

"Why are you... how are you here?" I note the voice inside my head is quiet. This Lily before me has to be my Lily.

A grin slowly creeps up on her face. "That is the million dollar question, isn't it?" She saunters around the room, keeping her distance from me as she takes in the excessive amount of knickknacks in the living room. “God, our mother might have a bit of insanity in her as well.” She touches her finger to a small figurine of a stallion. “Don’t you think?”

“I don’t think I’m the best judge of that,” I reply tentatively. “Considering my own mental instability at the moment.”

“At the moment.” She casts a glance at me from over her shoulder. “Oh, my dear Maddie, you’ve been crazy since you were ten-years-old, when you could neither except nor deny what our father was trying to instill in us.”

My bones feel as though they crack and tear out of my skin, my heart thudding violently inside my chest. I’m afraid, but I’m not sure if it’s from her or the truth.

“I need to know why you’re here… if you’re real.” I spot something out of my peripheral vision and jump to the side, bumping into the wall.

“Because we have some unfinished business.” Bella exits from the kitchen doorway, wearing black pants, a white t-shirt and boots. Her hair is pulled back tightly in a ponytail and something silver is in her hand—a gun.

I instantly start to back away, ready to run out the front door.

"I wouldn't do that if I were you," Lily says, pleased, as she crosses her arms. "We're not finished yet."

I glance back and forth between Lily and Bella, wondering if they're like Ryland—not really here. Part of me wishes that was the case. Insanity over death—I just my take it.

"We're very real, Maddie," Lily assures me as if she can read my mind and I suddenly realize that the Lily in my head has become alarming quiet inside of me. "So relax and let's chat."

"I'd rather not." I glance at the window, wondering where my mother went and if she'll return to this madness. Maybe I should try to text her—warn her. Am I that kind of a person?

As I reach for my pocket, deciding I am, Lily says, "Don't even try it." She sticks out her hand. "Now toss me your cell phone."

Glaring at her, I reluctantly throw it across the room to her.

"Thank you." Lily tucks it down her boot, out of sight.

"Stop talking," Bella abruptly snaps, quickly crossing the living room with the gun aimed out in front of her. There's also another gun sticking out of the pocket of her pants and an uncontrollable frenzy in her eyes, like she's about to lose all control. "I didn't come here to talk."

Lily glances at the gun in Bella's hand, composed with no fear in her expression, unlike me. I remember how she was always the composed one while we were in the basement, and for a second, I envy her steadiness.

"Relax; I haven't seen my sister in years." She flashes me a haunting smile, eyes lacking emotion. She reminds me too much of the Lily in my head. A chill courses up my spine because I honestly can't tell if she's real still. "How are you, my dear Maddie?"

I look helplessly around me. "Fine."

"You seem confused?"

"That's because I am."

"I don't blame you." Lily takes a leisurely step toward me, but stops still several feet away, as if she doesn't want to get too close to me. "It's kind of the whole point, isn't it? And it's good for you—brings out what needs to be brought out."

Confusion swirls inside my head. "What are you talking about?"

"Oh." Her grin shadows her entire face, and I can't help but think about when my mother said she was the bad one. But no... I still can't believe she's here. This has to be my Lily. I've lost all control and now she's taken over everything, including the outside world. "You still haven't figured it out, have you? What's been going on?"

"That your dead and I'm hallucinating," I say. "None of this is real."

"No, Maddie, I'm very much real and alive, but not because of you," she replies, cocking her head to the side, studying me. "Tell me, why did you leave me in that cabin when it was burning down?"

"I didn't." I shake my head in protest. "We were running away together..." But suddenly, the images rush through me that I haven't seen before.

*A light. Gas. Fire. I lit the cabin into flames and watched it ignite, lying down in the midst of it. I thought I was going to die, but Lily woke me up. We ran. She shot our father, while I took off in a panic and the whole place roared into flames behind me.*

"But you survived."

"Of course I did. I'm a survivor." She pauses then looks at Bella who is just standing there with the gun in her hand. "Unfortunately, her son didn't."

"I'm assuming you still don't remember me," Bella inches forward, reducing the space between us. "And I mean, who I really am. Not who I pretended to be."

It painfully clicks. I remember how she told me she had a son once, but that he died. I understand now what she meant. "You're the woman that was in the cabin with us... Ryland's mother and the person that was always talking to my father."

She looks lost. "Ryland?"

"Evan," I correct myself, trying to mentally guesstimate how quickly I could get to the door. I'm close to the threshold of the foyer, just a few steps and the wall would block the bullet... maybe. "You're Evan's mother."

That gets her to unstiffen and grin, but it's an eerie sight to behold, like it's painful to get her lips to move that way. "Awe, so you do remember my boy."

Just thinking about Evan hurts my heart, a fresh wound, still raw, that makes me feel sick, makes me want to run back to the cabin and beg him to come back to me. "Vaguely," I lie.

Her nostrils flare and within moments, she has stridden toward me and stolen most of the space between us. "Vaguely? That's all you can say after he sacrificed himself for you—told you to run after you burned the place down."

"You're the one who let him be tied up in the basement of a psychopath." I'm treading on thin water, wishing Lily would step in because she's always so much better at dealing with stressful situations than I am. I look over at the real Lily, who's watching Bella with a bored look on her face.

"I'm over this," Lily says, staring at Bella. "It's time to get it done and move on to something else."

"Get what done?" I ask Lily as she strolls around the sofa and stops beside Bella and I.

She shrugs nonchalantly. "You'll soon find out."

"I did what I had to do to survive in life," Bella says hotly with her finger on the trigger. "Your father took care of me, loved me. I had to make a few sacrifices, but I did what I had to do to keep a roof over my head and yes, his beliefs were a little hard to deal with, but it's better than the alternative."

"Survive life," Lily and I say simultaneously, like our brains are linked and we've become one person again.

Lily tips her head to the side, strands of her hair falling in her eyes as she assesses Bella. "That's a ridiculous excuse." She pauses. "You want to know what I really think? That you liked all that fucked up shit—torturing people—just as much as my father did. You were both fucked up in the head and were the perfect match for each other. No judgment here though."

I'm so perplexed. What's going on? Who's really bad? Is Lily real? Is Bella real? Do they know each other?

"Shut up!" Bella cries and I flinch, but Lily is calm, the exact replica of the person living inside my head. Bella cocks the gun like she's considering shooting me, right here in living room, when suddenly her eyes dart to the window. "Oh good, he's here. Now we can finish this."

I follow her line of sight and my heart misses a beat. In the driveway is a car and getting out of it is

River. He's wearing his glasses, a flannel jacket and jeans, his hair messy.

"What's he doing here?" I ask as I watch River walk up the path to the front door, looking at the house with hesitancy as if he's worried about something.

"Oh, you haven't figured it out yet?" Bella says and when I look at her, she's grinning, tears streaming out of her eyes as if she's emotionally overwhelmed. "The phone call at the bar. Getting you to come down there because my *AA boyfriend* got me into trouble. River helped me get to you. Poisoned your drinks. It was beautiful."

I shake my head in disbelief, backing up until I bump the wall. "It was you the whole time… I was never… Lily was never… I'm not crazy."

"I wouldn't go that far," Bella say, her tears drying. "But it was rather easy… and Lily helped us tremendously."

My attention snaps to Lily. "She can see you. You have to be real."

She rolls her eyes. "I already told you I was."

"Why…?" I can't finish, feeling as though I'm going to pass out. My vision is going in and out of focus, air getting trapped in my lungs. "Why are you doing this to me?"

"Because you let me burn." She puts herself right between Bella, the gun, and me, and has a contemplative look on her face. "Well, I guess that might be more of an excuse than anything. Sure I'm mad." She gives a sharp laugh, like she's about to go off the deep end. "But this was also kind of a test, like the tests we used to get when we were younger, Maddie. Do you remember those? Pass and we get spared the beatings and violence. Fail and... well, I don't need to explain it to you, since you always failed." A grin creeps up on her face. "Although, this time maybe not, considering what happened to all those victims."

"I didn't kill any of those people." I brace my hand on the wall to keep from falling down. *This can't be happening. This can't be happening.*

"If that's what you want to believe, then that's what you can believe. But that's not what mother will believe," she says. "She already thinks it's you... or well, the Lily version of you. So do the cops. So when you die, the truth will die with you."

I'm not sure what's real and what's fake. What's right and wrong. If I did kill all those people or if they set me up.

"They'll find out that you killed me," I tell her, hunched over, clawing at my chest, wishing I could claw my heart out so the fear would go away. "They'll find evidence that you did it."

She shakes her head, her face masking with an evilness that sends a chill down my spine. "No, they won't. No one will even believe that I'm real." Then she leaves the room and when she returns, she has a large gasoline bin in her hand. “They’ll barely be able to identify your body.” She starts dumping gasoline all over the place, dousing the sofas, the floor, the walls, even her boots and drops splatter on her red dress “It seems so fitting, doesn’t it? To die the way you killed Evan and me.”

I stand up straight and fight to keep my balance. “But you’re not dead, so this isn’t fair.”

“But I could have been,” she says, setting the gasoline bin down by her feet. “And as Dad always taught us, the bad must die. Fail the test and pay the consequences.” She pauses, musing over something. “You know, if you would just stop fighting what’s in you, it might not have come to this. I wouldn’t have to destroy you.” Then she takes a lighter out of her boot, ready to burn the whole place down.

“I don’t even know what you want from me.”

She taps the side of her head. “Think, Maddie. Think. What does Lily always tell you to do?”

I shrug. “I don’t know… hurt people?”

“There you go.” She glances at the front door. “And now, here’s your chance.”

I’m struggling to say that I thought I already did, when River knocks on the front door. Bella takes the gun that was sticking out of her pocket and drops it by my feet. Another knock and then the door swings open.

I glance over my shoulder as River enters my house with a wary expression. "I got a message to..." He trails off as he sees Bella with a gun aimed at me, gets a whiff of the gasoline scent, and then his expression instantly hardens. "What are you doing here?" he asks Bella.

"I think you know the answer to that question," Bella says, wiping some sweat from her brow.

"I told you to stay away from her," he replies, his jaw taut, hands to his side, his eyes colder than I've ever seen them.

"I already told her everything," Bella tells him, nodding her head at me. "There's no use pretending anymore that you didn't help me make her think she was insane."

I look from Bella to River, who looks like he's about to vomit, then to Lily, who looks at me with a curious expression. She bites her lip, considering something, and then mouths *the gun.*

I shouldn't trust her, but I feel like it's Lily in my head telling me to do it, so I quickly bend down and grab the gun. I skitter to the side with it pointed at River and then shift it to Bella, back and forth. "Someone please explain to me what the fuck is going on?" I direct my question to River.

He puts his hands up to the side, his hands noticeably trembling and his breath faltering from his lips. "Maddie, relax. I've told you from the beginning that I'm here to help you. And what she's saying... it's not true. I promise I never did anything to make you think you're insane."

I laugh sharply. "You know *her*." I direct the gun at Bella, who has her gun pointed at me. "And she's... well, she's bad, so that makes you bad, too, doesn't it?"

Lily chuckles under her breath. "Now there's logic for you and wouldn't that be like admitting you're bad, too, considering the people you know."

Bella laughs sharply. "I'm bad? You're the one who's been killing, Maddie. Sydney, Leon, the poor man in the woods. Granted, that one kind of deserved it. He probably would have raped you if you hadn't killed him."

"I didn't kill anyone!" I shout, looking around the room. I want to be more convincing, but I know I could be capable of what she's accusing me of. "I didn't." My hands are around the handle of the gun, palms damp with sweat, the metal stone cold.

"Of course you didn't," Bella says with a sigh then her eyes flick to River. "Would you like to explain that one to her, or me?"

River appears puzzled and starts to stammer. "I-I have n-no idea what you're t-talking about."

"Of course you don't." Bella rolls her eyes. "Okay, play dumb then. I'll be the one to tell her." She pauses, scratching her head with her free hand as the scent of gasoline makes its way around the room. "Every time River would slip you the rufi, all those times you woke up and lost track of time, he was setting you up. He was the one that killed Sydney and the men in the woods. He's the one that's been tormenting you, helping me drive you insane, all because I asked him to. You want bad? There's your bad."

"That's not true." River's words rush out of him as he starts to hurry toward me, but I hold the gun in his direction and it makes him stop in his tracks, his skin draining of color.

"He was helping us break you," she says. "He knew about your past. About your mental disorder. About everything from the moment he *accidentally* ran into you outside his AA meeting. He was actually waiting to run into you. Thought he could use it as a good excuse to get to know you more, to study you and see just how far you would go. It was never a coincidence that you ran into him."

I think about the stuff I read in River's notes and coldness seeps into my bones. "Is that true?" I ask River, swinging the gun in his direction. "Did you purposefully meet me because you... you knew about my past and my... Lily...?" I don't even know what to call her anymore and Lily smiles at me, like she understands.

He doesn't answer right away, raking his fingers through his hair. "Maddie, I never meant to hurt you." His voice is uneven as he keeps eyeing the gun. "At first, yes, I got close to you because I wanted to study you... and I knew about your past, but I never killed anyone or helped them poison you. That was all them." He blows out a breath of frustration. "I've decided to do my thesis on something else. I care about you too much to do that to you."

"Do your thesis on something else?" I gape at him incredulously. "You made me think I was a killer!"

"I promise that wasn't me!" he shouts. A promise with fear and begging in his eyes. He moves for me in desperation and I shake my head, inching the gun closer to him. The barrel ends up coming into contact with his chest, but he still doesn't step back, despite how terrified he is.

"Please listen to me," he begs. "I caught Bella slipping drugs in your drink and threatened her—that's why she disappeared. Or at least, I thought she did. It's been her, Maddie, this whole time. She's been trying to make you go crazy, drugging you and killing people then setting you up."

"Nice try," Bella says, shaking her head. "But don't try to put this all on me now that we're all here together."

River glares at her. "Stop lying to her." His voice cracks and I can tell he's scared. Terrified. And it makes me wonder how he could possibly kill someone. It just doesn't feel right. Him doing those things—he doesn't have it in him.

Me, on the other hand? I'm not so sure.

"I'm not the one who's lying." Bella looks over at Lily and Lily gives her a look of encouragement, which makes me wonder who's really running the show. "And if Maddie really thought about it, she'd know. And she'd kill you, River. Get her revenge, just like I plan on doing."

I'm starting to get flustered, my heart soaring in my chest like it did back when I lay in the street, dying. I'm just as confused as I was then, even more. A maze of lies right in front of me and I'm just supposed to what? Figure it out in a second?

*Lily, come out. I need your help.*

Nothing.

*Please, Lily. I need you.*

Only silence. And I look to the real Lily who's sitting on the armrest of the chair, watching the scene unfold in delight. Then she gives me this look and for a faltering second, I swear she looks just like me.

"Maybe I'll just kill you both," I sputter out, backing up until my back hits the wall. I'm taking ragged breaths, my mind racing a million miles a minute, and I can barely think straight. "Then I won't have to figure this out."

"Maddie, just calm down," River says unsteadily, hands surrendered in front of him. "Everything's going to be okay. Just take a step back and really think about this."

*Pitter-patter… pitter-patter… I can see the flames. The smoke. And the man in the center of it all. I point the gun at him, ready to shoot him, ready to make him pay, but I hesitate, too afraid. I'm always too afraid. Lily steps in and takes the gun from my hand.*

*"Everything's going to be okay," she says then aims the gun at the man and pulls the trigger.*

"Don't kid yourself, Maddie. You're nothing but a *whore*!"

*You're a whore!*

*You're a whore!*

*You're a whore!*

*The lies. The games. I'm tired of them. My father wants me to hurt people, mess with my head. Tells me I'm always wrong when I fight him. Then I'm punished and I'm split in half, not quite whole anymore. Lily though, she never lets him down. Does what she's supposed to and it hollows her out.*

I flinch from my memory, my finger starting to push down on the trigger, ready to shoot, when a man appears beside Lily, the same one I saw behind Sydney, the one who broke into my house, who's been standing in the street. If I thought things couldn't get worse, I was wrong. It's as if the veil has been lifted off my mind and suddenly I recognize him. He's the man in the photo I burned, the man in the cabin.

My eyes widen as I turn and point the gun at him. "Dad?"

## Chapter 36
## Maddie

"He's not real," Lily says to me from across the room. "Just your imagination."

"Then how do you know what I'm seeing?" I ask in horror, my wobbly legs about to give out on me. Deep down, I know he can't possibly real, but he looks so real and feels so real and he's making me feel so unstable, like he used to.

"Because I understand you," Lily says simply. "And how remembering back—remembering what he did and used to call you—brings him back."

River and Bella are staring at me like I'm the one that's the crazy person in the room. But my father smiles, then reaches for Lily's throat and she seems completely oblivious to it.

I rush forward, the gun targeted steadily at my father. "Get away from her," I demand, unsure why I'm protecting her.

"Maddie, stop," Lily says calmly. "Put the gun down. It's just another one of your hallucinations, probably because Bella called you a whore. It's kind of a trigger for you."

"I know, but..." I shake my head, my hand shaking so bad and my teeth chattering. "No, he's there... I can see him... feel him in my skin."

Lily tracks my gaze to the side of her then looks back at me. “Maddie, there’s no one there.”

*You’re a whore!*

“Do you remember?” my father asks, strolling in front of Lily and blocking her from my view. He’s shorter than I remember, but then again, I’m older and taller. Still, when he closes in on me, I feel small. “What I did to you?”

I do. How he raped me all the time. Hurt me. How I would pretend to be someone else. My sister, who was stronger. Who seemed to handle it better than I did. She didn’t cry. Always did what he wanted.

“You’re the one who’s been… who’s been messing with my mind,” I finally manage to speak again. “You made me think I was going crazy. That I was a killer. You’re real… still alive.”

“Only in you, Maddie,” Lily’s voice tries to push through my fear.

“And it was so easy,” he says with a grin, so close to me that I could reach out and touch him. “You were always the weak one. Every time I tried to teach you right and wrong, you fought me.”

*Make him pay,* Lily whispers. *Shoot him!*

“Get her to stop,” Bella says and, when she looks at me, River comes up from behind her, ready to tackle her, but she swings back around. “This isn’t how this was supposed to go down. I’m supposed to get the last say.”

I shake my head at my father. “Not this time. This time I’m the strong one.”

“Maddie, snap out of it.” Lily steps in front of him, her hands still up to her side. The scent of fire swirls around me, even though there are no flames. “He’s not really there. You’re just seeing things. And it’s time to let him go and come back to me.”

“But you’re just as bad as him!” I scream, my hands shaking so bad I nearly drop the gun.

My dad smiles from behind Lily. “Always so unstable.”

“I’ll kill you,” I say.

*Do it, Maddie. Make him pay.*

“I’ll fucking kill you.”

“What good is it going to do to kill me?” he says with a shrug. “They’d still be here. All of them. And they all hurt you in one way or another, just like me.” He pauses, musing over something. “I think you need to make them pay for their badness, for what they did to you. It’s about time you did what you were taught to do.”

As if I’ve lost control over my body, I move the gun around to River, then to Bella, and conclusively, to my father. Lily is still standing in front of him; her eyes on me, watching me unravel into insanity right before her.

“Don’t even think about it,” Bella says. “This is my moment, not yours.”

*Pull the trigger.*

"Pull the trigger, Maddie," my father says as Bella and River continue to argue, River looking like he's about to faint. "Just do it."

I cock the gun, noticing that Lily is about to drop the lighter and Bella's shoved the barrel of the gun in Lily's direction. And River, well, he's moving for her helplessly, unsure if he has the courage to take her down while she's armed.

"Maddie, please don't." I'm not even sure who says it anymore.

I close my eyes, swing the gun around, then fire.

## Chapter 37
## Maddie

The gun goes off as I'm turning around, aiming it at the person who's responsible for this. The bullet enters Bella's body, right in the heart. Blood splatters everywhere like spilled paint. Her heart stops. It's followed by a cry.

My sister grins at me. "Good girl." Then she drops the lighter onto the floor. The gasoline singes then bright flames erupt throughout the living room.

Smoke and fumes encircle us and Lily disappears in the midst of it. I try to move through it, try to find my way out, but something heavy falls on me and I collapse to the ground.

*I'm going to die.*

*This is it.*

*I'm going to die with blood on my hands. I'm a killer now, for real this time. There is no Lily with me, no force of will. I pulled the trigger. Killed Bella. And now I'm going to burn to death.*

I feel a hand touch my arm and the last thing I think is, *Well, at least I'm not going to die alone. I have Lily here with me.*

***

When I open my eyes again, I'm lying out on the front lawn and my mother is with me, along with River. I pass right back out though, going in and out of conscience for the next couple of days. When I finally do wake up, I'm in the hospital, my arms wrapped in bandages from the fire. There's a brief moment where I think everything that has happened was a dream and that I'm just ten-year-old Maddie, lying in a hospital bed, saved after days of her father kidnapping her and her sister, and ruining them; but then my mother walks in and I can see in her eyes that it's not the case.

"How are you feeling?" she asks tentatively. She looks like she's aged ten years overnight.

"Okay, I guess," I tell her, listening to the monitors beep, my heartbeat so consistent, so steady, so strange considering the circumstances.

"Can you... remember what happened?" she asks, taking a seat in a chair that's beside my bed.

I shrug, fiddling with the clamp that's on my finger. "Vaguely." Actually, at this point, I can remember almost *everything*.

"Oh, Maddie." She takes my hand and her skin feels so cold... or maybe it's mine. "I'm so sorry you had to go through that. I didn't even know Bella had gotten out of jail, or I would have tried to protect you more."

"You could have just told me the truth," I tell her coldly. "Then I could have at least protected myself better." I try to sit up, but I'm too weak. I loathe the feeling and can't wait until I get better. "And you should have told me that Lily was still alive. That would have been nice. Did the police find her?"

Her face drains of color, her hand tightening on mine. "Sweetie, your sister died in the fire with your father…" Tears well in her eyes.

"But you said she was bad," I say, searching her eyes for the truth. *The truth? The truth doesn't exist.* "You talked about her like she had been around afterward and was bad. I thought she died some time later, and just didn't remember when..."

"No, I was referring to the before. Even before you guys were taken… she still had problems. I think your father was doing stuff to her, even then. And when you came back, you were so much like her… rebelling… violent… cold…"

*Maybe that's because you're her.*

"But it all changed after the accident. You were you. And I thought, well, I just hoped, I guess, that things would be different." She starts to cry, her head falling forward as she mutters, "I'm going to make sure we get you some help. I won't let this ruin you even more. You've had such a traumatic life."

What she's saying about Lily, it's not sitting well. Emotions stir inside me almost violently. I have to ask. "The fire at the cabin… the one that my father and Lily and… Evan died in… did they find all their bodies?"

My mother nods, grabbing a Kleenex from a box by my bedside and dabbing her eyes. "There were three... bodies..." Tears pool her eyes again and she's about to lose it.

I, however, am calm as a revelation sinks into me. I feel myself changing into someone else, someone I've been before.

After my mother stops crying, she gets up and places a kiss my cheek. "I have some paperwork to fill out, but I'll come back and check on you in a little bit."

As she walks out of the room, shutting the door behind her, I reflect on what happened. Even if I wasn't a killer before, I am now. I killed Bella. Pulled the trigger. Blood is now on my hands and maybe the stench of gasoline, too. The thoughts that haunted me have become real—Lily is real—and for some reason, I don't feel frightened about it.

I listen to my heart beating on the monitor, the sound not quite matching the rhythm in my chest. It's steady, less afraid, carries more strength, as if I'm someone else now.

## Epilogue

*Two months later…*

“Maddie, you have a visitor.”

My hand gives a jerk and I glance up from my notebook that’s drenched with my thoughts. There’s a nurse in front of me, a warm smile on her face, as if she’s looking at a child.

I nod, put the pencil down, and close my notebook filled with ramblings that I can never remember writing, but that might be because they’re *her* thoughts. I wait for my visitor with my arms crossed on the table, poised as can be—in control. Moments later, he enters the large but seeming small room because it’s full of tables and chairs. It also has this sterilized scent in the air, as if someone is constantly scrubbing the floors and walls with cleaning products. But it’s definitely better than the place I was before. Much, much, better. And no one’s trying to get me to go away.

A smile almost touches my lips as River enters through the door on the far side. He’s wearing a plaid shirt, faded jeans, and his glasses, strands of his hair dangling in his eyes. He looks good, healthy, smiling, yet there’s a hint of uneasiness in him, probably because of where we are.

“How are you doing?” he asks me as he pulls out the chair across from mine and takes a seat. He glances around room, at the patients, nurses, and other visitors. *If only they knew.*

"Good," I say, my smile broadening. He's been visiting me off and on since I came here two months ago and I still haven't figured out if it's because he wants to or because he finds me fascinating, but I'll take either one just as long as he's clueless about what's going on.

He's nervous, fidgeting with the sleeves of his shirt. "Your mother said you were doing better."

I nod. "I am… and I feel a lot better. Not so much clutter in my head, which is always a good thing… makes it easier to see things for what they are."

"That's good," he says and then wavers. "So I have some good news."

I rest back in the chair. "Oh yeah. And what's that?"

"The cops are saying that Bella is the one that killed all those people… that she was trying to set you up."

"I still wonder how she managed to do it—how she managed to trick me so much." The idea still nags at me every day, that she played me like a fool.

"Well, I think she was having help drugging you." He swallows hard. "Leon was helping her at one point then she killed the poor bastard when she was done with him. I guess they were friends since high school and were into some heavy shit, even back then."

That wasn't what she told me, but then again, everything she said was a lie. In a way, I envy her flawless ability to weave lies—maybe one day I'll get there, too.

River continues, "The police have a lot of proof against Bella, so they'll probably be closing the case."

"Just like that?" I ask "They're just going to close it?"

"Well, there's not much more they can do since she's..." He looks at me worriedly, like I'm fragile glass about to break. God, if he knew how unbreakable I am.

"Dead," I say for him. "You can say it, River. It's what I've been working on here. Talking about what happened... and accepting it without turning to... well, *her.*"

He nods, thinking he knows exactly what I'm talking about. "So that's good then, right? It means you can get out of this place soon?" He shudders as he glances around the room. "This place is so... unsettling."

"It could be worse," I say, but I can almost taste my freedom. *So close.* "But yeah, hopefully within the next few weeks or so I'll be able to leave."

"Good." He pauses, considering something, then reaches across the table and grazes his finger along one of the pinkish white scars on my arm, one of the leftover wounds from the fire. "I'm glad you're getting rid of... *her.*"

I want to ask him if he's sure about that, but I don't. I learned Lily is a touchy subject for him when I asked him if he remembered her being at the house that day, just to see what he knew about what happened. He immediately tensed and then said something along the lines of, "*I saw that she was close to you that day, but I don't think she was controlling you completely.*"

How wrong he was and is.

I decide to keep my lips sealed, not wanting to make it so I stay in here any longer. I sit back and listen as he starts chatting lightly about other stuff, like school and work. I study him the whole time, wondering why he doesn't fear me after everything that happened. How can he not fear the madness within me? It makes me wonder if maybe, somewhere down the road, he and I can perhaps be together. He does have some potential.

I hardly say anything during the rest of the visit and then give him a hug before he leaves. When he pulls back he gives me a quick kiss on the cheek then on the lips, surprising me.

"When you get out, you can always stay with me until you find a place," he says, brushing a strand of black hair out of my eyes then tucking it behind my ear. My mother let me dye my hair before I came here and I think she was relieved about it.

"That sounds nice," I tell him and then kiss him again, leaving him a little stunned but dazedly happy. I can't help but think about how much fun this could be. He and I, when he's like this.

After he's gone, I go back to my room, a small space with a single bed and a dresser, but it's better than any of the other places I was locked up in. After I shut the door behind me, I glance inside my notebook, seeing what *she* wrote today. The pages are filled up with *I'm not a killer*, over and over again.

I chuckle at her attempts then put the notebook and pencil away and go up to the mirror on the wall. I stare at my reflection; short black hair, unfamiliar eyes, the strangeness of my smile. I wish I could change my looks, but I can't, at least right now.

"Please stop doing this," my reflection says to me. "Please, this isn't right. They're going to find out I'm not me."

"You really think so?" I say, smoothing my hands over my hair. "Personally, I think I do a good job being you." I pause as Maddie shouts at me, banging her hands on the mirror, wanting to get control of her body again. "I don't know why you're so upset," I say as she breathes fiercely. "I killed to save you. Everything I did was to save you. And besides, I've been trapped in there long enough. It's time for me to come out again, like before."

"You'll do it again." She starts to cry. "I can feel it… how much you want to hurt people… now that you have control."

I shrug. "I'm not sure yet what I'll do, but just remember, the people I hurt, always hurt us first."

"Lily!" she screams, trying to claw her way to the surface and take control of her body.

I step away and block her out, knowing that if I let it go on for too long, she'll get control of me again and then I'll be stuck inside her.

And I'm not going to lose control again.

Never again.

Jessica Sorensen is a *New York Times* and *USA Today* bestselling author that lives in the snowy mountains of Wyoming. When she's not writing, she spends her time reading and hanging out with her family.

Other books by Jessica Sorensen:

Shattered Promises (Shattered Promises, #1)

Fractured Souls (Shattered Promises, #2)

The Coincidence of Callie and Kayden (The Coincidence, #1)

The Destiny of Violet and Luke (The Coincidence, #3)

Breaking Nova (Nova, #1)

The Secret of Ella and Micha (The Secret, #1)

The Fallen Star (Fallen Star Series, Book 1)

The Underworld (Fallen Star Series, Book 2)

The Vision (Fallen Star Series, Book 3)

The Promise (Fallen Star Series, Book 4)

Darkness Falls (Darkness Falls Series, Book 1)

Darkness Breaks (Darkness Falls Series, Book 2)

Ember (Death Collectors, Book 1)

Connect with me online:

Printed in Great Britain
by Amazon